THE LION
OF MIDNIGHT

J D Davies

The Fourth Journal of Matthew Quinton

First published in 2013 by Old Street Publishing Ltd,
Trebinshun House, Brecon LD3 7PX

www.oldstreetpublishing.co.uk

ISBN 978 1 908699 27 5

Copyright © JD Davies, 2013

10 9 8 7 6 5 4 3 2 1

A CIP catalogue record for this title is available from the British Library.

Printed and bound in Great Britain

Typeset by Martin Worthington

For Anne, Janet, and Emma Bancroft,
and in memory of Peter (1969-2011)

Thy throne rests on mem'ries from great days of yore, When worldwide renown was valour's guerdon.
I know to thy name thou art true as before.
In thee I'll live, in thee I'll die, thou North Land.

From the Swedish national anthem

For God's sake, do not yield the ship to those fellows!

*Henry Dawes, captain of His Majesty's ship,
the* Princess, *17 May 1667*

The Swedish Empire in 1666

KINGDOM OF DENMARK & NORWAY

KINGDOM OF THE
SWEDES, GOTHS & WENDS

Stockholm

Lackö

N

S

Gothenburg

RUSSIA

The Baltic

COMMONWEALTH
OF POLAND AND
LITHUANIA

N = 'The Naze'
S = 'The Scaw'

100 miles

A NOTE ON TERMINOLOGY

Throughout this book, I have rendered Swedish, Danish and Norwegian names as an Englishman of the seventeenth and eighteenth centuries like Matthew Quinton would have done. Hence Gothenburg rather than Göteborg, Elfsborg not Älvsborg, Wrango not Vrango, Flackery not Flekkerøy and so forth. The one exception is the name of the King of Sweden. Matthew would undoubtedly have called him King Charles the Eleventh, but to avoid confusion with his own monarch, I have given the name as Karl.

Chapter One

The *Cressy* lurched again, the mighty waves of the German Ocean tossing her hull like a cork. The lantern hanging from the beam swung crazily, casting wild shadows over the chart weighted down upon the table. The ship's timbers groaned in protest. Salt-spray broke upon the stern windows as the icy wind's howl strengthened once more.

I braced myself anew, extending my feet to anchor myself against the table. I squinted tired eyes at the chart before me. The Naze of Norway: *there*. The Skaw of Denmark: *there*. Our course by reckoning, a confident line bisecting those two promontories before turning southeast to Gothenburg, our destination, *there*. But the line was a fiction, and had been for the thirty hours since the storm began. With a raging ocean and black skies above, observations of sun, moon and stars had been impossible, nor had there been any sightings of landmarks. The latter, at least, was a blessing; for in these seas, coming within sight of land might have been fatal to the *Cressy* and the two hundred and eighty souls aboard her. Yet with the wind so brisk and the current running so strongly, pushing us ever further north and east, I knew that we must be drawing more and more distant from our reckoning, ever nearer to the ship-killing shore of the Naze and the cliffs beyond it. 'Cliffs the size of cathedrals on that coast,' Seth Jeary had said to me but an hour before, and I had no cause to doubt that worthy old seaman, our ship's master.

God of England, God of the Quintons, I prayed, *keep us clear, I beseech thee.* Having survived one shipwreck, and witnessed the deaths of all but a handful of the crew that I commanded, I had ample cause for a rare outpouring of godly fervour.

There was a timid knock on the door of my cabin, and a boyish shout from beyond it: 'Light ho, Captain!'

'Where away?'

'Three points off the larboard bow, Sir Matthew!'

I threw a tar-coated sailcloth cape over my shoulders and staggered to the door, narrowly avoiding being flung against a culverin as a treacherous pitch rocked the ship. There in the steerage stood the boy Kellett, the only one of my captain's servants not to have been prostrated by seasickness, wet to the skin and smelling of brine. Yet he had a cheerful air about him as he saluted me; markedly cheerful, given that his life and mine might be ended by a great rock at any moment. The deck was wet from the waters breaking over the ship. All around us, my officers' tiny cabins resounded with a chorus akin to that of the lost souls in Hell. The loud groans of our chaplain, the Reverend Eade, were echoed across the way by the unmistakeable wails of Phineas Musk, notionally my clerk but truthfully my guardian, conscience and court jester, all in one. A violent dry retching from the conjoined cabins adjacent to Musk's tiny space indicated that the *Cressy's* mysterious passenger had nothing left to spew into his leathern bucket. The sound made my own stomach turn, but after five years at sea I was more a master of my gut than once I had been.

I made my way to the quarterdeck, where two of the hands helped lash me to the forward rail overlooking our main deck. It was a bitter, cold night: despite the gale, the rail was encased in hard frost. The roar of the wind outdid the broadsides of a hundred men-of-war. Kit Farrell, lieutenant, old friend and sometime saviour of my life, handed me his telescope and pointed away to larboard, into what still seemed to be an unforgivingly black night.

'I see no light, Mister Farrell,' I cried through the salt-spray breaking over our heads.

'There, Sir Matthew! A little more northerly!'

I rolled with the ship, steadied my elbows upon the rail, and squinted out into the terrible night. Nothing. But no, I caught a sudden glimpse of a pinprick, there in the trough between two great waves – and again, in the same position –

'I can't make out the coast', I bawled at the men around me. 'Are we upon the cliffs east of the Naze?'

'Light's too low upon the shore,' growled Jeary in his thick Norfolk speech, the cold giving shape to his breath. 'If we're lucky, it's on one of the islands outside Kristiansand, maybe Flackery itself.'

I knew from my waggoner that the isle of Flackery was one of the principal seamarks upon this shore: there were good, deep anchorages all around it, where a ship could ride out the worst of storms. Yet with no sightings and no bearings, we might just as easily have been in sight of *Ultima Thule* itself. And there were two other great dangers, quite apart from our ignorance of our position: the threat of the wind driving us onto unseen cliffs behind the turbulent waves; and – if the more credulous of the crew were to be believed – the huge sea-monsters that plucked men directly off the decks, perchance in league with the witches who were said to throng this coast in droves.

'Mister Jeary,' I demanded of the rugged old master, 'are there ever known to be wreckers on this shore?'

Jeary, chosen for this voyage because he had skippered many a Balticman through these waters, shook his sodden head in response. 'I've heard of such,' he bellowed through the gale. 'They say the *Hopewell of Yarmouth* was lured to its fate in these waters. Ten year back, that'd be. I've heard talk of many a Dutchman drawn onto the rocks hereabouts, too. One art the Cornish taught the world.'

John Tremar, on watch as a larboard lookout and part of the Cornish following that had been with me since my second commission, shot him a glance. The Cornishmen had a mighty name for placing false lights to lure unwary ships onto their rocks, there to be looted by the kith and kin of a large measure of my crew. But evidently the murderous trade was not unique to them.

I weighed our options. The ship pitched and rolled, throwing us all to starboard and port, fore and aft, as it pleased. The cold wind howled about me, icy spray lashing my face and oilskin. I looked up at the few pieces of canvas which we still had aloft. With the wind and current as they were, we could run off a little to eastward under reefed topsails, that was all; bearing away south by east for the centre of the great channel and weathering the storm was impossible. So we had no choice but to make a landfall and wait for the tempest to blow itself out, and the distant light offered us perhaps our single chance of doing so. The light might indeed prove false, put on a wrecking shore to lure a lucrative cargo into the clutches of Norwegian ship-thieves. But if it was a true light, and I ignored it out of fear of the other, what were the chances we would then find another lit anchorage further to the east?

I studied the light again, put down my eyepiece and turned. The eyes of all men upon that quarterdeck were upon me. They were true mariners all, men born to the sea. Each and every one of them would have his opinion of what we should do. Each of them knew the odds, each of them knew the consequences of the wrong decision. They were silent; there was no need for words. They knew, as I knew, that this was why a ship had a captain. The decision that had to be taken, the responsibility that had to be borne: *that* was what a captain was for. And they all knew full well that this captain had once got such a decision terribly wrong.

'Very well,' I said, 'we shall assume the light is true, and pray that it signifies a landfall at Flackery. Mister Jeary, we shall sound every quarter of an hour! Mister Farrell, summon all hands when we have consecutive soundings of eight fathoms or less!'

That done, I had myself unlashed from the rail. Swaying from side to side like a man sodden with an excess of gin, I returned to my cabin.

There I stared once again upon the chart. If the storm and the wreckers did not do for us, there remained the one other danger: perhaps the greatest of all. Kit Farrell, Seth Jeary, and any one of five score veteran seamen among the *Cressy*'s company could have studied the charts, seen the light, weighed the odds, and made the same decision I did, or chosen another. And every one of those other men would have based their decision solely upon the navigation of the ship, their reading of the charts and their knowledge of these seas. But only Captain Sir Matthew Quinton, one of the newest and youngest knights of His Britannic Majesty's realm, made the decision knowing full well that he was ordering his ship onto an enemy's shore, and knowing also what the consequences of that decision might be.

* * *

Dawn, some two hours after we had dropped anchor in five fathoms with good, firm ground, brought both relief and alarm.

True, we were in a wide channel between the frost-crusted shores of two, low rocky islands. The light, its fire now being extinguished in its tower upon an islet a mile away, had been true indeed, guiding us into this haven. The western isle gave us shelter from the worst of the wind, which was in any case diminishing by the hour. All should have been well for the *Cressy* and her captain. But by any measure, it was not.

It had been hidden at first, its bulk swallowed up by the blackness of the islands all around us. It was very nearly concealed entirely beneath the northerly point of the isle to westward. But there it was, and as the grey winter's dawn slowly illuminated the scene, I gazed out upon it.

'Big,' said Phineas Musk, his normally ruddy face pale from two days of sea-sickness. 'Too cursedly big for my taste.'

And for his captain's. It was big indeed, this great three-decked man-of-war, barely half a mile from our anchorage. The ship had already broken out her ensign at the stern: the white cross upon red of Denmark. And as Denmark encompassed Norway, this ship had a perfect right to be where she was, in her own home waters. Whereas the *Cressy* was an interloper. Worse, we might very well be an invader, for when we left the Nore the Danish king's declaration of war against us was expected daily. We should have sailed weeks before, but had been delayed by the endless prevarication and incompetence of the victuallers, and the ordnance, and the flibbertigibbet clerks of the Navy Office or the Lord Treasurer. Our mission was to escort back the mast-fleet from Gothenburg, the safe arrival of which was essential to our fleet's ability to sustain the war against the Dutch. England obtained most of the lofty pinnacles of pine that became the masts of men-of-war from the Baltic lands, Sweden above all. No masts, no ships, no victory: it was a simple equation, but the very stuff of life and death. The mast-fleet should have come home four months before, but had been forced to winter in Gothenburg because someone – unidentified, as is always the way in such things – had forgotten to send a ship to convoy them. Such, alas, is how England ever fights its wars.

The *Cressy* was a powerful ship – one of the largest fourth-rate frigates in Charles Stuart's navy. She mounted fifty-two guns, ten of which were demi-cannon firing thirty-two pound shot, along with twelve culverins firing eighteen-pound shot. But the leviathan beyond the island had an entire extra gun deck, and would be carrying at least seventy pieces of ordnance. The only saving grace was that the Danes, like the French and unlike ourselves, preferred not to cram enormous guns into every conceivable space: an English ship of that size would have mounted eighty or more, and would thus have sat several feet lower in the water.

There were men upon her upper deck. Many men. I did not doubt that they were at their quarters, awaiting their captain's commands to climb the standing rigging and unfurl her sails. If she had seen us first, she might already be cleared for action, her guns primed and ready behind their ports.

I lifted my telescope once more, and surveyed her quarterdeck. Ah yes, there he was, his own telescope levelled upon me. My counterpart, my alter ego, my enemy – call him what you will. The Danish captain, at any rate. A stout man, quite young, with his breastplate already fastened upon him. A man expecting a battle, then. Did he recognise me, perchance, from the pamphlets bearing my image that had flooded the market since my success at the Battle of Lowestoft, eight months before? Unlikely, for even if such had reached Denmark, the resemblance between the figure in the pamphlets and the captain of the *Cressy* was akin to that between a flea and an elephant.

'A three-decker,' said Kit Farrell, at my side, almost to himself. 'At sea in February. That can only mean –'

He was interrupted by a sudden flurry of fur upon the stair from the steerage. A tall, stout man of sixty years or so, sporting a vast and utterly unfashionable beard upon his square, florid, pitted face, and clad in an extraordinary wolf-fur coat, strode purposefully onto the quarterdeck. He looked out toward the great ship and the Danish colours flying from it, shook his head thoughtfully, and turned toward me.

'Well, then, Sir Matthew. This, perchance, seems to be the moment when we discover whether or not the Dane has finally declared war upon us.'

Our passenger, Peregrine, Lord Conisbrough, showed no sign of the indisposition that had laid him low for three days. Compared to the visage of his page, who followed slightly behind him – a callow youth named North – and to the ghastly countenance of Musk, the noble baron seemed the very picture of health. His passage in the ship had been announced by an urgent order from the Lord High Admiral himself, while we lay at the Nore, and awaiting his arrival was one of the many matters that had delayed our sailing. Conisbrough owned great estates in Sweden, it seemed, acquired while he served abroad during the late wars. There was no indication of which wars exactly (the last half century having seen more wars in Europe than there were countries, or so it seemed) and even less of whom he might have served. But one does not question the direct order of the king's brother.

In truth, Lord Conisbrough caused little trouble to the captain and crew of the *Cressy*. He graciously refused the captain's offer of his own cabin, making do instead with a double-cabin in the steerage – a notable sacrifice for such a large man, for even joining two officers' coops into one created a space no larger than ten feet by six. He dined with me on every night of the voyage, at least until the ever-increasing size of the waves did for his stomach, but although he was exceedingly good company, with a range of conversation upon every topic from the efficacy of ratsbane to the whoring of the French king, he was notably elusive upon the subject of his own past. Indeed, he was equally so upon the subject of his present: quite what had prompted a peer of the realm to examine the condition of his estates abroad in the depths of winter, and in the midst of a war, was never volunteered, and the honour of our respective stations prevented me from pressing him.

'He has not yet run out his guns, My Lord', I said. 'Nor has he demanded a salute.'

'Waiting to see what you will do, then, Sir Matthew. And who you are, as you have not hoisted an ensign. So precisely what do you intend to do?'

I looked him squarely in the eye. The question had consumed me since the Danish ship was first sighted. 'I intend to send a boat across to parley, my lord. Lieutenant Farrell, in the first instance, and Mister Jeary, who speaks a little of the Danish from his time in these seas. Thereafter, perhaps myself. If the captain is a man of honour, he will accept that we have invaded his master's territories out of necessity, not out of malice.'

'As the Danes claim Teddiman did at Bergen, Sir Matthew? I imagine they are now more than a little sceptical of English intentions, and of English promises, when it comes to incursions into their waters.'

There was the crux of it, of course. God knows how very different it had all seemed but eight or nine months before. Our war against the Dutch had begun so promisingly: the first battle, off Lowestoft in

June, had been a great and glorious victory. The Dutch flagship blown up, thousands of their men killed, their entire fleet put to flight... For his supposedly eminent part in that triumph, the young captain of the ancient *Merhonour* had been honoured by his king and born anew as Sir Matthew Quinton, an altogether more august being – aye, one even worthy of being immortalised in broadsheets. But the victory was soon overshadowed by recrimination and disillusion. The fleeing Dutch ships had managed to escape to fight another day, seemingly through the treachery of a craven courtier aboard the English flagship. King Charles, horrified by the slaughter that had come literally within touching distance of his brother and heir, our admiral the Duke of York, forbade his return to command for the remainder of the summer's campaign. Meanwhile the plague paraded the streets of London like a confident whore, drawing more and more into her boudoir, the lime-filled grave pits. At least a hundred thousand poor souls died, and the court withdrew first to Salisbury, then to Oxford, trying with little success to turn deaf ears to the siren voices that proclaimed the pestilence to be nothing less than divine judgement upon the immorality of Charles Stuart.

Yet news of the arrival of a fabulously laden Dutch return-fleet from the East Indies had fired anew the king's enthusiasm for the war. A squadron under Sir Thomas Teddiman was detached to intercept them in the harbour of Bergen, an accommodation to such effect having been made with the ruler of that neutral shore, the King of Denmark. Or so monarch, ministers and mariners erroneously believed – right up to the moment when the guns of Bergen opened fire on Teddiman's ships. In the aftermath of the battle, King Frederik denied knowledge of any prior accommodation with his cousin King Charles. Instead, he protested against a foul and unprovoked invasion of his territory, and prepared for war against our Britannic kingdoms. He was joined in this course by a far grander potentate: the Most Christian King Louis the Fourteenth of France, no longer able to avoid the inconvenient terms of a treaty of mutual defence that he had concluded with the Dutch some years earlier. That, then, was the most unhappy situation of England, and of those of us upon the quarterdeck of the *Cressy*, in those early months of the happy new year of 1666: as not a few pointed out, the date that contained the Number of the Beast. England was at war, or soon would be, with the entire coast of Europe from the Arctic to the Pyrenees, apart from a pitifully few miles of German and Flemish beach,

I looked away from Lord Conisbrough toward the menacing shape of the great Danish warship.

'My orders enjoin me to avoid conflict with the Danes if it can be avoided,' I said. 'But if the Danish captain wishes it, I will give him battle.'

My confidence was born of calculation. The more I considered the odds, the more firmly I came to believe that we could at least hold our own. We were smaller, but that would give us the advantage in manoeuvring in these confined waters. I would wager my fortune (not that it was substantial) upon my gun crews being able to outshoot the Danes; the Cressys were all volunteers, veterans of the previous summer's campaign and in some cases of the previous Dutch war too, whereas the Danes would have less experience and would all have been recruited very recently – since the debacle at Bergen – so the crew facing us was bound to be new and untried. And yet they knew these waters, and we did not. If the *Cressy* grounded upon an uncharted rock, even the least experienced gun crews on earth could batter us into matchwood at their leisure.

I do not know if Conisbrough was contemplating the same contingencies. He certainly studied the Danish ship intently for some moments, exchanged a glance with his page boy, and then turned to me. 'If I may, Sir Matthew, I believe I should make the visit to the Danish captain and seek to reach an accommodation with him. I speak their language well enough.' My face must have betrayed my bemusement. Conisbrough seemed to weigh his next words with especial care: 'My name also has a certain repute in these parts, Sir Matthew. It may not be without value.'

I weighed the issue. I had no idea of the basis for Conisbrough's strange boast, but surely it could do no harm to send him over to the Danish ship in triple harness with Kit and Jeary? The latter could report what he and the captain said to each other, while a peer of the realm might prove a useful buttress to Kit's authority as a commissioned officer of the King of England.

It was only much later, as the rotund and hospitable Captain Jan-Ulrik Rohde entertained us all in the great cabin of the *Oldenborg*, that I realised my mistake. Jeary reported that the first few sentences Rohde and Conisbrough had spoken to each other were in Danish, but thereafter they spoke exclusively in French. And neither my ship's master nor my lieutenant spoke that tongue, which I myself spoke with a fluency learned at the knee of a grandmother born and bred in the Val de Loire. Even so, the upshot seemed evident enough. Rohde confirmed that King Frederik had not yet formally declared war, and thus we had good enough reason to avoid hostilities here, in our tiny corner of the Norwegian sea. He even offered the *Cressy* a pilot, a local man of Flackery, but both Jeary and the Trinity House that had certified him competent for the voyage were confident that our master could guide us safely through the maze of islands and onto a true course for Gothenburg. Captain Rohde made a jest of it, hinting that I was fearful he was going to fob off upon me some madman who would run us onto the rocks. Thus we parted in good humour, and I prayed that the duplicity of kings would not soon make us enemies.

* * *

I was in my seabed, rocked by the motion of the moderating deep, trying to sleep but recollecting the day's events.

Consider my Lord of Conisbrough, my restless thoughts demanded. A mere passenger, bound for Sweden solely to assess the wellbeing of his estates? A mere passenger, whose very name and word seemed able to prevent a fight to the death between the *Cressy* and one of the King of

Denmark's mightiest vessels? We, your restless thoughts, think not, Sir Matthew Quinton. And now let us consider the words of Kit Farrell, words forgotten until the tolling of the ship's bell proclaims it to be one of the clock. 'A three-decker. At sea in February.' Aye, Kit, rare indeed. In England, to see a three-decker upon the brine before April is as rare as a sighting of the unicorn.

Upon that thought I rose, wiped sleep from my tired eyes, and walked to the great stern window. After a few moments, I became accustomed to the light and made out the hull of the *Oldenborg*, black and brooding upon the dark waters. The Danes were moving one of their greatest men-of-war during the depth of winter, a time when no realm ever sent its great ships to sea. One of the ships from Kristiansand, Kit had said, presumably moving down to Frederikshavn or Copenhagen to join the rest of King Frederik's fleet. True, the fact that she was more lightly armed than an English ship of her size made her more seaworthy in such a season, but that did not materially alter the case.

I stood until our bell rang again, taking in the full knowledge of what lay in front of my eyes.

Thanks to Conisbrough, we had no war today. But as God was my judge, the very fact of the *Oldenborg's* presence there, fully manned and fully gunned, meant that war with the Dane was coming. Add that to our war with the Dutch, and our war with the French, and as I stood upon the deck of my cabin in the *Cressy*, it seemed easy to believe that all too soon, we would be at war with all the world.

Chapter Two

Moses tells us that the span allotted to a man is threescore years and ten.

I, who have long surpassed that ideal, can testify that this is but the blinking of an eye. Yet how astonishing will it seem to future generations that almost entirely within my own lifetime, a great empire rose, flowered and perished? Why, even now there are young blades who find it inconceivable that barely twenty years ago, there was a glory and a legend that bore one name: Sweden. This land of rock and forest on the edge of Europe, where the sun for months on end never deigns to shine; this kingdom with few resources and less money; this realm of few people, and they made mad by cold and darkness – this same nation once bestrode Europe like a colossus. As a child, I learned and was enthralled by the tales of the hero-king Gustavus Adolphus, the Lion of Midnight, who conquered half of Germany, terrorised the Holy Roman Emperor and petrified the Pope before falling at the moment of his greatest victory. As a boy, I was intrigued by the myths and scandals attached to the name of his daughter Christina, the scholar-queen who favoured men's attire and finally gave up her throne for the love, not of a man, but of the abstract theology that some men call Popery. As a young man I idolised her successor Karl the Tenth, who marched an entire army across a frozen sea to crush Denmark and won vast swathes of new territory for the Three Crowns of the Swedes, Goths and Wends. And so the Swedish empire rose, driven by the Gothic legend that they, the Swedes, were invincible, and their Lion of Midnight would return to sweep popery and ignorance into the sea, bringing a new age of enlightenment to Europe. How incredible it seems now, even so few years after that entire empire crumbled to dust. Yet then, in the winter of 1666, the Sweden into whose waters the *Cressy* sailed was at the height of her power and fame, her armies and fortresses ringing the Baltic from Bremen to Finland, her sword-won territories controlling every great river that flowed from Germany into that sea.

We made our landfall at the isle of Wingo, upon which stood the beacon marking the entrance to the road of Gothenburg. With the wind at west-by-north, Jeary took us a little to the south and then due east for the small, low islet of Grytan, whence we turned north by east through the sea-gate. Stretching away to both starboard and larboard was a myriad of islands, some large, others little more than rocks. Many were dotted with rough fishermen's huts; here and there castles stood upon promontories, high-towered affairs with lofty pinnacles, so unlike our squat English fortresses. Every piece of land we could see was crowned with a thick covering of snow. The archipelago reminded me greatly of the western coast of Scotland, where I had finally confronted my destiny as a seaman. A few hardy fishermen were out in their little craft, and a large Lubecker passed us on the opposite tack when we were off the island of Branno, but otherwise the sea was empty. Few merchants would imperil their precious cargoes in a frozen, storm-wracked February, and the two principal nations who commonly plied these waters, ourselves and the Dutch, were at war with each other, multiplying the risks and thus the insurance costs. Since leaving Flackery we had sighted several small Dutch capers, optimistic privateering craft whose captains had evidently put to sea in the hope that some English skipper or other would be foolhardy enough to try and run home from Gothenburg before the spring. How their hearts must have sunk at the sight of the vast *Cressy*!

We made our way slowly through the archipelago. Here again, Jeary was confident enough in his knowledge of these waters to reckon we could dispense with the services of a pilot, although the busy throng of little craft that started to ply around us as we approached Gothenburg begged to differ. Each claimed to offer the services of the finest pilot in West Sweden, derided our folly in navigating these waters without his services, and proclaimed that we would certainly come to grief on any of the vast rocks that had mysteriously come into being since our charts were drawn.

I surveyed the scene from the quarterdeck, content to leave the conning of the ship entirely to Jeary. Phineas Musk and Lord Conisbrough were alongside me, looking out onto what for the noble lord was clearly a familiar spectacle: he named this island and that castle, identifying the owners of many of them. A surprising number seemed still to be the property of the former queen, Christina, whose abdication had evidently not condemned her to poverty. At length, I asked Conisbrough what I might expect in Gothenburg. After all, God alone knew when we would find a conjunction of wind and tide that would permit us to put to sea with an entire mast-fleet of eight ships, even if that fleet were ready to sail at a moment's notice – and knowing the nature of our English ship-masters and seamen, I doubted if that would be the case.

Conisbrough looked across to the distant shore of the mainland, a rocky strand of jagged cliffs and hills. For such a vast man, the eyes set within his ugly face were remarkably small, the eyebrows almost feminine. 'Gothenburg is a viper's nest,' he said slowly. 'The Dutch and English vie against each other, waging their own private war on this foreign sod. There are Dutch inns and English ones, and woe betide any man foolish – or drunk – enough – to enter the wrong door. Like most of the city elders, the *Landtshere* – that is the name for a governor in this country – namely, the noble Baron Ter Horst, favours the Dutch. He is no friend of the English. His father was a Dutchman, and the entire city was built up by the Dutch, less than half a century past.

But the Gothenburgers are shrewd. They know full well that the rest of Sweden detests the Dutch as being the age-old ally of the Dane, so they tread carefully. Sweden is neutral, so Gothenburg pretends to be neutral, but all know where the city's true sympathies lie.' Conisbrough turned to face me directly. He was a truly vast man; I was of a goodly height, one of the few men at his court able to look Charles Stuart in the eye, but I felt myself dwarfed by this hirsute titan before me. 'But trust not too far among the English of Gothenburg, Sir Matthew,' he continued, 'for our race in its turn is divided between royalists and the old Commonwealths-men, the Cromwellians, and all kinds of skulking fanatics who have made the place a safe haven.' Musk looked at him with unfeigned interest: an unexpected opportunity to crack a few round heads was suddenly opening up before him. 'Why,' said Conisbrough, 'Gothenburg even harbours a regicide, who walks brazenly in the open here and does not even fear lest the wrath of King Charles might put a blade in his belly.' Conisbrough's speculation was not outlandish: eighteen months before, one of the fifty-nine vile traitors who signed the late king's death warrant had been murdered at Lausanne by an Irishman shouting '*vive le roi!*' as he pressed the pistol to the rogue's head. Needless to say, our court (and my mother, who had her own very private reasons for detesting the regicides) had rejoiced heartily upon the tidings. 'Then, of course, there are the Scots,' Conisbrough said, 'who endeavour to profit their own enterprises, regardless of the war and regardless of the purchasers.'

'They sell to the Dutch?' I protested.

Conisbrough nodded.

'But that is treason!'

The noble baron smiled. 'Your Scot has an elastic notion of treason, Sir Matthew, especially if a goodly supply of florins might be in the offing. The Scots factors in the pitch and tar trades have greatly fattened their bellies by shipping cargo after cargo to Amsterdam since this war began.'

Musk nodded in vigorous agreement; he had little love for those whom now, since the late Union, we are meant to call 'North Britons' and embrace as our dear neighbours.

The king would hear of this, I vowed, feeling a sense of loyal indignation at such behaviour. Thus distracted and irritated by the perfidiousness of the North Britons, I entirely overlooked the real import of what My Lord Conisbrough had told me.

'Well then,' I said, 'I see I shall need to be on my guard in this Gothenburg of yours, My Lord. I pray our sailing with the mast-fleet is not unduly delayed, lest we become too embroiled in this northern Sodom.'

'Doesn't sound so bad,' said Musk. 'Sounds much like Colchester.'

'I have not yet told you the half,' said Conisbrough heavily. 'There are also the Danes, resentful of the Swedes' triumph over them in the late war and outraged by what they call our perfidy at Bergen. The city is full of them, for you know how close we are to their lands. They will seek an early blow against England to redeem the honour of their realms, you can be sure of it. And there are the Swedes themselves, of course. Their great victories have made them almost as arrogant as the French, but they have also become more peevish among themelves. Not a day goes by there without swords being drawn for and against the High Chancellor, or for and against a restoration of the late queen.'

'The late queen? Christina?' I said, with some surprise. 'But she converted to Catholicism and removed herself to Rome! Can there be Swedes who favour her return?'

Conisbrough nodded. 'She is a Vasa, of their own dynasty, unlike the German cousin to whom she resigned the crown. The child of Gustavus Adolphus, their hero king. Many will forgive her anything, even her religion, and there are even many true Lutherans who would rather see her back on the throne than the feeble dullard of a boy who occupies it now.' As Conisbrough implied, King Karl the Tenth had died suddenly at the height of his fame but six years before, leaving a backward child of four to succeed him. 'Indeed, some say Christina seeks just that,' said Conisbrough. 'You know she returned from Rome, a few years past, to assert her right to succeed young Karl if he should die? But the visit served only to remind her of how cold Sweden is. Ever since, she has not stirred from the Roman sunshine.'

Musk blew onto his hands. 'Can't say I blame her,' he said.

So this was our destination. A vipers' nest. I thought back to how grateful I had been when the Duke of York, Lord High Admiral of England, entrusted me with the command of the *Cressy*, one of the few ships of such size set out over the winter, as a reward for my gallant services in the previous summer's campaign. I recalled the delight of my wife – that is, of Cornelia, Lady Quinton, a title she deployed like a First Rate – at the prospect of the pay that would accrue to me for this voyage (it being common practice for the masters of merchant ships under convoy to provide 'gifts' to the captain of that convoy, quite apart from the wages that His Majesty might eventually deign to pay, many months in arrears). I had envisaged an easy winter's cruise, bringing back the mast-ships before our main fleet fitted out for the summer's campaign. I hoped for a good command – one of the vast new Third Rates at the very least – but as a knight and the former captain of a Second Rate, albeit a small and ancient one, I might even have some expectation of hoisting my own flag. It was a notable transformation for someone who could barely have told fore from aft just five years since; but Conisbrough's words, and our encounter with the *Oldenborg*, made much of my confident optimism fall away. Even setting aside all of the potential pitfalls that lurked ashore in Gothenburg, it was certain that by the time we sailed, England would be at war with Denmark, just as she was with the Dutch and the French. And I did not relish a second meeting the jovial Captain Rohde, this time at sea and with our battle-ensigns hoisted.

* * *

'Twenty fathoms and firm ground!' came the leadsman's call. Seth Jeary, at my side upon the quarterdeck, nodded in quiet satisfaction; that was the depth assigned to the main channel in our waggoners, so there seemed no danger of the ship being cast upon the exposed rocks that seemed to be encroaching ever nearer on either side. If the current were more leewardly, as it seemed it often was, we could not have got in; but the great seas that had struck us off Norway had abated. Jeary had his course set upon the tower of a distant church which the chart named as Arsdalen. Meanwhile I had my telescope trained upon an island a little way to the south of the church, upon which stood a large and very modern fortress. The batteries of very large cannon were clearly visible upon the ravelins and ramparts; batteries just as clearly manned and ready. From the great square tower in the fort's midst streamed the swallow-tailed yellow cross upon blue banner of the Three Crowns.

'The castle of New Elfsborg,' said Lord Conisbrough, who was also upon deck; still resembling a Viking chieftain in his great wolfskin covering. 'The principal seaward defence of Gothenburg.'

'Then we shall have to exchange salutes with it,' I said. 'I propose giving them eleven guns. Will they accept and return that, My Lord?' The matter of proper form in salutes was always of intense concern to a king's captain; to give more guns in salute than were merited, and to receive too few (or, most heinously, none) in return, would be a grave dishonour to the sovereign and nation that I served. A dishonour that could be answered only with a broadside and, if necessary, a war.

Conisbrough nodded. 'Eleven will suffice for New Elfsborg, in my experience, and they ought to return you three. That is the protocol I have witnessed before. But it is by no means certain to be observed. Ter Horst is a prickly fellow and no friend to the High Chancellor, so even if he has had orders to receive us properly, there is no guarantee he will do so. Much will depend on whether the captain of the garrison panders to him or fulfils his higher duty. If you so wish, Sir Matthew, I could go across and attempt to adjust matters.'

I pondered the courses available to me. I could send a boat across as Conisbrough suggested and negotiate an agreement over the number of guns to be given and returned; but in the Mediterranean three years before, when commanding the *Wessex*, I had witnessed just such a situation develop into a three-week stalemate with neither side able to agree, a farce that ended only when I sailed away shamefacedly and without my convoy. Moreover, was it not a diminution of both the person and the honour of his nation honour for a nobleman of England to demean himself and haggle with some low-born Swedish soldier? Better, I decided, to sail boldly toward this castle of New Elfsborg, give the Three Crowns the eleven guns, and place the onus entirely upon the captain of the fort. And if that became the onus for starting a war between England and a fourth great nation, then so be it.

'I thank you, My Lord,' I said to Conisbrough, 'but I think we will adjust matters in naval fashion. Lieutenant Farrell and Mister Blackburn!' I cried. Kit came up onto the quarterdeck from the ship's waist, stood before me and saluted. It was still curious to see him as a lieutenant, clad in breastplate, sash and sword, rather than as the bluff young master's mate I had first encountered four years earlier; but I, who had been entirely responsible for his elevation, was also not a little proud of my creation. Alongside Kit stood the ship's gunner, a brisk, lively fellow of fifty or so named John Blackburn who had served in the artillery train of the King's army during the civil war and claimed to have personally fired the shot that breached the walls of Bristol.

'We have no guarantee of a return of our salute from the Swedish castle, yonder,' I explained, 'and equally no guarantee that they will accept our eleven as sufficient. So we would be advised to prepare for any eventuality. Thus we shall clear for action, but as quietly as possible, Mister Farrell. We shall man the larboard guns, Master Gunner, but there must be no unusual bustle upon the upper deck. The Swede must not see that we are prepared to do battle.'

My old friend frowned. 'Sir Matthew, should we not at least discover whether they are prepared to return our salute?'

I record his words as he spoke them. Nowadays, such questioning of a captain's direct order publicly, upon his very quarterdeck, would probably place the lieutenant squarely before a court-martial. Then, sixty years ago, there was still a freer intercourse between captains and their officers. The latter were readier and more able to proffer advice, and the former had not yet given themselves the god-like airs and graces that they assume these days. The young Sir Matthew Quinton certainly had not. No; I remember the words so vividly because this was the first time that Christopher Farrell, whose station in life was entirely of my creation, ever sought to contradict me.

As it was, my answer was equable. 'We dare not risk what the French call an *impasse*, Mister Farrell. We could lie here for a fortnight, sending our boat back and fore, and at the end of that time, still have the same outcome as if we sail past their guns upon this tide. And the delay might have cost us the moment to bring out the mast ships. From now on, every week – every day – will see more and more Dutchmen and Danes upon the sea. Our necessity and our honour alike impel me to resolve this question of the salute at once.'

Kit still seemed unconvinced, but he was too good an officer and too firm a friend to argue the matter. He went below, and almost at once I heard the Cressys clearing the decks as silently as they could manage. Even the Cornish managed to restrain themselves from singing as loudly as was their wont, contenting themselves instead with quietly humming some strange tune of their land.

'Mister Farrell and I share an opinion of the honour of the salute,' said Musk in his customarily gruff manner. This was what passed for discretion from Phineas Musk: his way of informing me in public that I was being an obstinate stickler for a principle that in private he would proclaim to be unworthy of using to clean his breech.

I tried to tell myself that neither Musk, a low-born rogue, nor Kit Farrell, a plain tarpaulin, understood that for the heir to Ravensden, honour was tangible: so real, so potent, that it seemed almost alive. But I saw something in the eyes of Lord Conisbrough, who was of a lineage at least the equal of my own, and it did not suggest that he agreed with my notion of honour.

The *Cressy* had taken in most of her sails. We moved through the waters at barely walking pace. Those waters now carried rafts of ice down from the Gothenburg river; rafts that bumped into the hull of the *Cressy* like visitors knocking loudly upon a door. The larboard battery of eight-pounders upon the upper deck was manned by the gun crews who would fire the blank rounds in salute to New Elfsborg, which drew ever nearer. What the men on the castle walls could not see was the scene below, on the covered main deck, where my men crouched over the demi-cannon and culverins of the larboard battery.

Closer, then closer still. The eyes of the men on the upper deck turned nervously in my direction. Conisbrough and Musk at my side, both inscrutable. Kit Farrell in the waist, doing his duty but clearly thinking that a Captain Farrell would be handling the matter differently. A nod to Gunner Blackburn, and the foremost eight-pounder fires and recoils, the smoke hanging over the deck in the light airs. Then the next gun gives fire. Then the next, and so along the battery and back to the forward gun until we have fired eleven times.

A stillness in the air. From the ramparts of New Elfsborg, not a movement; no gun fired either in salute or in anger. The captain is calling my bluff. Very soon, I will have to decide whether to accept an insult to the king's flag or to fire in earnest, with God knows what consequences. Conisbrough says nothing, but his whole body indicts me, insisting that I should have followed his advice and permitted him to go over to the castle and negotiate an agreement.

Apart from the shrill call of the sea-birds and the wind in our remaining sails, there is silence; and that silence seems to last for ever. We come level with the castle island. Through my telescope I see the man who must be the commander of the garrison, armoured and cloaked, his eyepiece trained just as intently upon me. The guns upon the frost-encrusted ramparts remain silent. We are almost past the island. I wish my friend Francis Gale, vicar of Ravensden, is with me upon this voyage, for his prayers had proved mightily efficacious in the past –

A puff of smoke upon the lower rampart, followed by the sound of the blast. That moment of uncertainty when one waited to see if a ball would throw up a water spout in the sea, or tear through a sail, or through a man –

No ball struck us. A second gun fired, and a third. No more. The castle of New Elfsborg has returned the *Cressy*'s salute. Honour has been satisfied. Captain Sir Matthew Quinton walks to the quarterdeck rail and orders Lieutenant Christopher Farrell to stand the men down. Two young men look upon each other afresh, and critically.

* * *

We bore up into a large bay of brade water behind the castle island, where our charts showed ten fathoms and a good roadstead, and there dropped anchor. This was some way short of the town of Gothenburg itself, which lay upstream, but the young officer on the boat that came out to us from New Elfsborg informed us that the river was frozen over a little way west of the town; besides, I wished to remain in an anchorage that gave me sea-room in the event of unforeseen circumstances. This caused no little grumbling among my crew, who knew that the further out from the city we moored, the less likely their prospects of leave. But in the light of Lord Conisbrough's account, I was of the opinion that adding a large cohort of Cornishmen – ferociously loyal to me after several voyages together, but still the most violent and volatile souls upon God's earth – to the potent brew of troubles already extant in Gothenburg would be akin to tossing a lighted candle into our powder room.

The next morning, the *Cressy*'s longboat took Conisbrough and I ashore, making landfall on the south side of the estuary beneath the ruins of the Old Elfsborg castle. This shore was one of the principal anchorages of the port, and was thronged with moored shipping: Lubeckers, Hamburgers, some Scotsmen, but above all the ubiquitous Dutch in their flyboats, some already deeply laden and awaiting a fair wind for Holland, most high in the water and presumably hoping for a thaw that would allow them to go up to Gothenburg to load.

Phineas Musk, restored to his customary condition after the travails of the voyage, eyed the serried ranks of our enemy with calculation. 'They'd make a pretty bonfire,' he said at length, his words forming a little cloud in the chill air.

'Perhaps we'll catch a few of them at sea on the return voyage,' said Kit, at his side upon the wale in front of my privileged position at the stern of the longboat.

'Easier to put a torch to the lot of 'em here,' said Musk.

I smiled. 'You have a pretty disregard for the laws of war, Musk. Neutral waters, remember.'

'War is war,' Musk replied, 'and show me the man who invented the notion of "neutral". Was there "neutral" in the war between the Philistines and the chosen people? I think not.'

There was a laugh from Peregrine, Lord Conisbrough, seated beside me; his attendant, the nervous, silent youth North, was further forward, toward the bow of the boat. 'Pray God the king never sees fit to make you an ambassador, Mister Musk,' said Conisbrough merrily.

Ours was a short voyage, but a bitter one; we could get no nearer to the town by virtue of the frozen channel upstream of the castle, and the presence in the water of great lumps of ice made the oarsmen's task onerous. I had never seen the likes of John Treninnick and George Polzeath, stout Cornishmen both, gasp for breath, but that was their condition long before we reached the shore. I prayed that none of them suffered frostbite, for although all wore self-knitted woollen mittens with which to grip the oars, I doubted that garments appropriate to wet Cornish winters would suffice in this harsher northern land.

Several horsemen awaited us at the jetty. One, a stocky and cheerful young major of the governor's retinue, bowed with an exaggerated flourish and made an extravagant apology in flawless French on behalf of the most noble Landtshere, Baron Ter Horst, who regretted that urgent business precluded his greeting us in person. Nevertheless, he looked forward to entertaining us shortly in his city of Gothenburg, where he would pay proper respect to the esteemed representatives of His Britannic Majesty.

As we mounted, Conisbrough murmured, 'I expected Ter Horst to keep us waiting for days.'

'Surely he is merely doing what any loyal viceroy of the Swedish King ought to do, My Lord?'

'And that is the troubling aspect, Sir Matthew. The Landtshere's sole loyalty is to his own aggrandisement; for him to behave as a loyal viceroy ought to do is out of character He hates the English, yet he is making every effort to show us honour. We should be upon our guard, I think.'

We set off for Gothenburg. This was almost as treacherous a voyage as the *Cressy*'s through the archipelago; the land was covered in snow, the grey clouds threatened more, and the road was little more than a ribbon of ice stretching across a treacherous, undulating landscape. Yet my horse took it in his stride, as though he and I were upon a gentle summer's stroll through the meadows of Ravensden. Conisbrough rode a little way ahead of me, conversing animatedly in Swedish with the young major, while Musk and Kit were a little behind, discussing how old England was brought low by the seemingly universal presence of corrupt time-servers in all parts of our public affairs.

We rode around the side of a great hill crowned by a stout castle, and there before us lay Gothenburg. It resembled many a town or small city of the Netherlands; unsurprising, as it had been planned and built by Dutchmen. It was a new foundation, the major explained, of no significance at all but a half-century before, when King Gustavus Adolphus decided to build it up as Sweden's gateway to the west. Surrounded on three sides by moats, ravelins and bastions, and on the fourth by the great river, the town consisted principally of grid-patterned streets of two-storeyed buildings, some of brick but more of timber, the whole bisected by canals. Three edifices stood out: two churches, one squat and English-looking, the other with a fine thin spire in the German style; and a large, long, red-brick structure that the young major called the Crown House, a kind of arsenal. It was within that building, he said, that the young child Karl had been proclaimed King following the sudden death of his warrior father. The slight breeze brought to us a powerful smell of wood-smoke and tar.

'Look there, Sir Matthew,' said Kit, riding up to my side, 'the mast ships.'

He pointed out into the great river that ran to the north and west of Gothenburg. Many ships lay within it, but one group was unmistakeable: eight vessels moored together, two by two, deeply laden and with their upper decks piled with large wooden beams that would one day form yardarms. Below decks would be even greater lengths of timber: the future masts that would propel the *Cressy* and her like to victory over England's foes. That is, once the mast-fleet was released from the vast sheet of ice that encased it and all the other ships in the Road of Gothenburg.

'We shall summon the ships' masters after we are done with the governor, Lieutenant Farrell,' I said. 'Although God knows what we shall discuss, for our sailing is evidently entirely in His hands.'

My heart sank. My intention had been to sail within days, to be back in England well before the start of the new campaign against the Dutch. This plan now seemed to lie in tatters, confounded by the unremittingly vicious snow-bearing north wind that assailed my face. Kit Farrell knew me well enough to divine my thoughts.

'Thaws can come on fast in these waters, Sir Matthew. Faster here than on the Thames above London Bridge, for certain. We could still be away within the month – if the masters are ready, that is.'

I was not reassured. 'Kit, you know as well as I the depths of prevarication and incompetence that our merchant skippers can plumb. It will be a miracle if we sail this side of doomsday.'

'Come, Sir Matthew, these men have been trapped here for months, through the whole of the winter, for want of a convoy. Surely they will be ready to sail upon the thaw?'

Kit was by far a more experienced seaman than I, despite being of the same age, so I deferred to his opinion. But privately, I held to my doubts.

We rode through the outer lines of fortifications and came to the south gate of the city, a fine structure bearing a statue of the late King Gustavus Adolphus within a niche in the wall. Brass cannon poked out of the embrasures atop the ramparts. Guards came to attention as we passed through the gate unchallenged, much to the disgust of the long queue of ordinary citizens seeking admittance. Within the ramparts, Gothenburg was a very Amsterdam in miniature, narrow houses rising from narrow streets on either side of a frozen canal. The narrowness of our way forced us into single file, and the young major shouted back to me that we were fortunate: if the canal had been clear and the stevedores able to work upon the stranded barges, it would have taken us hours to get through the throng. As it was, the conditions had driven all but a few hardy and well-wrapped souls from the street. Yet other eyes were upon us, glimpsed occasionally looking out of windows or from shadowy doorways. In those eyes I saw a gamut of human emotions: utter unconcern, curiosity, suspicion. And rather too often for my comfort: hatred.

At the head of the canal, and at right angles to it, was an even broader waterway, lined by warehouses and grander houses. We rode across a wooden bridge that could be opened to allow the passage of shipping – not that any of the craft frozen within the ice had any prospect of moving until a thaw came. Some of these were quite large, and one flew an ensign that I recognised at once: a red field with a blue canton bearing the cross of Saint Andrew. A Scotsman, then, and a privateer by the look of her, mounting some twelve guns. Her shrouds were crusted in ice, like those of every other vessel stranded in that great canal, but unlike the others, she was not entirely deserted: a stout man with no left leg stood upon the deck, gripping his crutch tightly, seemingly impervious to the cold and staring brazenly at us as we passed. On the far side of the waterway was the large German church that I had spied from outside the city. We rode beneath its walls into the broad public square that lay beyond it, dismounting before a large building that resembled many of the town halls I had seen in the Low Countries. The stairs leading up to the door were guarded by an impressive body of pikemen.

The major led us up into the heart of the building, into a large chamber beneath a fine wood-vaulted roof. Two great fires made it blessedly warm. Several dozen well-dressed men and a smaller smattering of women stood around, regarding us curiously: burghers and other dignitaries of the city, Conisbrough whispered. In the centre of the room stood a round, jowly creature in a breastplate crossed by a sash of blue and yellow. In truth he looked about as unlikely a military man as Phineas Musk, whom indeed he vaguely resembled.

'Ter Horst,' said Conisbrough in a low voice. 'Still as self-satisfied a worm as when I last saw him.'

The major stepped forward and made an announcement in Swedish, evidently proclaiming the entry of the 'Baron Konigsburg' and a creature called the *riddare* Matthias Kven-don.

The jowly personage stepped forward, smiled, and embarked upon a long speech of welcome in a high, thin voice and bad French, remarking upon his delight at this re-acquaintance with his old and dear friend the noble Lord Conisbrough, the honour done to his city by the presence of the famous Sir Matthew Quinton, who had distinguished himself in arms so mightily, and his earnest desire to be of service to the most esteemed King Charles. As Ter Horst droned on and on, my attention wandered. I noticed that the same was true of Kit, but in his case, his attention had wandered toward the only young woman in the room, a comely creature with fine yellow hair and a smile that revealed her at once as the daughter of the Landtshere. Moreover, she seemed to be returning Kit's interest in her with an ample measure of her own.

I was only dimly aware of Ter Horst's peroration. '... and thus, my dear English friends, I rejoice that I am in a position further your great king's stated aim of reconciling old foes, of putting behind you the divisions and enmities of your land's troubled past.'

There was a pause. I glanced at Conisbrough, whose expression was unreadable. Ter Horst seemed quite inordinately pleased with himself. His other guests smiled knowingly at each other in anticipation of whatever spectacle was to come.

A door opened at the far end of the hall, and a man stepped forward. He was perhaps of my brother's age or a little older: a thin man with a sallow, unremarkable face and a calculating expression, clad in an ordinary black raiment. To me the features were unknown, but for those older than I, that was evidently not the case. I was aware of a growl from Musk, behind me. I saw Conisbrough's eyes narrow. He said one word: 'Bale'.

I felt a shock as intense as any I had known in battle. It was as though the air had been sucked out of the room and the icy wind outside had hammered its way through the very walls. I felt myself sway. I looked into the eyes of the newcomer, and he into mine.

I was looking upon the face of the man who had killed my king.

Chapter Three

I had seen the document. My brother and my uncle showed it to me in the muniment room of the Parliament house, a few days before the king's coronation. I had read the words. By the time I came to the warrant's grim peroration, I was in tears at the enormity of it, the rank injustice, the sheer affront against natural order and the law of God:

> ... he hath been and is the occasioner, author, and continuer of the said unnatural, cruel, and bloody wars, and therein guilty of high treason, and of the murders, rapines, burnings, spoils, desolations, damage, and mischief to this nation acted and committed in the said war, and occasioned thereby. For all which treasons and crimes this Court doth adjudge that he, the said Charles Stuart, as a tyrant, traitor, murderer, and public enemy to the good people of this nation, shall be put to death by the severing of his head from his body.

I had looked beneath those words, and seen the fifty-nine signatures that ordered the severing of the head of the Lord's Anointed. I had read the first of the names, ahead even of the confident scrawl of 'O Cromwell'. A single, fateful, fleeting word, the shortest of signatures.

Bale.

John, Lord Bale of Baslow, was the only peer to have subscribed his name to the death warrant of King Charles the First, Saint and Martyr. By virtue of his rank, he signed first of all those hell-bound devils, the most evil men in the entire history of the kingdom. John Bale killed a king, and by so doing he had become the foulest of traitors to my rank and kind, the nobility of England. My mother brought me up to detest the regicides; upon my tenth birthday, she made me swear that if ever I encountered one, I would imperil life and limb to avenge our slaughtered sovereign. I needed no encouragement, although I did not know then – did not know until very recently – that my mother's wrath was born in part of having once been the slaughtered sovereign's lover. As it was, to every one of my friends, to every cavalier in the land, the regicides were the greatest anathema, the most notorious murderers ever to walk the earth. Many had already met righteous justice in the courts and upon the scaffolds of the restored King Charles the Second; those like Cromwell who had avoided such retribution by inconveniently dying beforehand were exhumed from their grand tombs, given a posthumous execution and cast into common grave-pits. Others had been tracked down and despatched by loyal agents of truth and retribution. But a few were still at large, and now I, Matthew Quinton, breathed the same air as one of them.

'What monstrosity is this, Ter Horst?' growled Conisbrough. 'How dare you insult His Majesty so?'

The Landtshere feigned perplexity. 'An insult, My Lord? How can it be so, when I merely seek to implement your king's own policy? And surely you, My Lord Conisbrough, have especial cause to embrace My Lord Bale –'

Still stunned by the dread apparition before me, so few yards away, I did not fully comprehend what Ter Horst had said to Conisbrough. I was thinking only of my oath to my mother, an oath given a new and powerful impetus by the astonishing knowledge I had acquired so few months before: that the king whom Bale had put to death was my mother's lover, and perhaps the father of my brother Charles. My heart screamed at me to draw my sword, cross the room and bury into deep into the foul murderous heart of John Bale –

'– but remember, My Lord, I am the Landtshere of Gothenburg, and thus bear the full authority of the King of the Swedes, Goths and Wends in this city. There will be no disharmony, no ill words and above all no violence here, in my own quarters. Is that not so, My Lord?'

Conisbrough's face was a mask. 'As you say, My Lord Ter Horst.'

He bowed to the Landtshere, and reluctantly, I joined him. Ter Horst smiled and moved away to greet Bale. Conisbrough turned to me and led me to the side of the hall.

'How Ter Horst will have enjoyed that,' he said. 'See how greatly amused he is by our discomfort, and what sport his people make of us. This whole occasion has been nought but one great joke at our expense.'

'What can we do, My Lord?' I demanded urgently. 'This is the gravest dishonour imaginable, to ourselves and to our king!'

'Think I'll just slip outside to piss,' said Musk. 'Might be a long one. Long enough to still be there when that king-killing fucker comes out.'

'A noble aspiration, Mister Musk,' said Conisbrough, 'but it cannot be so. You see why, Sir Matthew, do you not?'

My feelings still raged within me like a sea-storm, but I was clear-headed enough to perceive the truth. 'For us to kill Bale would play into Ter Horst's hands,' I said. 'It gives him an excuse to persecute all the English in Gothenburg. Perhaps even to prevent the sailing of the mast-fleet. All to the advantage of his friends, the Dutch.'

'More, too,' said Conisbrough wearily, 'but that is sufficient for now, I think.' He looked across the room. Having made his point, Ter Horst had left Bale and moved off to join his own coterie, who were clearly highly amused at our embarrassment. Conisbrough nodded. 'Very well,' he said. 'I think it is time to disappoint the noble Landtshere.'

To my surprise he strode boldly across the hall, making directly for Lord Bale. The regicide watched his approach intently, a cold smile upon his villainous face. Conisbrough gestured toward a vacant space at the other side of the room, and after a moment's hesitation Bale turned and followed him. The two noblemen of England fell into a whispered but evidently urgent conversation.

'To be a fly upon the wall behind them,' said Musk. 'As if a fly could survive in this damnable city of ice.'

I looked around the room. 'But that would not be the only wall to be a fly upon, Musk.'

Musk followed my gaze to where Kit Farrell was attempting to find some sort of *lingua franca* in common with Ter Horst's daughter, apparently with some success. 'Hope she's not got her father's sense of humour,' said Musk, gruffly.

A sudden commotion at the other end of the room made me turn. Lord Bale was irate, but his eyes suggested more than mere anger: even from a distance, it was easy to see that he was tearful, not simply enraged. He stabbed a finger angrily at Conisbrough. 'We will meet next in Hell, My Lord!' cried the regicide. He pushed past the giant figure of Conisbrough and pushed brusquely through the throng toward the door directly behind me.

I know not what instinct impelled me, but I stepped directly into Bale's path. I was aware of Ter Horst's and Conisbrough's eyes upon me, respectively urging and decrying the rashness upon which I must have seemed intent.

The regicide stopped barely a yard from me. Confused from his quarrel with Conisbrough, he looked at me blankly. Then he frowned. 'You will be Quinton,' he said. The voice was old beyond his years, and tired.

I knew not what to say. I could not take in the enormity of it all. I was within a sword's length of this most vile, most unforgivable of sinners. Suddenly I was aware that somehow, unconsciously, my hand had come to rest upon the hilt of my blade. All I had to do was draw and strike. None of Ter Horst's men were near enough to stop me. In one stroke I could end him, fulfil my childhood promise to my mother, and earn the undying gratitude of my king and my country.

For what seemed a very eternity, Matthew Quinton and John Bale stared each other out.

Strangely it was Conisbrough's page, the boy North, who burst the bubble. I had not been aware of him near my side, but like every good attendant, he knew his master's mind well: he spoke exactly the words that Conisbrough himself would surely have spoken, were he in North's place.

'Not here, Sir Matthew. Not now.'

I was overwhelmed by an apprehension of the enormity of the moment. I had been perhaps a heartbeat away from dragging England into war with Sweden. What lesser outcome could there be for the cold-blooded murder of a man granted sanctuary by the Landtshere of Gothenburg, under that dignitary's very roof? And that act of murder would surely also be suicide for he who wielded the blade. My mother might have been proud that I died so, but my wife would have been inconsolable.

John Bale sensed my condition. He looked upon North curiously, nodded, and said calmly to me, 'No, Sir Matthew Quinton, not now. But we will talk, you and I. Count upon it.'

He brushed past me, his right arm touching mine. The arm that wielded the pen which signed the death warrant. The shock ran through me like a lightning bolt, and my hand shook.

As Bale left, I struggled to comprehend his words: *we will talk, you and I*. Not *fight*, which was surely the only and inevitable outcome between a king-killer and a cavalier. Instead, *talk*. But what, under heaven, Matthew Quinton and John Bale possibly find in common to talk about?

Phineas Musk stepped up to me. In such circumstances, I was never entirely certain whether he came to see how I fared or to reprove me for not acting as he would have done.

'Should have gone for that piss,' Musk said. 'I'd be out there now. With a blade.'

I took a deep breath and looked my old retainer in the eye. 'And I have no doubt, Musk, that it would have been the last piss you ever took. Bale will have his own bodyguard, of that you can be certain, even before one reckons upon Ter Horst's soldiers.'

I remembered what Conisbrough had told me of the rival gangs that stalked the streets of Gothenburg. In such a hell-hole, a man like John Bale would only be able to walk abroad with a small army at his back; and if the place was as full of malcontents as Conisbrough said it was, Bale would find footsoldiers enough. As the tumult of my thoughts subsided I gave thanks for my prescience in denying immediate shore leave to the Cressys, although I knew I could not long delay the moment when my stout lads poured ashore to add to the heady brew that was Gothenburg. It was easy to make Phineas Musk see reason and not bring on the diplomatic crisis that I myself had very nearly precipitated; I doubted if I would have the same success with drink-filled Cornish seamen whose fathers and brothers died loyally and heroically in the service of the king whom Bale had murdered.

Conisbrough and Kit Farrell joined me, the former intimating that we should withdraw and thus deny Ter Horst the pleasure of further sport at our expense. Kit seemed downcast at that, and it was not difficult to divine the cause of his displeasure. He stole a long backwards glance at the maiden Ter Horst, who returned his farewell with a wistful smile.

* * *

My intention had been to summon the mast-ship masters to attend me on the *Cressy* on the following day, but the unanticipated brevity of our reception by the Landtshere meant that even a winter's day in Sweden still had several hours of daylight left to it. Moreover, following my febrile encounter with Lord Bale I felt a deep need for the reassuring certainties of the sea-business; even a gentleman captain of King Charles could feel a sudden and overwhelming need to feel a deck beneath his feet. I had been unsettled more than I could say by my encounter with the regicide, and there was still a part of me that felt I had betrayed my mother and my king by not executing the villain there and then. Thus I determined to visit the mast-fleet immediately, and sent Kit ahead to forewarn the masters. Conisbrough and his page left us, apparently intending to secure rooms at an inn known to be favourable to English king's men. Musk and I pressed on, passing the stranded Scots privateer and following the directions Conisbrough had given us to the west gate, close to the boom that by night sealed the entrance to the Great Canal. Uncharacteristically Musk said nothing throughout our journey, seemingly intent on keeping his footing upon the treacherously icy roadway; but he had known me since I was a child, and no doubt sensed the strange conflict that was raging within me.

We emerged through the walls of Gothenburg, past the export warehouses filled with pitch and tar and the import sheds brimming with Spanish leather, Cadiz salt, Syrian textiles and Scottish wool. As we walked out onto the narrow strip of land that fronted the river, a grand paradox presented itself. What should have been a wide and busy waterway was transformed instead into a great white field, a grand carpet of ice. Men walked upon it as though strolling in a pasture. Stalls had been set up near the clusters of stranded ships, selling wares that seemed to range from roasting chestnuts and fish to aquavit and wolf-furs.

'A veritable frost fair,' said Musk. 'Remind me, Sir Matthew. Just when did you say we would be back in England?'

'You are impudent, Musk,' I said, without conviction.

'So your grandfather told me. And your father. And your brother. Your mother too, while we're about it. But it seems to me that pointing out your mast fleet is stuck fast in the ice can't be impudence, Sir Matthew, not when we can walk all the way to it, which seems to me to be that which learned men call a *fact*. Might that not be so, Sir Matthew?'

I did not answer Musk, but it was impossible to deny the force of his argument. The ice was as solid as the paved floor of Westminster Abbey.

We approached the mast ships and could now clearly see the principal difference between them and ordinary merchantmen, which loaded their holds through hatches in the upper deck: instead, the mast ships had two large ports cut in their sterns, immediately below the windows of their masters' cabins, through which the vast wooden pinnacles could be loaded horizontally.

Kit came out to meet us. He was attended by a small guard of men, each bearing a musket and looking upon me suspiciously. My lieutenant saluted and said 'The masters await you aboard the *Thomas and Mary*, Sir Matthew.'

'And their temper, Mister Farrell?'

Kit smiled. 'Akin to the weather, Sir Matthew. Inclement.'

We boarded the *Thomas and Mary*, the largest ship of the fleet. Kit led Musk and I below to the master's cabin, a low, dark space which bore only a passing resemblance to the captain's cabin of a man-of-war. Eight men stood within. Their expressions told me at once that this would not be an easy encounter.

'Friends,' said Kit, who would know how to mollify these tarpaulins if any man could, 'I name Sir Matthew Quinton, the heir to the most noble Earl of Ravensden and captain of His Majesty's ship the *Cressy*!'

If the introduction was intended to impress, it evidently had little effect. The eight looked me up and down appraisingly, but the hostility did not leave their visages. At length, though, one stepped forward. He had a great gut but no left arm. 'John Gosling. Master of the *Thomas and Mary*. Here, Thomas Crafts of the *Hopewell*, Tom Simpson of the *Last-offe Merchant*, Dick Noble of the *Charles*, Tom Tyndall of the *John and Abigail*, Nathaniel Adams of the *Gloucester*, Jack Tilford of the *Delight*, Joss Burlingham of the *Unity*.'

'I greet you all,' I said, assuming my most knightly air. 'I commend you upon the state of your ships and the preservation of your cargoes through what must have been a trying winter.'

The one named as Tyndall, a short and beetle-browed fellow, snarled 'Aye, only trying 'cos you wasn't here four months ago.'

Kit glanced at me, but I ignored the disrespect. 'His Majesty and His Royal Highness regret the exigencies of the service did not permit the earlier despatch of a ship to convoy you home –'

'And which exigency would that be, then?' snapped Tyndall. 'That there was no money for a convoy, or they simply forgot about us?'

This time Kit did not wait for a signal from me. 'You will speak with due respect to Sir Matthew!'

Gosling, evidently the spokesman and a more moderate man, scowled at Tyndall, who fell silent, but not before I thought I heard him mutter to his neighbour, Adams, some remark about 'fucking butterfly gentleman captains'. 'Our apologies, Sir Matthew,' said Gosling. 'But we have been as impatient to sail as Sir William Warren has been to receive our cargoes.' The great timber merchant, this; a man whom I had encountered only by reputation, but who was said to have tricked our Navy Office, notably the bustling Mister Samuel Pepys, into signing a vast mast contract on terms most favourable to himself.

'Just as the navy has been impatient to receive them from Sir William,' I said, I trusted in a pleasant and reassuring tone. 'But if you please, Master Gosling, I would have some notion of the size of your cargoes.'

Gosling shrugged. 'The inventories are open for your inspection, Sir Matthew.' He gestured toward a small mountain of documents and sailcloth-bound books upon the cabin's much-repaired table.

A man-of-war captain dealt daily with a monstrous pile of paper: lists, letters, musters, inventories. I needed no more. 'No doubt, Master Gosling. But in summary, please?'

The man looked at his fellows as if to suggest I had asked him for the moon. 'Five hundred and twenty-six masts, Sir Matthew. The best Swedish spruce and fir. The biggest mast fleet to sail for England in many a year. The most, seventy-one, aboard the *Delight*. The tallest, one of twenty-three hands and two of twenty-two, here on the *Thomas and Mary*. Most of the masts of sixteen and fifteen hands.'

'And there'll be no more,' said the man who had been introduced as Burlingham.

'Aye,' said Gosling, 'that's likely.' My face must have been blank, for he continued 'You'll not have heard, then, Sir Matthew? But the news would have reached England after you sailed – if it's got there at all. There's to be an embargo on all cutting for seven years. Conserving stocks, the Swedes say. But we know different.'

'Their Chancellor's in the pocket of the French,' said Noble of the *Charles*. 'And before he announced the embargo, the French duly bought up all the remaining stocks. 'Twas a miracle Sir William got his hands on a consignment this big. But there'll be no more, so you brave captains had best take down the Dutch ere long.'

'Now the Danes are coming into the war too, they'll cut off the supplies over in Danzig and Riga,' said Gosling. 'So we'd best hope the ice melts soon and you get us home safe, Sir Matthew. Without our cargo, you'll have no navy by the end of summer – or at any rate, no ships with masts that can bear a sail.'

I glanced at Kit, but he had no comfort for me. This was dire indeed. During the great fight off Lowestoft in the previous summer, I had witnessed at first hand the awful frequency with which masts were felled in battle. I recalled the crack of great timbers, the roar as yards, shrouds and canvas fell to the deck. Our foes, the Dutch, fired high on the uproll to achieve precisely that end. In a nutshell, then, the number of replacement masts aboard the fleet, together with those in the dockyards, meant that the fleet could fight perhaps another two large actions, maybe three, before all of our great ships became mere immobile hulks. The previous war had seen seven battles, and then we were fighting only one opponent, not three.

'Well then,' I said, aware that in such a case a king's captain ought to show bravado rather than self-doubt, 'we shall do just that, my friends. When the ice melts, the *Cressy* and her captain will indeed see you safe home to England. You have my word upon it.'

* * *

By the time we emerged from the cabin of the *Thomas and Mary*, night was falling fast. The cold was already as bitter as any I had ever experienced, but Gosling counselled that it would be yet worse within an hour or two.

'To attempt a return to the *Cressy* before morning would be folly, Sir Matthew,' said Kit.

'Aye, folly,' said Musk brusquely. 'I have mutiny in mind if you even suggest it.'

'Very well,' I said heavily; the force of their argument was undeniable. To risk the unfamiliar road back to where the *Cressy*'s boat was berthed, in winter darkness and the extremity of this unimaginable cold, seemed indeed the very height of folly. 'We shall seek out My Lord Conisbrough and his vaunted friendly inn –'

My attention was taken by a sudden glimpse of light on the far shore, less than half a mile away. I walked across to the starboard side of the ice-bound *Thomas and Mary*'s poop, the better to make out the unexpected sight. Kit, Musk and Gosling joined me at the rail.

'Three fires?' I said, chiefly to myself. 'They seem to be upon the ice, Mister Gosling.'

'Strange, Sir Matthew,' said the mast-ship master. 'There is but little habitation on that shore. I have not seen fires in that quarter on any of the nights we have lain here.'

As we watched, dark shapes seemed to move in front of the flames. It took a few moments more for the truth to strike me. The flames were coming nearer. I could hear a distant but unmistakeable sound of hooves: the hooves of galloping horses.

I turned to Kit, but he had already divined the question I intended to ask him. 'We are under attack,' he said bluntly.

Gosling bawled for his men to assemble on deck at once with swords and loaded muskets. The other seven mast ship captains emerged, heard

Gosling's hasty explanation and ran to the ladder that let them down from the side of the ship onto the ice. Orders were barked to the nearest ships ahead of us in the ice, the *Charles* and the *Unity*; we heard the repeating cries to the further ships in the line. As frantic English voices broke the calm of a Swedish winter night, I primed my pistols and awaited our foe.

'Riders are taking an almighty risk, going at the gallop upon ice,' said Musk as he snatched a musket from one of the *Thomas and Mary*'s crew and began to prime it as though he had not a care in the world.

'There are no riders, Musk,' I said. As I squinted my eyes against the dark and the cold, I was more and more certain of what confronted us. The flames moved at a constant forward speed behind the galloping horses, which could be glimpsed from time to time as silhouettes against the fiery light. But the flames also had a different momentum, horizontal, then upward –

'Fuses,' I said. 'Barrels of powder lashed to rafts of wood, pulled by horses desperate to flee from the flames.'

A crude weapon, impossible to guide with any accuracy – but with so little distance between shore and target, and the eight mast-ships moored close together in ranks of two, the attackers did not need to concern themselves with precision. Our ship-masters' natural urge to cluster together for mutual security had created a vast and surely unmissable target. The horses must have been held until they were in a frenzy, then sent off toward the mast ships with cracks of the whip. Instinct would make them seek out the gaps between the ships, but that, in turn, would swing the deadly rafts around, bringing them close enough to the hulls for even an approximately adjacent detonation of the powder barrels to wreak considerable damage.

The thunder of hooves upon the compacted ice grew louder. The beasts neighed frantically, desperate to escape the terror they drew behind them. Gosling's men lined the rail, levelling muskets and attempting clumsily to load and aim a couple of six-pounders, but these were clearly men unused to their weapons. Kit ran to instruct the gun crews, but I cursed my decision to leave my men aboard my ship. If only I had brought a leavening of the Cressys with me –

A great flash of light, a thunderous roar, and the rightmost fire-raft blew itself apart, perhaps three hundred yards short of the ships. I heard the terrible death-agony of the horses pulling it, but thankfully was spared the sight by the vast cloud of smoke that rolled toward us.

'A poorly set fuse,' said Kit. 'God be thanked –'

His words were cut off. Nervous and afraid, a few of Gosling's men reacted to the blast by opening fire at once. Their fire was crude and aimless.

'No man fires but upon my order!' I cried. Gosling glared at me, but neither he nor his men dared usurp the authority of a Quinton warrior knight. 'All of you – take aim upon the nearer horses! The horses, not the raft!'

Obeying my own command, I levelled my own pistols toward the nearer threat. The other raft and its horses had pulled away well to our left, heading for the middle of the mast fleet. The men there would have to shift for themselves.

'Steady, lads!' I cried. 'Check you're truly primed, check you're not firing your ramrods! Hold your fire – hold – hold – *give fire!*'

The guns of the *Thomas and Mary* belched out. I fired my two pistols at once, feeling the pain in my shoulders as the weapons kicked back. The smoke stung my eyes and filled my nostrils. Our fire had been ragged; these were no musketeers of the Duke's Regiment, that much was certain. And as my eyes cleared, that impression was confirmed. The horses had been hit, had slowed and were stumbling, but still they were coming on toward the ships. The fuse behind them showed no sign of joining its fellow in detonating early. And now the deadly cargo was perhaps no more than a few dozen yards away –

'*Give fire!*'

I turned to see Kit Farrell play the part of gun captain and apply a lighted match to the linstock of the nearest six-pounder. The gun spat a great tongue of fire and recoiled viciously across the deck, trapping the leg of a man who was too slow or stupid to get out of the way. The fellow's cry of agony was echoed in an instant by an almighty explosion as the oncoming raft of powder barrels was struck by Kit's shot and blew to kingdom come. The blast was close enough to send wood and horse flesh alike crashing into the hull of the *Thomas and Mary* and the men upon her deck. Something struck me and span me round. Off balance, I fell heavily to the deck. I must have been stunned for some moments, for I was suddenly aware of Musk shaking me. As I opened my eyes, I saw barely a foot away upon the deck that which must have struck me: the left half of a horse's head, its single eye staring unblinkingly at me.

I climbed unsteadily to my feet in time to witness the explosion of the other raft. Without a captain and lieutenant of the navy royal to direct their fire, the other ships had never stood a chance of repelling the assault upon them. I could not see the full impact of the blast; the ships immediately ahead, the *Charles* and *Unity*, were intact, so the raft must have struck the vessels ahead of them. The fireball carried aloft ships' timbers and human limbs alike. I had seen ships blow up at the Lowestoft fight the year before, and knew that although damage had been done, the stricken mast-ship had not been destroyed. But this was still the crisis; if the fire was not controlled upon the damaged ship, or if it reached its powder magazine, it might start a reaction that could destroy the entire fleet. We could not cut cables and move the ships apart: we were all embedded in the ice as firmly as well-founded houses in good honest earth.

'It'll be the *John and Abigail*,' said Gosling. 'Tyndall's borne the brunt.'

I recalled the rude fellow who had taken issue with me so recently in Gosling's cabin. 'Keep a half-dozen men with you in case of another attack, Captain Gosling,' I ordered. 'The rest, with me to the *John and Abigail*.'

Kit, Musk, Gosling's men and I climbed down onto the ice and ran forward, past the inert hulls of the *Charles* and the *Unity*. As we passed the latter we could see the damage to the *John and Abigail*, and I gave thanks to God that it was not as bad as it could have been. Much of her starboard midships planking had been staved in by the blast, but her frames seemed intact. Tyndall might have been an insolent scoundrel but he evidently knew his business: he already had chains of men bringing up leathern buckets from his hold to douse the small fires that had broken out upon his deck and precious masts, and was giving brisk orders to the parties of fresh men arriving from the other ships. The *John and Abigail*, and more importantly the entire mast-fleet, would be spared.

'We could search back to the shoreline, sir, following the horses' tracks,' said Kit as we drew breath under the stern of the damaged ship.

'Our assailants will have long gone, Lieutenant,' I said, 'and if they have not, I do not propose to divide the force available to us here in case they make another attempt upon the ships.'

'Bale, it'll be,' said Musk, gasping for breath. Running was not his accustomed condition. 'That vile regicide and his Dutch friends. Satan's infernal imps, the whole damn crew of them.'

As Kit organised the crewmen from the *Thomas and Mary* and those from other ships who were not engaged in fire-fighting into a defensive picket, I gave thought to Musk's words. Bale. He was the likeliest suspect, of course. This scheme to destroy the mast-fleet might have been crude in its execution, depending upon the paths taken by terrified horses and the notoriously random timing of powder fuses, but there was clearly intelligence in its conception. To launch the attack only when all of the captains were gathered together aboard one ship was inspired; it ensured confusion aboard the leaderless ships. Yet our assailants must have known the meeting was taking place, and that could only have been betrayed to them in one of two ways. Either they had been sent the intelligence by a sympathiser in the mast-fleet itself, or they were cognisant of my order to meet with all the captains. Perhaps they had even followed me from the Landtshere's residence. For another catalyst had undoubtedly inspired the timing of the attack: me. The arrival of the *Cressy* meant that the time available to our enemies for an attempt on the mast-fleet had suddenly decreased dramatically; when the ice melted we would sail at once, and our foes were aware of that simple fact. But such an immediate attack also sent out a very clear warning to the *Cressy*'s captain. Be on your guard, Sir Matthew: you do not impress us, for see how we greet your arrival?

The assault upon the mast-fleet, the impudence of Landtshere Ter Horst, the malevolent presence of Lord Bale: all demanded a response. And as I stood upon the ice, watching the last remnants of the last fire-barrel burn itself out, I knew precisely what that response should be.

Chapter Four

I made my way from the captain's cabin of the *Cressy*, through the steerage, and up onto the quarterdeck. Behind me came those with whom I had just been in conference: the Lord Conisbrough (accompanied as always by the pale youth North, who spoke not a word), Captain Gosling as representative of the mast-fleet masters, Lieutenant Kit Farrell, Seth Jeary and Phineas Musk, nominally taking the record for my journal but as ever acting as my confidential advisor, my very own Father Joseph. Then all of the ship's warrant officers bar the ancient cook and the carpenter: Blackburn the gunner, Eade the chaplain, Hallam Everett the purser, and, thanks be to God, Martin Lanherne the boatswain, the leader of my Cornish following, whom I had been able to put into the post in exchange for the incontinent eighty-year-old veteran who served as the *Cressy*'s shipkeeper while she lay in ordinary.

It was the morning after the attack on the mast-ships; Kit, Musk and I had snatched a few uncomfortable hours of sleep upon pallets in the hold of the *Thomas and Mary*. Dawn brought a true reckoning of the damage caused by the ingenious fire-raft attack. Five men had been killed, all of them aboard the *John and Abigail*. Another five were maimed. But thankfully the ship itself and its precious cargo had survived. The thickness of the ice and the compacted snow on top of it had prevented any damage below the waterline, and Tyndall's quick response had ensured that although there was a gaping hole in its hull, the ship was not irreparable. I had already sent across Wat Haydon, the capable carpenter of the *Cressy*, and a number of his crew to assist with the repairs. With them had gone Julian Carvell, the sometime Virginian slave who now served as my coxswain, and twenty men to provide a guard upon the mast-fleet.

Upon the quarterdeck of the *Cressy*, swivel guns were now fastened to the ship's rail, and the sakers and eight-pounders were fully manned. Muskets had been distributed to the best shots among the crew, several of whom stood at both the larboard and starboard rails, as keen-eyed as any redcoat. Others were stationed in the tops, a perilous and mightily uncomfortable quarter upon such a bitter day. I doubted whether the assailants of the mast fleet would dare attempt anything similar upon the might of the *Cressy*, but the show of force would serve another purpose. The captain of New Elfsborg would certainly report the news back to Ter Horst, and I wanted the duplicitous Landtshere to hear of a *Cressy* bristling with guns and clearly ready for war.

I turned and looked out upon the waist of the ship, which was filled with most of the men of the *Cressy*. All wore as many clothes as they possessed; most had their Monmouth caps pulled well down over their ears, and there was barely a man not in woollen mittens that he had sewn himself. My men were cold and longed to be below decks – or, better, before a log fire in some tavern or in the arms of some naked wench – so there was an powerful imperative upon the captain to keep his speech as short as possible.

'Cressys!' I cried. All eyes were upon me. 'You know me. You know I have a fatherly concern for each and every man of you.' I looked directly at Luke Ollerenshaw, the ship's cook, at seventy-three by far the oldest man in the crew and thus capable of being his twenty-five year old captain's great-grandfather. His shipmates jostled him good-naturedly, and I heard a laughing reference to 'old father Quinton yonder'. 'Thus I have sought to spare you the manifest temptations and vices of the city of Gothenburg.' There was some growling at that; I knew from Kit and Jeary that the failure to grant immediate leave and an opportunity to explore those selfsame temptations and vices was a matter of discontent at the mess tables. 'But it seems I was mistaken, my friends, and you were right. See what my folly nearly brought upon us! Why, our enemies have even dared to make an attempt upon the masts that will propel our noble fleet to victory over the Dutch, the French and the Danes in the coming campaign! All because they had not seen the true might of the *Cressy* – the might of you, her crew!' That brought forth a cheer, albeit only a thin one; many were unwilling to stop breathing upon their hands, despite their mittens. 'So I intend to begin grants of leave immediately, mess by mess, for a day at a time.' A far louder cheer, and even a few hands punched into the air. 'We must keep a strong crew aboard lest our enemies attempt something upon the ship itself, but I have no doubt that a mess which overstays its allotted time ashore will be reproved in the very gentlest manner by that which it is meant to relieve.' Members of not a few rival messes glowered at each other. 'But I tell you this, men. Ashore, you will behave yourselves as true Englishmen. Thus there will be no thieving, no raping, no beatings of the good honest townsfolk of Gothenburg.' I leaned forward, assuming what I trusted was my most serious air. 'And if you take too much of the drink of these parts, and enter into brawls – oh, sirs, I assure you the wrath of your captain will be boundless! A man provoked, say, by the insults of a greasy Dutchman or a damnable Covenanting Scots rebel – or a man who came to blows with any acolytes of the foul regicide Bale – or an entire mess that took it upon itself to knock the heads of some of the noble Landtshere's guards – why, such men, upon the incontrovertible sworn testimony of a sufficient number of stout and loyal Englishmen, could expect the utmost severity, even up to perhaps three lashes!'

I let the words hang in the frozen air. A few of the more quick-witted and those who knew well their captain's humour, like the renegade Moor Ali Reis and the Scot MacFerran, caught my meaning at once, smiled knowingly and whispered reassurance to those around them. But there was much murmuring elsewhere, with some at the back of the crew, the men furthest toward the forecastle, seemingly convinced that I had warned them of thirty lashes. And in those more innocent and less brutal times, thirty lashes was very nearly the harshest punishment that even a court-martial ever bestowed.

'Let me be clear,' I cried. 'I want every man of every nation in Gothenburg to know that in this place, and at this time, there is a power that will not brook the scurvy assaults of foreign knaves and English traitors. There is a power abroad in Gothenburg that will uphold the honour of king and country, of captain and ship. We know the name of that power, do we not, men? The power bears the name of the battle where the flower of England, your very ancestors, cut down the arrogant pride of the rapacious foreigner. It is the name of Cressy!'

The lads at the foot of the quarterdeck rail cheered loudly, and as the acclamation rolled back toward the forecastle, so a chant began to issue forth: at first a menacing bass growl, then louder, more rhythmic, a battle-cry as terrifying as any employed by a barbarian horde against a Roman legion or by English archers against proud French knights on the very field from which the ship took its name.

'Cressy! Cressy! Cressy!'

Lord Conisbrough leaned over to me and whispered 'I pray you know what it is that you do, Sir Matthew. It seems to me you have cried havoc and let slip the dogs of war.'

'Blood. Cracked skulls,' murmured Musk, who seemed to have entered some kind of delectable private reverie of his own.

'My Lord,' I said, 'I have sailed with many of these brave lads for three or four years now. I can think of no finer body of men to stand up for the honour of England, or to send a signal to our foes that they attack us again at their peril. As you told me earlier, My Lord, Ter Horst will not place a guard around the mast fleet – no doubt pleading strict neutrality, that he cannot guard our ships without granting an equal right to the Dutchmen in the harbour – and we should not give the man the satisfaction of even applying to him for one. So let us make sure that he and all our other foes in Gothenburg know that we are more than able to defend ourselves.'

Still the chant of 'Cressy! Cressy!' went on.

* * *

Half a glass later, the crew had dispersed and the first of the messes, as selected by Kit Farrell and Jeary, were going into the boats to make for the shore and twenty-four hours of drinking, whoring and fighting: the time-honoured litany of the English upon a foreign strand. Lord Conisbrough, too, made to go ashore at once, and Kit sought to accompany him, as he explained to me somewhat awkwardly during an audience in my cabin.

'I would – that is, I wish – Sir Matthew, I believe it might be advantageous for me to become better acquainted with this town of Gothenburg.'

His evident embarrassment made me merry. 'With the town, Lieutenant, or with one particular young lady of it?'

Kit blushed. 'Magdalena – the maiden Ter Horst – and I –'

I laughed and raised a hand. 'Kit, I would be the last man to stand in the way of your endeavours with the lady. Remember that I, too, found a foreign maiden in a foreign port – one who could speak not a word of English. Now she is the Lady Quinton, so who knows where you and your Magdalena might end? I take it she does not share her father's antipathy to we English?'

My lieutenant still blushed like a small boy caught stealing from an orchard. 'No, Sir Matthew. Nor any other of her father's inclinations. Thank you, Sir Matthew,' he whispered.

As he departed, Phineas Musk entered with a sheaf of papers in his hand; even he could not put off indefinitely the tedious duties demanded of a captain's clerk, despite knowing full well that his captain shared his aversion to the endless manifests and musters that required his attention.

'Never thought I'd see that one lovestruck,' said Musk with a backward nod toward the door through which Kit Farrell had exited.

'I trust it does not end badly, Musk,' I replied. 'End it surely will when we sail, but I fear her father's duplicity may play a part in it.'

'Could see it the other way, of course,' said Musk.

'The other way, Musk?'

'Friends at court, Sir Matthew. Might it not be to our advantage to have friendly eyes and ears in Ter Horst's house?'

Musk never ceased to astonish me: he, the very rudest of men, ever more inclined to the fist than the quill, could when he wished be as perceptive and Machiavellian as the king himself.

'Yes, Musk. Yes, indeed. I had not thought of that.'

He piled the papers unceremoniously onto my sea-table. 'A veritable feast today, Sir Matthew. The pay book to check and countersign, the new muster book to compare with the last one we made up before we sailed, the inventories of the gunner's and boatswain's stores to be examined. And Purser Everett craves audience when we are done, that you may countersign his letters of credit and bills of exchange so we may commence revictualling the ship.' Musk piled misery upon misery without a glimmer of a smile on his face. 'But at least you have some letters, too. Delivered to Sir William Warren's factor not three days past. Should have been delivered to us in Solebay, but missed our sailing. Then got put on a Danziger from Lynn which made a faster passage through the storm than we did. The letters first, I presume, Sir Matthew?'

'Indeed so, Musk. The letters first.'

There were a half-dozen or thereabouts. One was from Mister Pepys, the Clerk of the Acts to the Navy Board, enjoining me both to report on the sailing qualities of the *Cressy* following her recent refit at Woolwich and, entirely needlessly and pompously, to take especial care of the preservation of the mast fleet; as if a king's captain, already set to the task by his Lord High Admiral, would deliberately neglect such a duty! There was a missive from my Uncle Tristram, the unlikely Master of Mauleverer College, Oxford, reporting among many other things an item of news from the foreign gazettes which he thought might of interest to me in my voyage: namely that Christina, former Queen of Sweden, was said to have left her sumptuous residence at the Palazzo Riario in Rome to recover her health in the Apennines. (Tristram being Tristram, he speculated at length upon the likelihood that this was merely a euphemism for her eloping with her alleged lover, Cardinal Azzolino.) Then there were two letters from my dear Cornelia, both of them holding forth at some length upon the iniquity of the landlord of our rented rooms in Hardiman's Yard near the Tower and making distinctly unsubtle suggestions that these quarters were no longer appropriate for a knight of the realm and his lady.

I put down the second of her letters with a sigh. 'Lady Quinton seems determined to have me seek out a suitable new residence for us upon my return to England, Musk.'

'They tell me the King wants to sell Nonsuch Palace,' said Musk. 'My Lady would think that suitable.'

Of my young servants standing against the bulkhead, the feeble Ives and Upton remained impassive. But the lively Kellett smirked, and Musk shot him a glance akin to that of the Gorgon.

'Perhaps His Majesty can use the proceeds to pay me the prize money I am still owed for taking the *Oranje* in the Lowestoft fight,' I replied gloomily. 'What sort of devils incarnate are Admiralty lawyers when they can take eight months – eight months *at the very least*! – to determine whether or not a Dutch man-of-war, taken in battle in a state of formally declared war, is a lawful prize?'

'Be of good cheer, Sir Matthew. If we've now got war with the French and the Danes as well, who knows how many prizes you might take on this very voyage?'

Musk's attempts to make a man feel cheerful were well-intentioned, but his general demeanour of unremitting gloom meant that they were delivered with the air of a gravedigger who whistles a cheery air as he works. Hence I shook my head sadly. 'If we ever sail, Musk. And what prospect of prizes can there be when all I am to do is husband a gaggle of ungrateful tarpaulins back to England?

Consumed by such miserable thoughts, I looked again at the remaining heap of papers upon the table. My heart emulated Drake's leaden coffin and plummeted straight to the sea-bed of my soul. An afternoon and evening chained to the inkpot, straining my eyes by dim candlelight, seemed particularly unattractive when the mast-fleet might still be under threat and a vile regicide stalked the streets of Gothenburg –

Well, just so. A captain had a duty to keep his papers in order, but he also had a much higher duty. A duty that was now surely presenting itself in a most timely and convenient fashion. I brightened.

'Musk,' I said decisively, 'I think I should be ashore. To ensure that the Cressys are following my orders to the letter. To set an example. To be on hand if there are any difficulties. Mister Jeary can have the ship.'

The old man smiled. 'Had been hoping you'd say the like, Sir Matthew.'

* * *

We reached the southerly King's Gate of Gothenburg shortly before sunset, but the guards were already making ready to close the passage for the night. They were inclined to exclude us, but my loftiest tone and some of Musk's ripest abuse brought forth a young ensign who spoke good French and brought both his men and himself to a crisp salute for this English knight. The streets of the city were blessedly quiet: that is, there was no evidence of a battle royal between my Cressys and the citizenry, or with John Bale's coterie, or with the Landtshere's guards, or with the crew of the *Nonsuch* of Kinghorn, Captain Andrew Wood (that, according to Gosling, being the identity of the Scots privateer in the Great Canal, which had docked there in the autumn to repair damage sustained in a fight with a Dutch caper in the Great Belt).

'Strange, the way shadows form and dance on the snow and ice,' said Musk suddenly; an unusually contemplative comment for him. 'If he didn't know it was just shadows, a man could swear he was being followed.'

I said nothing, but I had the same uncomfortable feeling. More than once I glanced behind us, but none were in sight but the occasional townswoman, drunken boor or inquisitive dog. Yet the snow and ice created sounds, too, and echoing the crunching footfalls that Musk and I made, albeit further away, there seemed to be –

I endeavoured to dismiss the thought, but did not entirely succeed.

We came at last to the Sign of the Pelican, a large inn over toward the Saint Erik bastion, where Lord Conisbrough was well known and had taken rooms for the duration of his time in Gothenburg. It was owned by an Englishman of good repute and stout loyalties, he had said, and so it proved. As Musk opened the door, I could have sworn I was transported into the likes of the George in Bedford or the Swan at Biggleswade. The principal space was filled with English voices, many of them familiar and tinged with Cornish. Perhaps twenty Cressys turned, registered my presence, and saluted either conventionally or by raising their tankards. The minute but formidable John Tremar stepped forward. I had elevated him to a boatswain's mate for this voyage, and he took the responsibility seriously. Up to a point.

'Sir Matthew,' he slurred, 'Mister Musk. God blesh you both.'

'Tremar,' I said. 'All is well?'

'All well, sir. Landlord's a good man. Of Somerset, so better at least than a Devon whoremonger, and loyal to the king.'

The good man duly presented himself. He was of middling height, a lean fellow with a few wisps of hair remaining on a head that at one time had received a mighty blow from a blunt instrument, judging by the indentation on the right side of his skull.

'Lukins, Sir Matthew. Peter Lukins. Been in Gothenburg these twenty year, had this inn the last ten. Had the honour to know your brother, the noble Lord Ravensden, when he was here in the company of Lord General Brentford and poor Lord Montrose. And the Lord Conisbrough as well, of course.'

I glanced at Musk, who shrugged. He evidently knew what I had not, until this very moment: that my brother had been in this land before me. Moreover, he had been here with Ruthven, Earl of Brentford, the toothless and invariably drunken Scottish general to whom King Charles the Martyr had once entrusted the supreme command of his armies, and James Graham, Marquess of Montrose, the legendary military genius who nearly won back Scotland for the crown before being betrayed by his own side and summarily executed. What could have brought a Marquess and two earls, including a former Lord General and perhaps the greatest hero of the Cavalier cause, to meet in this frozen northern fastness?

'And when would that have been, Lukins?'

'Why, Sir Matthew, the year Forty-Nine. After His Late Majesty was shamefully done to death by traitors, one of whom stalks this very place to this day.'

Sixteen Forty-Nine: so much led back to that fateful year, which had begun with John Bale appending his signature to a large sheet of paper. I was but nine years old, learning my Latin grammar at school in Bedford (most reluctantly) and history, science and much else besides upon the knee of my Uncle Tristram (with unrestrained enthusiasm). My twin Henrietta and I knew that our brother, twelve years our senior, was somewhere beyond England's shore, condemned as a reprobate, malignant and traitor by the Rump Parliament that ruled the land with an iron fist. But Earl Charles was never spoken of by the two formidable dowager countesses, my passionately Anglican English mother and devoutly Catholic French grandmother, who warred incessantly over our religion, education and most other things; our only knowledge of his doings came from the occasional scraps fed to us by our vivacious fifteen-year-old sister Lizzie. I remember her whispering that Charles had been at the Escorial, and had seen King Philip; and on another occasion that he had been at the Louvre, and seen Cardinal Mazarin. But I could not recall her ever mentioning Sweden. If Charles had been here, it was one of the most closely guarded of my brother's many secrets.

Musk had already scuttled off, ostensibly in search of ale, for he knew full well that I would soon be tasking him to reveal all he knew about the time in 1649 when the Earl of Ravensden and two other of the royal Stuarts' most prominent supporters all came together here, in Gothenburg. But it occurred to me at once that Conisbrough, the man who knew this country and this town best of all, was likely to know much more.

'Bale will come to his judgment, Lukins,' I said. 'But tell me – is my Lord Conisbrough within his rooms?'

'No, Sir Matthew. Went out shortly after one with that page of his.'

I sighed. Nothing in this Gothenburg seemed straightforward. So there was nothing for it but to take some refreshment –

Suddenly I heard the sounds of a distant commotion. Even before I could buckle on my sword, the sound was no longer distant: raised voices, shouting urgently in a language I did not understand but which had to be Swedish, the clanking of weapons and armour, the thunder of large numbers of men running upon the hard streets.

'Think we've found the rest of the crew,' said Musk, returning with a tankard of ale in his hand and giving voice to the silent fear that was already taking hold of me. I had unleashed the Cressys upon Gothenburg. Even at that time, there were already prominent captains and admirals who thought it folly to grant leave at all, and nowadays their views prevail. Perhaps this was the first moment in my life when I sympathised with that draconian stance upon the issue. For what if I had misjudged my men, and they had committed some terrible crime?

I ran into the street, followed in short order by Musk, Tremar and the rest of our men. Soldiers bearing blazing torches were running toward us, and at first I thought my dreadful premonition had come true. But something was not right. If these men were seeking battle with a mob of rampaging Cressys elsewhere in the city, their behaviour seemed strange. They were not moving as a body, all in the one direction: at every alley, two or three men broke away and began thrusting their brands into doorways and dark corners. These were not men looking for a fight. Rather, they were looking for something, or someone.

Behind the main body of soldiers came a smaller party of half-a-dozen. There was Ter Horst, talking urgently with two officers; there Lord Conisbrough's attendant, the boy North; there Kit Farrell at the side of the shapely and not unappealing figure of Magdalena Ter Horst, who was covered by a sable-lined cloak.

'Lieutenant!' I cried.

'Sir Matthew! I had not expected you to be ashore – I have sent word to the ship –'

Ter Horst nodded curtly to me and hurried on with his subordinates; whatever he was about, he had no intention of sharing it with me.

'What is it, Kit? The crew?'

'No, Sir Matthew. Lord Conisbrough is missing. Mister North, here, reported it to the Landtshere barely a half-hour ago. I happened to be present –' he glanced coyly at the maiden Ter Horst, who could not understand a word he was saying – 'and joined the search. I encountered Carvell and some others of the larboard watch and have sent them around the city to give the word to the rest of the ticket-of-leave men. It is not a large place, sir. With the Landtshere's men and our own scouring the streets, it is only a matter of time before he is found.'

'Dead or alive,' said Musk bluntly, 'that is the question.'

North was shivering, but whether from cold or fear was impossible to tell. 'Mister North,' I said, 'how did My Lord come to be missing?'

'He left me shortly after two, Sir Matthew,' he said, avoiding my eyes. 'We were to meet at four, beneath the statue of King Gustavus in the main square. But he did not appear. I waited an hour, though I knew My Lord is never late.'

'Did he tell you where he had gone?'

'No, Sir Matthew. And that was unusual.' The miserable North was almost whispering and nearly in tears, seemingly overwhelmed by the enormity of what was happening. 'My Lord Conisbrough took me everywhere with him. He confided entirely in me.'

'He knows the city,' said Kit. 'He knows many people here. It is possible he could be with one of them – that for some reason he has been detained and could not meet with Mister North at the allotted time –'

Magdalena Ter Horst looked at Kit admiringly, but in entire ignorance of his speech. He was right, of course: Conisbrough knew the city well, better than any of us and perhaps even better than Ter Horst. But I also thought upon Conisbrough's own account of the dangerous enmities that lurked in Gothenburg. He was a vast man, an unmistakeable and immediately recognisable figure. Such a man, alone in such a place...

Then I recalled the regicide Bale's words. *We will meet next in Hell, My Lord!*

A man ran toward us from one of the side alleys, and both Kit and I put our hands to our sword-hilts. But the figure was unmistakeable, even if only as the shadow we saw for a moment before the man himself emerged before us: John Treninnick, the ape-like monoglot Cornishman who had the strength of five men. He could not speak his message in words we would comprehend, but his gestures were clear enough. He pointed urgently back down the alley whence he had come, toward one of the small canals that ran at right angles to the Great Canal.

It was only a matter of yards away. As I ran out of the alley I saw a small group upon the canal wall, holding blazing torches out over the frozen expanse. There were two or three Swedish soldiers and a half-dozen of my men, Julian Carvell and George Polzeath at their head. Carvell nodded downward, toward the ice.

I looked down, onto the frozen surface of the canal.

In one place, close to the bank, the ice had evidently been broken, and that recently. But the bitter cold had already frozen the surface water once more into a thin film of ice. Polzeath thrust forward his blazing torch to enable me the better to see into the hole.

I shivered uncontrollably. Perhaps it was the cold; perhaps it was the spectacle I beheld. There, framed beneath the ice, pressed against it like a child making faces in a window, was the unmoving head and the unblinking eyes of Peregrine, Lord Conisbrough.

Chapter Five

'This interview is concluded, Sir Matthew,' said the Landtshere of Gothenburg.

'But My Lord –'

Ter Horst bowed his head very slightly, turned upon his heel and left me staring at his departing arse. Being rumped by kings was intolerable enough, but to be rumped by this mere functionary, this jumped-up jackanapes, this *Dutchman* –

I turned and glared at Kit Farrell. 'You still tolerate the man? You can abide being in his house?'

My friend scowled. 'Are the sins of the father visited upon the daughter, then, Sir Matthew? And is he not right, that it is just as likely My Lord Conisbrough was killed by a Dane, a Dutchman or some other fanatic of our country's own making?'

Thus we both left the Landtshere's residence in bad temper. Ter Horst had rejected out of hand my demand for the immediate arrest of John Bale on suspicion of the murder of Peregrine, Lord Conisbrough; as, in truth, I entirely expected him to do when I marched post-haste to his door after ensuring that my erstwhile passenger's corpse was brought out of the canal and placed respectfully in a coffin following the removal of the all-too-apparent cause of death, a cheap dagger protruding from his back. But what I had not expected was the Landtshere's amused disrespect for the cause of the King of England, wrapped in silken but empty words of sympathy and reassurance. Nor had I expected Kit's evident affection for the Ter Horst girl to effected this unwelcome independence of mind on his part. Yet as we walked back in silence toward the Sign of the Pelican, I had to admit to myself at least a little of the justice of the other case. In truth, there were dozens, if not hundreds, of suspects for the murder of Lord Conisbrough and the attack on the mast-fleet alike. Was my condemnation of John Bale based upon evidence and the balance of probabilities, or upon my revulsion at the different and rather greater crime that he undoubtedly had committed? I prayed for some of the wisdom of my uncle Tristram, who was well versed in the law, but precious little of it seemed to enter into my thoughts.

With both Kit and I lost in such thoughts, we paid too little attention to our surroundings. It was another bitterly cold night, and there were few people on the streets. Built on the Dutch grid pattern, Gothenburg had a particular foible if the wind blew hard from the north-east, as it did that night: a man could walk for yards in perfect stillness, only to be struck by a sudden blast of the harshest and iciest of gales when he came to the junction of two streets. The force of just such a blast shocked me from my sullen contemplation: shocked me from it in time to see six men, all with dirks drawn, in the shadows at the street corners, three to one side, three to the other. Kit and I drew our swords and took up the stance of true guard, our rapiers held below the waist.

Two of the villains came for me at once, two from the other side for Kit. They were ugly, dirty brutes, the sort of desperate cutpurses one finds in any alley in any land. Evidently they were practised with the dagger, and were not fazed by encountering a proper sword. They attacked at once, one for the groin and one for the head, hoping that I could not defend against both; but swiftly turning my hilt and bringing my blade down, then sharply up, I deflected both of their blades with ease. Subtle now, they moved apart, hoping to make it more difficult for me to mount a similar defence against a simultaneous thrust at my sides. This might have succeeded against an incompetent, one of those buffoons-about-town who wear swords only for show. But Matt Quinton knew the principle of divide and conquer. I struck fast and hard, four quick steps forward through the icy slush, thrusting directly for the man on my right. He ducked aside and down, but my blade still struck home, albeit glancing his shoulder rather than impaling his chest. No matter. It gave me time enough to swing to my left in time to parry the rush from the other villain, who came at me most violently. The sight of my blade, extended and ready to meet him, gave him pause, and he began to circle back toward his wounded companion.

As I swivelled upon the icy street, I brushed falling snow from my eyes with my left hand and caught a glimpse of Kit, who was more than holding his own. A rapier, a gentleman's weapon, was still a relatively new weapon for Lieutenant Farrell, yet he ducked and stabbed, parried and lunged, with the dexterity of an Italian. In those few seconds of grace that were granted me to spectate, he executed a dazzling *trompement* and stabbed one of his foes in the thigh, though not deeply enough to disable him.

My own opponents had regrouped and were now joined by the two brethren who had hung back thus far. The wounded one took his left hand from his bleeding shoulder, wiped off the blood upon his damp breeches, and came at me one-handed, his companion at his side, the two fresh men a little behind them. They had learned from their initial mistake. Now four blades together aimed at one point, my heart. I could hope to deflect one, or two, but four? I sprang back, but my shoes slipped upon the ice and I very nearly overbalanced – without conscious thought or gaze, I brought my sword up and heard it strike steel –

When I looked again, my assailants had backed off once more. Somehow, I know not how, I had managed to deflect their attack, but whether I could do the same with another was moot.

A sudden cry – I glanced aside, and saw one of Kit's foes fall to the ground, clutching his stomach. Blood flowed into the ice and snow upon the ground. Kit had his remaining opponent in an armlock and was endeavouring to slit his throat with the blade in his free hand; but his very success meant that he was in no position to aid me against the final attack that had to be imminent.

My assailants were advancing abreast now, all four blades exposed against me. I backed against the wall of the house on the corner, my sword threatening each of them in turn. But these were odds that not even the great Cyrano would favour –

The roar of the musket and the explosion of my rightmost assailant's chest came as one. The shock of the unexpected blast fazed Kit's opponent, who ceased his resistance for a moment; and that moment was all Kit needed to inscribe a deep smiling gash into his throat. Pushing away the corpse, my friend charged furiously at the next rogue in the enemy line. His blade pushed deeply into the man's side, and the creature sank to his knees, a stare of astonishment upon his face.

I breathed hard and swallowed, trying desperately to stop myself fainting. Julian Carvell, wielding a still-smouldering musket, came up with Musk, Ali Reis and three more of the Cressys. He essayed a perfunctory salute. 'Sir Matthew,' he said in his familiar Virginian drawl. 'Mister Musk, here, reckoned you needed some assistance.'

'You followed us, Musk?'

The old scoundrel shrugged. 'Simply took the same road, Sir Matthew, a few yards behind. Seems to me this is the sort of town where a man's back is mightily exposed, and a tempting target for those inclined to plunge a knife into it.'

'I thank you, Musk. Once more.'

Kit was attempting to interrogate the man upon his knees, but it was clear there was little time in which to glean his secrets; the man's blood was flowing like a flood tide down his side, forming a growing red-black puddle in the slush.

'Who is your master?' Kit barked in English, repeating the question in Dutch. The man stared at him with cold contempt. Ali Reis, who acquired languages as easily as other men acquire warts, already knew enough Swedish to repeat the question in that tongue, but met an equally blank response. The man swayed, and it was clear his time was nearly done.

'*Qui est votre maître?*' I shouted in desperation. The man fixed a stare of contempt upon me. The stare turned blank, and he fell forward into the snow.

'We had best away, Sir Matthew,' Kit exclaimed, 'the Landtshere's guards are certain to be here soon.'

Half-walking, half-running, weapons at the ready, the small army of Cressys scurried along the frozen streets of Gothenburg toward the one place of safety within the city walls. The inn of the Sign of the Pelican already resembled a military camp. Treninnick, John Tremar and four other Cressys, armed with an astonishing collection of muskets, swords and half-pikes, patrolled in front of its door. Within, Cressys mixed with loyal Gothenburg English and Scots, talking in low tones of the ghastly slaying of the Lord Conisbrough and muttering dark threats indiscriminately against Roundheads, Dutchmen and Swedes alike. Two of the mast-ship skippers, Crafts and Tilford, sat within a corner booth; Kit made for them, seemingly finding the company of his fellow tarpaulins more appealing than that of his friend and patron. I was unconscionably hungry and could think only of eating a hearty meal before resuming the search for Lord Conisbrough's killer. But the hour was already very late, and God alone knew how such an expedition could make progress in the light of the antipathy of the Landtshere of Gothenburg –

Conisbrough's page, the youth North, stepped before me.

'Sir Matthew,' he said hesitantly, 'I congratulate you upon your most fortuitous escape, sir.'

'Thank you, Mister North, though fortune must give precedence to the fighting skills of my men, notably Lieutenant Farrell.'

'As you say, Sir Matthew.' I made to move away, but he reached out and gripped my arm with unanticipated force and urgency. 'A word with you, perchance?'

My reply was impatient; I had too many concerns to worry myself with those of this insignificant stripling. 'Do not be fearful, Mister North,' I said sharply, 'we will not abandon you to the Swedes, though your master be dead. You may keep your berth aboard the *Cressy* for safe passage back to England.'

'No, Sir Matthew. That is not my business.' There was now an unexpected determination about North's tone that made me scrutinise him properly. 'I would speak to you in private and in confidence, upon a matter of the very highest import.'

North's pale, childish face bore an unaccustomedly old look. Impatient as I was, something about his expression made me humour him. The innkeeper had a small room vacant toward the rear of the building; windowless and putrid, it was clearly not a favoured haunt of his customers. But it would suffice to despatch whatever insignificant troubles distracted this pageboy.

'Well, then, Mister North, be brisk and direct, I beg you. What is this matter?'

'First, Sir Matthew, I require your oath that you will not divulge what I am now going to tell you until such moment as I permit it.' Great God, this was too much – a Quinton did not prostrate himself to the whim of a schoolboy – 'Believe me, Sir Matthew, it is necessary.'

Still I resisted. I felt the indignation rise in me like a tide. 'For a mere page, Mister North, you demand too much.'

He nodded, and looked me directly in the eye. 'Men like myself are called upon to play many parts, Sir Matthew. That of a page is merely one of them. Indeed, it was the very part that I played in life until not too many years past. Page to My Lord Arlington, before his lordship divined that I might serve him better in another capacity.'

Arlington. That was a name well known to me; aye, and the harsh, unsmiling face accompanying it, with its hideous plaster-covered sword-cut upon the bridge of the nose. Henry Bennet, Lord Arlington, the king's principal secretary of state, chief intelligencer and God alone knew what else. His path and mine had crossed in the summer before, when a byzantine plot of his making had almost led me to grief.

I looked anew at Lydford North. Indeed, I now looked upon him properly and intently for the first time, and I saw that the feeble youth of our outward voyage had been something of an illusion. There were faint lines about the eyes that betrayed a man, not a boy; and those eyes were deep and penetrating. Perhaps, then, the scar upon the temple was not some school-time graze, but evidence of a more manly wound.

Somewhat unnerved, I raised my hand and swore upon my honour and that of the noble house of Quinton that I would keep Lydford North's secrets until the day of revelation. An oath that I now break by relating it: both North's cause and his bones have been dust these many years, and if there is to be a judgement upon me for breaking it, then I shall know it soon enough.

At my 'amen', North nodded. 'I have played a part, Sir Matthew, but so did My Lord Conisbrough. He was upon a mission of the utmost importance to His Majesty and to England's prospects in the present war.' The words were difficult to digest, but at once, they made sense: so much about the dead Conisbrough had marked him out as a man of far greater consequence than that to which he pretended. 'Consider our condition this new year, Sir Matthew, with an imminent triple war against the Dutch, the Danes, and the French. We would struggle to prevail against any single one of those enemies, Sir Matthew. A combination of two threatens us with defeat. War with all three might presage the very destruction of the kingdom –the very end of old England.' This was a dire litany, but I knew better than to protest against it; such talk was common in London before we sailed. 'Thus we need allies to divert our foes. Above all, Sir Matthew, we need a great power in the west as an ally, one whose very name will strike terror into our enemies. Spain will not favour us while we support Portugal's war against her, and we cannot forsake that as long as we have a Portuguese princess for our queen. Besides, endless decades of war have brought Spain low – De Witt and King Louis will simply laugh at the threat of Spain. Which leaves one land, and one only, where England might find the friendly power it so desperately needs. The one land with the name to afright England's foes.'

'Sweden,' I said slowly. 'You and Conisbrough were to engineer an alliance with the Swedes.'

The scheme was breathtaking in both simplicity and ambition. If Sweden, with its mighty army and navy, entered the war on England's side, Denmark would be hamstrung. The Dutch would be forced to divert entire squadrons to defend their own vital Baltic trade and would have to move their army to their eastern border to guard against invasion from Sweden's province of Bremen. Thus whatever opaque scheme King Louis of France was playing out in this war would most surely be stymied. Sweden the mighty, Sweden the invincible. The Lion of Midnight roaring alongside its cousins, the three lions of England. Of course. I looked upon Lydford North with newly found respect.

North smiled dismissively. 'I was merely an attendant, Sir Matthew, as you have observed. My Lord Conisbrough, though – who better as a secret envoy to the Three Crowns than a personal friend of the late King Gustavus? My Lord knew intimately all those who now hold power in Sweden – the Queen Regent, the High Chancellor –'

'Then his death is doubly unfortunate,' I said, sadly. 'His Majesty will have to despatch another envoy to complete his mission. Or if you truly have the confidence of Lord Arlington, Mister North, then perhaps you could undertake it yourself?'

North's expression was curious. 'I am a mere functionary, Sir Matthew – a boy, a nobody. Or so I would be perceived, I fear.' His tone suggested that his perception of himself was rather different; in that moment, Lydford North chafed to be a man of years, and at the very least a viscount. 'By the time a new envoy could be selected, and prepared himself for the expedition, and had a ship appointed for him – Sir Matthew, you know as well as any man the speed at which our English government moves. By then months will have passed, the moment will have been lost, and perhaps England will already be overrun by the armies of our foes.'

The dread had begun as the slightest dryness in my throat. By the time North concluded, it was a pounding within my head. For I could see beyond his logic, and knew full well what was in his mind.

'I have my duty,' I said tentatively. 'It is to the mast-ships. They are in danger here – who knows when another attack on them may be attempted? Besides, Mister North, I gave my word to the masters that I would see them home, and I cannot disobey the Lord Admiral's order to bring them safe back to England.'

'Nor shall you, Sir Matthew,' said North smoothly. 'But you have a higher duty too, as a knight of the realm and the heir to one of England's most illustrious titles. It is a duty that your honour, and your high birth, demands of you – that your king would demand of you, were he present.' A confident youth indeed, to divine the wishes of absent Majesty! And a relentless youth, too: 'You must take Lord Conisbrough's place, Sir Matthew. You must undertake the secret embassy to Sweden.'

'But I know nothing of diplomacy! I cannot speak Swedish – and I must bring back the mast-ships –'

North smiled, but it was a smile from the same mould as Charles Stuart's: the crocodile smile of the arch-dissembler. 'The Swedes are excellent linguists, Sir Matthew. Not English, of course, but all of them have the German, in which I am fluent, and most have French, as do you and I. The High Chancellor, Count De La Gardie, is one such – indeed, he is the grandson of a Frenchman, as, I believe, are you.' A French woman, in my case; and my paternal grandmother, the erstwhile and formidable Louise-Marie de Monconseil-Bragelonne, would not have taken kindly to having her name taken in vain by such a stripling. 'The embassy need not delay the sailing of the mast-fleet by more than a week or two,' North continued, 'given that the ice shows no sign of melting. All that is required is for a man of rank to open proceedings face-to-face, thus displaying our sovereign lord's respect for his child-equal King Karl. The more detailed negotiations will take longer, but they are invariably delegated to those of lesser rank.'

'Namely yourself,' I said.

'Namely myself and my Swedish counterpart, whosoever he may be, another nonentity whom history will forget.'

'But how can this mission be accomplished so speedily? Surely the Swedish court is at Stockholm or Uppsala – the other side of the country? In a winter such as this, will it not take weeks to travel in just the one direction?'

'True,' said North, seemingly indefatigable in his argument, 'and thus we can discount the audience with the young king and the Queen Regent that Lord Conisbrough expected to have to endure. But that would have been merely for the sake of protocol, Sir Matthew, and in my experience, protocol can always be adjusted.' Experience! And yet I, who had fought against the combined armies of Marshal Turenne and Oliver Cromwell when I was barely eighteen, should have been the last man to dismiss the possibility that Lydford North had started young, and experienced much. 'No, it was always intended that the real business would be transacted with the true power in Sweden – the High Chancellor, De La Gardie. He favours the French, but not blindly so – he is amenable to argument, and even more so to money. It happens that the High Chancellor has an estate barely a hundred miles from here, where he is building a quite remarkably grandiose palace,' said North easily. 'It is no inconvenience to His Excellency, and naturally arouses no suspicion, for him to be resident there. He has business in these parts – or so he has told the Queen Regent. Thus even now, with the land frozen, you can be there and back in days. Two or three formal but secret audiences, Sir Matthew. That is all that will be required.'

I felt my heart's beat. North was so plausible, and yet this was truly *terra incognita* for Matthew Quinton. The oath I had sworn meant I could consult no-one; none at all, apart from this strange creature, at once impossibly young and impossibly old, that stood before me. 'If we encounter unforeseen delays – if, then, the masts fail to reach England,' I said tentatively, 'the navy could not fight one battle –'

'Sir Matthew,' said Lydford North sharply, 'if we do not have the Swedish alliance, there may be no England to fight for.'

For the only time that I could recall, I wished with all my heart that my brother was in my place. Charles Quinton, Earl of Ravensden – a man of undoubted rank, a man who had negotiated with kings, cardinals and criminals alike, a man used to acting the part that was required of him. Dear God, Charles would have known how to answer this upstart North. Charles would have known how to disport himself in secret negotiations with the ruler of another land, especially since he was already familiar with the land. Charles would not have dreaded – *did not dread* – the prospect of failure, and with it the possible wrath of Arlington and King Charles the Second. But my brother was not in that low, dark room at that moment. In his place was young Matt, acting the part of Sir Matthew Quinton, whoever he might be.

And yet...

Yes, and yet. True, I had a responsibility to the mast-fleet that lay ice-bound within the road of Gothenburg, but perhaps I had also been given a God-given opportunity to ensure that it would not be the last such fleet to reach England in the present war. If the High Chancellor had ordered the embargo on new supplies, was it not at least possible that he could be persuaded to reverse that policy by the envoy of His Britannic Majesty?

There was another vista before me, too. Landtshere Ter Horst had refused to sanction the deportation to England of the vile regicide Bale. Might not the intercession of King Charles's ambassador with King Karl's High Chancellor ensure that the wretch finally came to the righteous and divinely ordained sentence of hanging, disembowelment, the burning of entrails, castration and quartering?

At the very least, that would make my mother happy: especially if she was able to watch.

'Very well, Mister North,' I heard myself say, 'you have your ambassador.'

Chapter Six

We buried Peregrine, Lord Conisbrough, after the English fashion, that is, by torchlight in the evening, the service being held within the great German church upon the broad canal that bisected the town. The Swedes found this perplexing, as it is their custom to leave their dead unburied for months, if not years, until the ground unfreezes sufficiently to dig graves and they have saved enough lucre to be able to afford a grand interment for the deceased. It was with only some difficulty that we had persuaded the pastor of the German church, a sullen Brandenburger, to permit a Baron of England the honour of a grave beneath the floor of his south aisle.

Thomas Eade, the chaplain of the *Cressy*, delivered an adequate and thankfully brief eulogy, and led us briskly through the funeral service: the bitter cold of a Swedish winter night was repelled not a jot by the walls of the German church, broad but relatively low by English standards, nor by the blazing torches within, so many of those within the congregation, myself included, were visibly shivering. I could see my breath rise in little clouds before my eyes. My teeth chattered. My hands were gloved, but I seemed to have precious little feeling in them. And yet I kept my eyes upon the coffin – the very large coffin – upon its bier before the altar, mourning the man who lay within.

'Now is Christ risen from the dead,' Eade proclaimed, reciting the words in his flat Westmorland tones, 'and become the first fruits of them that slept. For since by man came death, by man came also the resurrection of the dead...'

As Eade droned on, I reflected that my old friend and comrade-in-arms Francis Gale would have made a rather better fist of the interment. Indeed, I had not realised until that moment how much I missed Francis's counsel and steadying presence at my side. Certain it was that he had a God-given duty to tend to his flock in my home parish; his last letter had spoken of the ever-increasing insolencies of the dissenters in our part of Bedfordshire, among whom a certain Bunyan held a particular sway. Even more certain was the unbridled wrath that could be expected from my mother if Francis forsook that duty once again to serve at sea alongside me. But I knew I could handle my mother, and vowed there and then that I would take Francis to sea once more in my next command.

Thus lost in my thoughts, I was briefly unaware of a sudden commotion at the back of the church, by the west door. North, sitting to my right, had already turned to face it, and I, too, inclined my head in that direction.

'By Heaven, the presumption!' hissed North. 'The killer comes to mock his victim!'

Within the west door stood John, Lord Bale, surrounded by a dozen or so supporters who were clearly heavily armed.

There was confusion in the church. All heads were turning westward. There was much angry murmuring, especially from the Cressys. Phineas Musk, in a pew across the nave, had his hand inside his jerkin, and I knew for certain it would be resting upon the hilt of a knife. The prospect of a pitched battle upon holy ground seemed imminent indeed, and my honour would not permit such a desecration. Which meant but one thing, if we were to avert bloodshed –

'North,' I said sharply, 'with me. Now.'

I stood, and with Lydford North at my side, I strode up the nave toward the west door, my hand outstretched to command all Cressys to remain where they were. Bale looked upon my approach curiously, but stood his ground. The men of his little army tensed, their hands going to concealed weapons.

I halted before the regicide. 'In the name of God,' I said, 'what is it that you do here? Why do you show such disrespect to the dead, and dare show your face among those who mourn?'

Lord Bale did not answer immediately. Instead, he looked me up and down appraisingly before greeting me with perfect courtesy. 'Sir Matthew.' His attention turned to Lydford North, who seemed barely able to contain his rage. 'And you will be Arlington's creature. I am surprised the noble lord sends one so very young to kill me.'

This took me aback, but it clearly had no such effect upon Lydford North. There was no denial: rather, there was a grim half-smile of acknowledgement. 'You killed My Lord Conisbrough,' said North, 'as you killed the king. I shall merely be the instrument of God's righteous judgment upon you.'

'The killing of Charles Stuart I have no choice but to acknowledge,' said Bale casually, the murder of a monarch reduced to a mere matter of fact. 'But I did not kill Conisbrough. You can believe that or not, but having murdered a king, as you would put it, why would I not admit my guilt for the very much lesser killing of a baron?' There were angry cries behind me, and again I raised my arm to quell the revolt.

'Then what is it that you do here?' I could not bring myself to bestow the correct dignity of 'My Lord' upon this villain.

'Two reasons. First, Sir Matthew, I tell you to your face that the noble lord, there, was killed not by me, but by another. There is a dark force abroad in this land, an enemy to us all -'

Lydford North scoffed at that. 'You are the only dark force here, John Bale. And you will perish at my hand, that I swear.'

'This,' I demanded contemptuously, 'would be the same dark force that sought to kill me upon the streets of this city so very recently? A dark force that you yourself have unleashed?'

Lord Bale ignored North; his eyes were fixed upon me alone. 'Believe whomsoever you wish to believe, Sir Matthew Quinton. I have been here for six years, you for barely six days, and I now know this land nearly as well as did the noble lord, yonder. I say there is an evil at work in this benighted realm of Sweden – an evil that transcends the petty quarrel of Cavalier and Roundhead. Yes, those who tried to kill you served it, but they did not serve *me*.' He nodded toward Conisbrough's coffin. 'And if you seek proof that I did not kill he who lies yonder, consider my second reason for wishing to come here tonight.'

'That being?'

'Correct me if, in my absence, the present King Charles's Parliament has passed new laws to the contrary,' said Bale heavily, 'but as I recall, it has always been customary in England for a man's closest relation to be the chief mourner at his funeral.' I glanced at North, but his face was impassive. 'Conisbrough was my good-father,' Bale continued. 'His daughter is my wife, although I have not seen her these six years. Why do you think I chose Gothenburg as my place of exile, when I could have lived out my days in warmer climes? I have been under his secret protection all this time, despite his detestation of my part in the High Court of Justice.' Thus the malcontents termed that illegal monstrosity, the sham-court which condemned a King of England to death by beheading. 'He hated me and the fact that his daughter loved me, but I loved and respected him, Sir Matthew. Believe it or not, for that is your prerogative, but for me to kill Peregrine Conisbrough would be akin to killing myself. Our quarrel at the Landtshere's was brought about by our differences over the future of one dear to us both.' Bale's eyes narrowed. 'And that, gentlemen, is the crux of my innocence. For think upon this. What man would kill his own son's grandfather?'

With that, Bale nodded curtly to me and turned, making no acknowledgment at all of Lydford North. With Wood and his guards flanking him, he walked out into the bitter Swedish night. Through the open west door, I saw that the snow was falling again.

* * *

I was in my great cabin aboard the *Cressy*, making final preparations for the embassy to the High Chancellor. Or rather, Musk was making the preparations, commanding such-and-such to be placed within my travelling chest and such-and-such to be removed, ordering my young servants Ives and Upton hither and thither, while addressing me with only a modicum of greater respect.

'Will Sir Matthew really be requiring a *third* sword upon the journey? A good snowfall will do for Sir Matthew's better hats. Lady Quinton will be displeased if Sir Matthew ruins yet another pair of French breeches –'

'Enough, Musk, in God's name!' I was still not best pleased with him for concealing from me the knowledge of my brother having been in Sweden; I had tasked him with the matter during our journey back to the *Cressy*, but he pleaded innocence as only Phineas Musk could. 'Forty-nine was a desperate year,' he said, 'and My Lord was employed much upon missions to garner support for the new king. Sweden, Denmark, Holland, France, Spain – wherever there might be a prince willing to lift a finger for one of their own kind. I knew no more than that, Sir Matthew. Spent most of that year barricaded in Ravensden House so as the rude mob didn't pillage it. One week all I had to eat was one old dead rat I found behind a close-stool.'

Young Kellett suddenly burst into the cabin without ceremony. Musk rounded on him and was clearly prepared to fire off one of his most ferocious bellows, but the lad forestalled him. 'Mister Farrell's compliments, Sir Matthew, and he requests your immediate presence upon deck. Lookouts have sighted something untoward, sir.'

More than a little relieved to be removed from both Musk's evasiveness and his vision of domestic organisation alike, I made my way to the quarterdeck. Kit and Jeary were at the starboard rail, their telescopes trained on a craft moving toward us through the islets of the archipelago. Both turned and saluted as I approached, and Kit at once offered me his eyepiece.

'A galley,' he said. 'Large one. But whose?'

I focused on the fast-approaching vessel. I had seen galleys before, of course: those of the French, the Ottomans, the Venetians, the Knights of Malta and the Barbary corsairs in the Mediterranean, as well as those of the Sallee rovers off the west coast of Africa. In those seas, they were to be expected. But here, in the icy waters of the north?

'The Danes still have a few,' said Jeary gruffly. 'Perhaps the Swedes, too, although I have never seen any of theirs. They were once common in these waters. Not so nowadays.'

'Most likely a Swede, then,' said Kit.

'Most likely,' I said.

'The Swedes have a galley-dock upstream, beneath the old Elfsborg castle,' said Jeary. 'She'll probably be making for that.'

I continued to watch the galley. She was lower and beamier than those I had encountered in the Mediterranean; a long slender hull with a single bank of oars and some sort of shed-like wooden structure covering where the quarterdeck would have been on a warship. Three large cannon were mounted as bow-chasers overlooking the beakhead. She flew no pennant or ensign. And as I watched, I felt a growing sense of unease. The galley's bow wave seemed to be growing; I knew the water would be spilling over the ram hidden under the waterline, below the beakhead. I counted in even time to thirty as I watched the sweep of her oars into the water, then counted the same again. I lowered my telescope. There was no mistaking it now.

'The oarsmen are increasing the rate,' I said. 'She's picking up speed. Why would she do that, if she means to come to an anchor or go up to the galley-dock?'

Kit, Jeary and I looked at each other in the same moment, the same thought evidently in all our minds. And we could not move. Even if some magic could be found to bring up our double anchors in the blink of an eye, there was not a breath of wind upon the waters.

'Surely the Danes would never dare,' said Kit. 'Attacking us in Swedish waters? Risking war between themselves and this country?'

'Did we expect them to fire upon us at Bergen?' I replied.

Not the Danes, boy, a voice in my head seemed to say; and indeed, it would surely have been madness, if not suicide, for King Frederik to order an attack on the kingdom that had utterly humiliated his own only a few short years before. But then I recalled the ingenious, desperate attack on the mast-ships, and also I heard John Bale's words: *There is a dark force abroad in this land, an enemy to us all.* Perhaps the regicide was right after all.

'Sir,' said Jeary urgently, 'should we clear for action?'

I looked again at the distance between us, calculated the speed of the galley, and recalled the demonstrations of the speed of such craft that I had witnessed in the Mediterranean. There had been a Venetian galley off Ithaca that astonished me, seeming almost to fly across the sea –

'No time,' I said. 'We will never clear and run out a broadside before she is up with us. And what if she is a Swede after all? But man as many guns as we can upon the upper deck, Mister Farrell. Break out swords, muskets and half-pikes. Trumpeters, there!'

Purton and Drewell, the ship's two young trumpeters, emerged hesitantly from the tiny hutches in the poop that constituted their cabins; they had only just returned from ashore and were evidently attempting to sleep off the effects. But they saw to their duty with a vigorous, if not entirely note-perfect, rendition of a shrill clarion-call. Meanwhile Kit was at the quarterdeck rail, barking orders to Lanherne, Carvell and as many of the ships' petty officers as were within earshot. And all the while the galley came on, relentlessly, seemingly faster and faster, heading directly for our starboard quarter, apparently intent upon ramming.

Cressys spilled out onto the upper deck, each more bewildered than the last. At last men were coming up from the armoury clutching armfuls of weapons. Phineas Musk emerged from below, too, and thrust a familiar scabbard into my hand.

'Third-best sword,' he said. 'Already packed the other two.'

We had men along the rail now: a makeshift force, unlikely to mount anything more than a token resistance if the galley was truly intent on ramming and boarding, as it surely seemed to be. Its bow wave was formidable now, and despite myself, I had to admire the spectacle. The oars cut the water, emerged, swung forward and cut again with almost immaculate rhythm –

'Sir,' cried Kit, 'the starboard eight-pounders in the waist are primed and ready to fire upon your command! Sir Matthew?'

A Dane, or a Swede? But if the latter, why mount what could clearly only be interpreted as an attack upon us? Unless it served John Bale's unnamed 'dark force' –

I drew my sword and raised it, ready to give the order to fire. The galley was approaching us at a rate that would have been unbelievable for a ship. She was already closer than the range at which I would have opened fire on a certain enemy – surely closer than the distance at which she could safely stop before striking us –

I can still barely credit what I saw next. The galley's rows of oars suddenly jammed down hard into the water, then pushed sharply in the opposite direction. As the headway came off her, the starboard bank of oars was swiftly drawn inboard, allowing only the foremost oars of the larboard to propel the vessel. The bow swung over, and the galley came in sharply alongside us. In that moment, a blue-and-yellow swallow-tailed pennant broke out at her ensign staff.

I lowered my sword very slowly, lest an over-eager gun-captain misinterpreted a swifter descent as the order to give fire. As I did so, Phineas Musk jabbed a corpulent finger in the direction of the galley.

'That captain,' he said, his voice quivering a little, 'is a bedlam-man. A booby. A crackbrain. An addle-head.'

'I tend to agree, Musk,' I replied, my throat unconscionably dry.

'Nevertheless, he is coming alongside. Let us take the precise measure of his lunacy.'

* * *

The captain of the galley was piped aboard with due ceremony. However, it took me a moment to realise that the strange creature setting foot upon the deck of the *Cressy* was indeed the man responsible for the impressive manoeuvre that I had just witnessed. He was not quite a dwarf, but he was one of the smallest men I have ever encountered: small, and to my eyes impossibly old, his tiny face an undulating mountain range of warts and folds of leathery flesh. His breaths, irregular, loud and consumptive, resembled an ancient blacksmith's bellows.

I recovered from my perplexity in time to observe the correct formalities of doffing my hat and bowing, although my very lowest bow would still have brought me nowhere near the height of the ancient little man.

'Quinton,' I said in French, 'captain of His Britannic Majesty's ship the *Cressy.*'

'Glete of the galley *Fortuna*, in the service of His Majesty the King of the Swedes, Goths and Wends,' the newcomer replied in both flawless English and a high, gasping voice which reinforced the impression that I was dealing with some kind of demonic imp.

'Y– you are very welcome aboard, Captain Glete,' I said, unsettled by the man's contradictions.

'General,' he replied, promptly adding another, 'Lieutenant-General Erik Glete. Galleys don't need fucking *sailors* to command them, Captain Quinton. No concern for the wind. Point the fucking thing the way you want it go and get the idle buggers below to row like the devil.'

'Sir Matthew Quinton,' I said. If the astonishing, wheezing little creature that was Lieutenant-General Erik Glete could rest upon his dignity, then so could I.

He looked me anew; and of course, for him that meant looking a very long way upward.

'Fucking hell, King Charles is knighting *children* now?'

There was barely suppressed laughter throughout the side party of Cressys. Musk was red-faced and pretending to have a coughing fit. I decided that it would be best to remove this peculiar peasant-mouthed creature from the public arena as rapidly as possible, and conducted him down to my cabin. Seated at my table, attended by my young servants and taking a long draught of the finest Ho Brian wine we had aboard the ship, General Glete became somewhat less abrasive.

'Your command of English is – is quite remarkable, General,' I said, putting it as neutrally as I could. 'How came you by it?'

'During the late wars, of course! War is the best education a man can get – killing and whoring as well as acquiring a half-dozen languages.' Glete did not wait to be served, snatching the Ho Brian bottle from Upton and pouring himself a large measure. The wine seemed to settle his chest; the death-rattle in his voice subsided. 'Fought with men from all parts of your isles. Scots, Irish, Englishmen. Better fellows by far than some of the other shit-headed bastards we served with, the French above all.' So, then: Glete had learned the very particular English of the barrack-room and the soldier's campfire debauch. All was clear. 'And I came up through the ranks, Sir Matthew. Was just a sergeant when the wars began. Was one of those present at the side of our veritable lion, King Gustavus, when he perished upon Lutzen field. Ended the wars a general, charged by Queen Christina herself with the command of the *Fortuna*, Sweden's finest galley. Now Sweden's last galley, alas.'

'There are no others?'

The tiny man shook his ancient head vigorously. 'A few small craft, here and in the Stockholm archipelago, but none worthy of the name galley. Thirty years ago, Sweden had two dozen like the *Fortuna*, the Danes the same. But fashions change, Quinton. The seamen cried up ships, for they have the commands of them and provide the crews, unlike galleys that are manned by soldiers alone, apart from the occasional pilot to keep us out of shallows and off the rocks. But what use would ships like this be amidst the islands and shoals of the archipelagos?' He glowered, as though blaming me personally for the decline of the galley. 'And our soldiers of today are not the iron men I fought with at Lutzen, Wittstock and all the rest. They somehow find it beneath their dignity to pull upon oars, complaining that it makes them but the equals of French convicts and Barbary slaves.' He sighed, and once again his chest wheezed alarmingly. 'Yes, fashions change, and I trust I will live long enough to see them change back again.'

Glete did not, even though he lived far longer than the few weeks the state of his chest seemed to presage; but I have. My old friend Jack Norris told me that when he commanded in the Baltic a few years ago, the entire sea swarmed with galleys once again. It seems they were favoured particularly by my old acquaintance the Emperor Peter of Russia, who thus forced Sweden and Denmark to build them anew.

'Your crew is certainly capable of impressive oarsmanship,' I said.

'Forgive the vanity, Quinton,' the little general replied airily. 'We have no duties to speak of beyond endlessly cruising around these fucking interminable islands, sometimes catching a Danish spy or two, sometimes a smuggler. A chance to show off before a great ship of one of the world's mightiest navies and her famous captain was not to be missed. And I thought perhaps you might indulge an old man with a tour of inspection of such a proud and glorious craft, hence my presumption in presenting myself upon your deck.'

I had thought of reprimanding Glete for the near-suicidal nature of his simulated attack upon the *Cressy*; after all, how could he have been certain that I would not open fire on him? But his generous compliments to myself, my ship and the cause I served quite deflated me, and besides, I could not in conscience deny a man who seemed to be not long for this earth. Instead I raised a glass and proposed a toast to His Majesty the King of the Swedes, Goths and Wends.

'Aye, God bless the boy king,' said Glete reflectively, 'and God bless Her Majesty the Queen.'

'You know them both, I take it – young King Karl and his mother, the regent?'

He looked up at me contemptuously, and his throat rattled quite alarmingly. 'Shit and fuck, Sir Matthew, you think I refer to that fat ugly Holsteiner sow Hedwig Eleanora? Mad bitch. Worst temper I've ever known on a woman. Queen Regent of Sweden, my arse.' I was taken aback; privately I had doubts about the suitability of England's royal consort Catherine of Braganza, but I would never have betrayed them thus to a foreigner I had only just met. 'No sir,' Glete continued, 'I refer to Queen Christina, the once and, I pray, future sovereign of these realms. May she see the folly both of her abjuration of the faith of her glorious father and her resignation of the crown.' With that, he raised his glass in salute, then drained it.

The late Lord Conisbrough had warned me that many Swedes thought thus, but Glete was the first I had knowingly met. And Christina had appointed him to command this galley, which meant he must have encountered her. 'Tell me of her, General, for she has always been something of an enigma to we Englishmen. In my country, we are not accustomed to having rulers who resign their authority on a point of philosophical principle.'

Glete sighed. 'Not only an enigma to Englishmen, alas. Her Majesty was – *is*, there in her Roman fastness – the wisest and kindest ruler that ever drew breath. Once, we had a young soldier in the crew who lost an eye to a snapped hawser. She had her own physician attend on him for weeks, and provided him with a generous bounty out of her own pocket. She is a paragon, Sir Matthew.' Glete shook his head sadly. 'If she had married her cousin Karl rather than handing him the throne, and borne a line of new Vasas, Sweden would now be the happiest land upon Earth. As it is, dissension is everywhere. The peasants, the very backbone of this realm, are oppressed. De La Gardie and his favourites drain the treasury.'

I calculated that an opinion upon the High Chancellor from one who must have known him might be of some value to the Britannic ambassador who was shortly to pay court to him.

'Yet surely you serve the Chancellor, General.'

'I obey none but High Admirals of Sweden, anointed sovereigns of The Three Crowns, and God Almighty,' said Glete haughtily. 'Certainly not that worthless puffed-up windfucker De La Gardie and his fawning turd-spawn here in Gothenburg, Ter Horst.'

The general's education in English had evidently been thorough indeed. And his veneration for lawful monarchy put a thought into my mind.

'I take it then, General, that you know Ter Horst permits sanctuary to a most heinous enemy of my master King Charles? One of those who signed the warrant ordering the execution of his sacred father, of blessed memory?'

'Of course. The man Bale. Another stain upon Sweden's honour, that such a fucking obnoxious creature should be allowed to walk free upon her soil. But that is the way of it, in these reduced times.'

I acknowledged General Glete's remarks with an approving bow of my head. As I conducted him on his tour of the *Cressy*, I found myself calculating in ways of which my uncle and perhaps even young Lydford North would have been proud. *If we are to bring John Bale to a reckoning*, I thought, *we require allies in this strange, hostile realm. And methinks I have just acquired one.*

Chapter Seven

We set out the next morning from the east gate of Gothenburg, leaving Kit Farrell in acting command of the *Cressy*. My doubts about forsaking her and the mast-fleet were mollified somewhat by the fact that there was no sign of a thaw. Quite the opposite, in fact. It seemed even colder than it had been in the preceding days, and there had been a fresh fall of snow in the night. But I was leaving behind a city where a regicide was at liberty and the murder of Lord Conisbrough remained unresolved, governed by a scheming Landtshere who wished England ill (and who had acceded to my request to seek audience with the High Chancellor with evident bad grace, no doubt believing my purpose was to denigrate him before De La Gardie). Thus I rode out through the gate and across the long fir bridge that traversed the moat with a heavy heart. Who knew what further villainies might be committed in this vile place while I was absent?

The entire party was upon horseback: myself, Lydford North, Phineas Musk, a sullen captain named Larssen from the Gothenburg garrison who spoke virtually no French, six Swedish dragoons, and the same number of my men, chosen partly for their competence on horseback and partly for the trust that I had in them. These were Lanherne, who had once served as a despatch rider in the late king's western army during our civil war; Carvell, who it seemed had ridden frequently in the Americas; Ali Reis, our renegade from the Algerine corsairs, even though he was more familiar with fleet Arab stallions than the great beasts preferred in northern climes; MacFerran, who had spent much of his young life in the west of Scotland riding bareback upon garrons; and two men who had served me well the previous summer aboard the *Merhonour* and were said to be steady horsemen: a gangling Wiltshireman named Stacey and a taciturn Suffolk man named Britten. None of my young servants accompanied me. Kellett had been keen to do so, but a winter journey in an unknown land would be difficult, and I did not relish explaining to his mother, a friend of my sister Elizabeth, that her precious boy had been frozen to death in a snowdrift or else consumed by wolves. We also had four packhorses, although they were not heavily laden. Transporting the equipage necessary even for a confidential ambassador could easily have justified a coach or two and some carts, but such would have slowed our journey considerably and I, for one, was determined to return to Gothenburg as quickly as possible to fulfil my duty to the mast-fleet.

We were setting out at dawn. The winter days were still short and the roads treacherous; North's advice, presumably derived from Conisbrough, was that we might manage twenty English or three Swedish miles in a day (there being roughly seven of one to one of the other) but I was determined to reach Lacko in four days, not five, and insisted upon a brisk pace from the start. As it was, the local horses that we had hired from the Sign of the Pelican coped admirably with the snow and ice that covered the road, which at times was almost indiscernible from the white wastes all around us. The road east from Gothenburg soon took us into a barren, uneven country, littered with great, strangely-shaped stones pushing above the wave-crested snow like islands from a sea. At times we passed through rocky defiles striated with what looked for all the world like the cuts made by a giant sharpening his sword upon the bare stone; frozen waterfalls adorned the grey-brown rock faces, as though that same giant had moved on to sculpt fantastical shapes out of the ice. Clad in furs as we were, we looked very much like men from an earlier time, picking their way uncertainly through a savage, hostile landscape and eyeing the rocks warily in case bloodthirsty trolls suddenly sprang from them. Thick forests of fir trees lay beyond the snow-covered open ground on either side of the road, cloaking much of the land. I looked upon them enviously, calculating how many great masts they could produce. God alone knew why the High Chancellor had ordered an embargo, for this country seemed to have enough trees to fit out every navy in the world a thousand times over.

As our Swedish escort had predicted, shortly after nightfall we came to a *dorf,* or village, with a mean, low-roofed inn that could accommodate us for the night. The building was of timber, as was every house in the village and its church, too. Our coming attracted much astonishment from the local peasants: I think they would have been startled enough by the sight of such common Englishmen as Musk and myself, but they looked upon the brown turbaned features of Ali Reis and the black skin of Julian Carvell with a frank admixture of curiosity, suspicion and downright fear. The Swedish captain barked at them and they retreated to their hovels or the farthest corners of the inn, the one saving grace of which was a multiplicity of large, blazing fires. The Swedes were famed for their generous hospitality to visitors, and the landlord made us welcome enough, gleefully practising the one English word he knew – 'Krom-vell!' The place provided but mean fare, though: thick beer that was too strong for our modest English tastes, together with lean broiled beef and a peculiar kind of bread. Ali Reis, listening intently to the innkeeper and his other customers so as to improve his grasp of yet another language, swore they were saying that this beef came from a rotten cow that had been found dead in a ditch, and indeed, it was vastly inferior to a fine roasted English rump; but after a day upon a hard road, it tasted like a very plate of ambrosia. But none of our hungry palates could take to the bread, which was as well. When Ali Reis asked what it contained, he was told that it was made of the bark of a tree mingled with chaff and cemented with water. Musk turned pale and ran outside; loud and prolonged sounds of retching followed. He eventually returned by way of making an inspection of our quarters, reporting miserably that the beds were of straw and that we would have to be at least four to a room. As it was, I was so exhausted and saddle-sore that I slept solidly for near six hours, ignoring the discomfort and even Musk's snoring upon the adjacent pallet.

Thus was established the pattern for our journey: rise at dawn, ride as hard and far as the road and our horses allowed, eat and sleep at invariably poor village inns, with not a stone building in sight apart from rare glimpses of distant lordly towers. Apart from the occasional howl of a wolf or a sighting of a white hare – for in those parts, hares' fur turns white in winter, a singularity which convinced the credulous Britten that the entire land was bewitched – we went for miles without a hint of life anywhere in this strange, unsettling landscape. We met few travellers going in the opposite direction, and none overtook us. It was so bitterly cold upon the road, with frequent (if blessedly light) snow showers, that it proved impossible to hold a conversation of any sort for any length of time. Musk inflicted upon me his thoughts on a range of matters, from the crumbling condition of the Quinton properties to the King's unaccountable retention of the Earl of Clarendon as his chief minister; but for most of the time he rode almost, but not quite, out of earshot, complaining endlessly to members of our escort about the cold, the discomfort of his saddle, and the miserable nature of this realm of Sweden.

Lydford North said little to me during the early stages of our journey, seemingly preferring his own company, but on the morning of the third day he rode up beside me. It was a bright day, the low sun casting beams through the trees and making the snow glisten. We were riding along the side of a frozen lake upon which a few peasant children were skating and playing while their fathers gathered wood among the trees that lined the shore.

'We have been fortunate, Sir Matthew,' he said. 'No blizzards, no blocked roads. God willing, we will reach Lacko by nightfall tomorrow.'

I stared critically at the youth. So very young, and yet so strangely influential; and perhaps menacing, too. A menace that needed to be addressed.

'Tell me, Mister North,' I said, 'was Bale correct? Did My Lord Arlington send you to kill him?'

'Sir Matthew,' he replied innocently, 'do you take me for a common assassin?'

'With due respect, Mister North, that is not an answer.'

He glanced across at me and spoke slowly, choosing his words carefully. 'My orders are to return John Bale to England, preferably alive, to face the rightful wrath of His Majesty against those who put his father to death. But if such a course proves impossible...' He shrugged. There was no need to complete the sentence.

'And Lord Conisbrough was privy to your mission? To kill or at least arrest his own good-son?'

'No,' North replied emphatically. 'Conisbrough detested Bale's part in the murder of the king, but complicity in his execution would have driven a knife into the hearts of My Lord's daughter and grandson. He told me that often enough. Perhaps he suspected that I had a secondary purpose which was kept secret from him, but he never hinted that he possessed such knowledge. And in that sense alone, of course, his death is a convenience. I am not entirely certain where his loyalties might have lain if I had revealed my true intentions.'

Conisbrough's death a *convenience*? I shivered, and was not entirely convinced that the cause was the bitter Swedish winter. I prayed that I never made an enemy of Lydford North.

'Then you will pursue Bale, once your negotiations at Lacko are complete?'

He seemed genuinely surprised by the question. 'Of course, Sir Matthew. Is it not my duty, given me by God and Lord Arlington? Is it not striking down John Bale the debt we owe to all those who died before our time, in the cause of the blessed saint and martyr?'

I kept my peace. North was but three years younger than I, yet those three years might as well have been an eternity. For I was just old enough to remember the war among the English, albeit only barely: its sounds, its smells, its fears, the sight of turtle-back helmets and mourning weeds. Conversely, Lydford North was just too young. His generation could remember only the rule of the swordsmen, not the apocalypse that had brought them to power. Thus I was not entirely confident in his assertion that the shades of countless thousands of cavaliers, my own father among them, would have regarded this brash, very certain youth as a suitable standard-bearer for their vengeance.

To divert him, I asked him to tell me more about the man we were soon to meet, the High Chancellor of Sweden.

'Ah, now there's a tale, Sir Matthew. My Lord Arlington was quite effusive upon the subject. He has an interest in Sweden – although of course nominally it comes under old Morice – and he met De La Gardie once, in France.' In name Arlington was the southern secretary, concerned principally with France and Spain, while the ineffectual northern secretary Sir William Morice ought to have had responsibility for England's relations with Sweden; but as I knew from my dealings with the man, Arlington was not one to pay much regard to such niceties. And as I now knew full well, Arlington's creature North had even less regard for other inconvenient niceties, notably the rule of law and human life. 'There were rumours that De La Gardie was Queen Christina's lover, which was the true cause of his rise to power,' North continued conspiratorially. 'Arlington thought the rumours were true. Conisbrough did not, and of course, he knew both the Queen and the Chancellor personally, so I give greater credence to his opinion.' So, then: young North was prepared to think independently of his puppet-master. 'At any rate, it is of no consequence now. The previous King Karl's will named De La Gardie High Chancellor of the Three Crowns, thus making him Sweden's ruler, and that is the reality we confront.'

A flock of birds took wing suddenly from the snow-tipped trees away to our left, flying southward across the leaden grey sky. The land all around seemed as bleak and empty as ever.

'You think we can succeed in persuading De La Gardie to bring

Sweden into the war on our side?' I asked.

'His inclinations are with France, but the factions and opinions within this realm are complex,' said North. 'The High Chancellor has to take account of the opinions of the Queen Regent, and she is no friend to King Louis. And most of the old nobility are against De La Gardie. They see him as a low-born upstart, promoted above his station, and hanker after Sweden's glorious olden days of victory. Peace does not suit these people.'

'So if De La Gardie is to retain power, he will eventually have to give the nobles what they want. Another war. Ideally, our war.'

'Quite so, Sir Matthew. Sweden has ample cause to hate the Dutch – has always done so. The Dutch are allied to the Danes, and De La Gardie and his generals know the Danes will strike for revenge one day. The complication, of course, is France. King Louis will want to do his utmost to ensure that Sweden does not do what we hope it will do, namely join the war on our side. Who knows what inducements he will offer De La Gardie – indeed, might already have offered him?' He sighed. 'It will be difficult, Sir Matthew. If truth be told, we might not succeed. Then England will have to stand alone against the dreadful alliance that stands ranged against us. But strange things can happen in this world, can they not? Who would have imagined that the Most Christian King would go to war on behalf of a coterie of merchandising Calvinistic republicans? And you were in exile with our own king, Sir Matthew. When His Majesty celebrated Christmas in his Flemish garret in the year Fifty-Nine, could he – could you - have conceived it possible that barely six months later he would ride into London in triumph?'

Well, then: perhaps young Lydford North, whom I had taken for at best an obstinate young blade and at worst a fanatic, had something of a realist about him after all.

I barely had time to digest that thought before MacFerran rode up at a gallop from the very back of our straggling party. 'My pardon, Sir Matthew, Mister North,' he said in his near-unintelligible west Highland tongue.

'MacFerran? What is it, man?'

'We're being followed, Sir Matthew. Certain of it.'

* * *

I took MacFerran's words seriously. He had grown to manhood in the far west of Scotland, in country not dissimilar to this, chasing the deer and avoiding the factors of the Earls of Argyll, who claimed ownership of those same deer. But as I looked all around me, I saw nothing: only the endless expanse of snow, rocks and trees.

'Whereabouts, MacFerran?'

'In the woods to the left, Sir Matthew. First thought I noticed something a few hours ago, but reckoned it might have been wolves. Can't be anything but men, though. Two riders, I'd say, perhaps three. And they're good, Sir Matthew. North wind would bring any sound from that forest down to us, but they're taking care not to break branches. There'll be less snow on the ground under the trees, so there's less to muffle sounds of movement, too.'

I looked away toward the trees, but could see no sign of movement other than the rustling of the branches in the breeze and the occasional fall of snow as a bough shook. Two or three men would hardly attack more than a dozen, all of us heavily armed; besides, the wide expanse of open ground between the road and the forest would expose any advance against us in an instant. So our followers had to be just that: men sent to follow, to observe, and no doubt to report our movements to some distant and concealed presence. Yet to what end? Although the mission that North and I were upon was a close secret, our journey itself was not. We had left Gothenburg publicly, the Landtshere had been informed that we were bound for Lacko to seek audience with the High Chancellor, and there was but one direct road from the city to the castle. John Bale would surely have been relieved to see us leave Gothenburg, and would hardly have had cause to send men after us; unless, that is, he was playing some hidden game as sinister as Lydford North's. But there was the one remaining possibility, one that I did not wish to contemplate. If Bale spoke true and there really was a mysterious dark force at work in Sweden, might not our concealed followers be the agents of it?

'Thank you, MacFerran,' I said. The good and loyal Scotsman raised a finger to his forehead in salute and returned to the rear of our line.

'You believe him?' North asked.

'I believe him. MacFerran has the keenest eye and the sharpest instincts of any man I have known.'

'A mere *Scot*, Sir Matthew? But if you say it is so... You will inform Captain Larssen?'

'No, I think not.' North looked at me sharply, but I was certain of my reasoning. 'Larssen is a dullard. He will either dismiss MacFerran's report out of hand, in which case there is nothing to be gained by relaying it to him, or he will assume we are in imminent danger of attack by massed legions, in which he case he will either order a search of the woods or divert us to the nearest garrison for greater security. And if he reacts thus, Mister North, then just how many days are likely to be added to our journey?'

North was clearly unconvinced, but I was a warrior, and he was not; I was a knight, and he was not; and I was an ambassador of the King of England, albeit one of North's own creation, and he was not. So he kept silent.

Through the rest of that third day I had MacFerran report to me at hourly intervals. The men were still there, he said, betrayed only by an occasional rustling in the trees or a sudden bird flight. Musk, who had resumed his place at my side, was for going off into the woods with MacFerran and two or three others to put paid to them, but I rejected his counsel. Our followers were bound to notice even one man breaking away from the party; such occurred frequently when calls of nature impelled each of us in turn to fall behind, dismount and go behind a rock, but it would be a rather different matter to detach several men simultaneously and surreptitiously. Those in the woods were protected by the same simple fact that defended us from them: any advance one way or the other across the broad open space between the road and the forest would be seen at once. I had no doubt that our followers would have melted away long before Musk and his putative killing party could reach them, and in any case, attempting such an action was also certain to be noticed even by the lumpen Captain Larssen, and then stymied in favour of his own preferred course.

That night we found shelter in a village near the shores of Lake Vanern, a mighty body of water which also lapped the walls of De La Gardie's castle of Lacko, still some twenty-five English miles distant by Larssen's estimation. The Swedish captain had initially proposed pressing on through part of the night in order to reach Lidkoping, which he claimed to be a respectable city some ten miles nearer our destination, albeit on a more easterly road. The counsel held some appeal, for it would bring us to Lacko more quickly and thus enable me to return to Gothenburg the sooner; but I had to weigh that against the advantage that night would give our followers and any reinforcements that they might have lurking among the Swedish wilds. As it was, I set my own guard for the night, two men at a time beginning with MacFerran and Britten, the duty watch to be relieved every two hours. If Larssen thought this strange, or an indication of lack of trust in him and his men, he said nothing to the effect.

The inn was better than any we had yet encountered, providing a good repast of well-cooked venison; this was the High Chancellor's land, we were told, and he did not tolerate hovels or poor hospitality. I even had a chamber to myself, albeit a small one, but sleep proved elusive. To my concerns about being followed or about what might be transpiring in Gothenburg during my absence were added troubling thoughts of Cornelia. My wife never coped well with my absence, and although this voyage was as a row upon the Thames compared with my previous expedition to Africa, I knew she would be finding it difficult: especially in winter, when London and the court had fewer diversions to offer. Now, it shames me to say that I even felt pangs of suspicion and jealousy. Cornelia was as loyal to me as I had always been to her, that

(

I did not doubt. Yet somehow I could still envision her in the arms of some plausible courtier or young blade –

I shuffled beneath my bedding of animal furs, unable to get comfortable or to dismiss the thoughts that crowded in upon me. It was in that moment that I heard the shouts outside the inn: the shouts of angry men and women, many evidently running through the village. I drew my sword and went down, through the main body of the inn, and out into the rough space outside that passed for a main street. Shouting men bearing burning torches aloft marched hither and thither; they seemed to bear sufficient weaponry for a regiment.

'Who forms the duty watch, Mister Lanherne?' I demanded.

'Stacey and Ali Reis, Sir Matthew,' said Lanherne, nodding toward the two men who were evidently checking the side of the inn. 'The Moor believes the Swedes are crying up an attack by wolves. Larssen and his men have gone to assist them.'

I relaxed my grip upon my sword. Wolves might be a threat to the village, but they were no direct threat to myself or my party. I had feared some attempt by our mysterious followers before we reached Lacko; if such was to take place, it had to be tonight.

The rest of our English company emerged into the cold air. Musk shivered, looked around contemptuously, and blew onto his hands. Lydford North at once sought my report, and on being told the cause of the alarum, he merely turned upon his heel and returned to the warmth of the inn. But MacFerran furrowed his brow and appeared troubled. I asked him the cause.

'Rare for wolves to attack a village at all, Sir Matthew. Very rare, unless your Swedish wolf is from a different mould to his Scots cousin.'

Shots rang out, accompanied by further great shouts and men and boys running about.

'Pity the wolf who attacks this village,' I said. 'It resembles a garrison.'

Which, of course, was precisely what it was: Sweden's mighty army was drawn directly from its peasantry, who remained ready for the call to arms when they returned to the land. Most of the older men of the village would have fought half way across Europe, against some of the most formidable armies of the age. A mere wolf or two would be child's play to them, and useful practice against the day when the Lion of Midnight would take up arms again and drive all before it –

'*Down*, Sir Matthew!' cried MacFerran.

The young Scot threw himself at me, knocking me off balance. In the same moment I heard the familiar crack of a musket firing. The ball struck a timber strut of the hut directly behind me. If I had remained standing where I was, it would surely have lodged in my chest.

Carvell and Britten ran in the direction whence the shot must have come, but it was very dark and they did not know the land.

'Perhaps an attempt to shoot a wolf,' said Musk, albeit without much conviction.

I got to my feet. 'MacFerran?'

The young Scot shook his head. 'Saw the glow of match, Sir Matthew. Know the sight well enough from night stalking. Thanks unto God that flintlocks have not yet reached these parts.'

'An attempt upon my life, then?'

'It was a deliberate aim, from a man standing stock still. Not the action of a man pursuing a wolf and loosing off a shot upon the run.'

'And you did not see his face?'

'I am sorry I did not, Sir Matthew.'

'Merciful Heaven, MacFerran, you have nothing to be sorry for! You have performed prodigies upon this journey, and you have just saved my life! The first vacant petty officers' post on the *Cressy* is yours, and a guinea from my own purse.'

The young Scot's eyes widened. 'Thank ye, Sir Matthew!'

But MacFerran's pride and delight could not conceal the uncomfortable truth. If he was right, and I had no cause to doubt him, then someone wished me dead. They had failed, but nothing was more certain than that they would make the attempt again. I was a marked man.

Chapter Eight

We pressed on early the next morning. Once again, I told Larssen nothing of the previous night's events. As we rode north-east, glimpsing the frozen lake Vanern from time to time through the trees to our left, I reassured myself that if any of England's enemies had somehow got wind of my new status and the true purpose of my visit to the High Chancellor of Sweden, then any attempt upon me would have to be made before I reached Lacko. Within De La Gardie's own palace, guarded by some of Sweden's best troops, I would surely be invulnerable; and once the negotiations began, then whatever their outcome, my mission would be accomplished. Our mysterious followers (who had now disappeared, MacFerran said) had surely bungled their best chance of preventing King Charles's confidential ambassador to King Karl from mooting an alliance between England and Sweden.

Towards evening the track emerged at last from the forest, and there, quite suddenly, was the castle of Lacko. I have seen Stirling and I have seen Hohensalzburg; I know Windsor well, the grandest fortalice that England can offer. But I have never forgotten my first sight of Lacko. The great white walls and towers seemed to rise from the very midst of the vast lake of Vanern: it was only as we came nearer that I perceived the spit of land upon which the castle stood. Surrounded by the snow-crusted ice of the frozen lake and the snow-topped trees that enclosed the lake on all sides, the white palace was an astounding sight, a veritable fortress of winter. High towers with the lantern-like domes favoured by the northern races stood at each corner of a great, square, red-roofed palace. An incomplete palace, at that: scaffolding stretched along parts of the south and east walls. The light was fading as we rode across the spit and through the low outer court toward the gatehouse. Blazing torches and braziers were already lit both on the wayside and atop the castle walls. Bright candlelight shone forth from many of the windows; the High Chancellor clearly was not a man to stint on heat or light, nor, indeed, on anything that might serve the interests of aggrandising his property.

Guards came to attention as we passed through the gate into the heart of the castle, but otherwise there was no pomp to mark our entrance. A formal, public embassy would have entailed a vast procession, pomp, and a lengthy ceremony of welcome, the whole dictated by a rigid series of protocols that were clearly set down and meticulously observed by all nations. Thankfully, a secret embassy entailed none of those trials, but certain formalities had to be kept up: the court of the High Chancellor of Sweden was like that of any other great minister or monarch in Europe, a seething cauldron of faction overrun with the spies of every other great minister and monarch. It would be impossible to keep secret the fact that Sir Matthew Quinton, a captain in the King of England's navy royal, was visiting the most noble Count de la Gardie, and thus due honour had to be paid on both sides. As for the cause of Sir Matthew's presence in the palace of Lacko: why, surely that could be nothing more than a formal protest at the attack upon the mast-fleet and against the Landtshere of Gothenburg for his harbouring of the regicide Bale and his dilatoriness in the pursuit of the murderers of Lord Conisbrough? North was confident that the Dutch, French and Danish spies within the palace, for some of each kind there were bound to be, would come to that entirely reasonable conclusion.

Thus after we dismounted in the courtyard of Lacko we were led up into a square, warm chamber distinguished by the fine Mechelen tapestries upon the walls. Here we were given time to warm ourselves before the fire, to eat braised beef and drink Rostock beer and Rhenish wine, while de la Gardie's steward, a pernickety and ancient creature with atrocious French, informed us of the great honour that the High Chancellor bestowed upon us by entertaining us at all, let alone immediately, of the many pressures upon his time, etcetera, etcetera. At last, he showed us through into the first of a series of reception rooms, each filled with gaggles of men and women who fell silent as we passed, whispering in Swedish as soon as we were past them. Some were evidently displeased that their own suits to the High Chancellor were being delayed by the unwelcome importuning of mere *engelsmän*, a word I heard muttered disapprovingly several times during our transit. Then there were the others, those who stood alone at the sides of rooms in corners, silent and appraising. No doubt the spies of our enemies could be counted among their number.

At last we came to a set of high lacquered doors, guarded by two pikemen. The doors opened at our approach, and we were admitted into the great room that lay beyond. The principal feature of the hall was above, forcing one to look up: thirteen huge painted angels adorned the roof, quite outdoing the splendid battle paintings and allegorical scenes that covered the walls. The hall was lit by candles set high up on the walls, their flickering light illuminating the vast space but dimly. The great room contained two men, and two alone, both upon the dais at the far end: no courtiers, no attendants, no guards. The emptiness was unsettling. The shoes of both North and I clacked loudly upon the lacquered floor as we strode toward the dais, the sound echoing through the vast hall.

I have approached many royal thrones during my inordinately long life, but few were as grand as that upon which sat a mere commoner, albeit one who bore the office of High Chancellor of the Kingdom of the Swedes, Goths and Wends. Count Magnus De La Gardie's chair was elevated upon a grand dais with purple trappings decorated with what had to be his armorial bearings, an extravagant concoction of quarterings with crossed cannon in the outermost cantons, spears, helmets and sword-bearing rampant lions galore. The far more ancient arms of Quinton of Ravensden seemed positively modest in comparison.

The High Chancellor was a tall, square-faced man of middle age and considerable girth, although one could guess that in his youth he had been fastidiously elegant: he wore his hair, which was still largely golden although now streaked with white, down over his shoulders as the Cavalier blades of our civil wars had once done, and his moustachio was neatly trimmed. He wore a tunic and breeches of black trimmed with cloth-of-gold as well as a sash of blue-and-yellow similar to, but far broader and richer than, that worn by Landtshere Ter Horst. Lydford North had never met the High Chancellor, but Lord Conisbrough had, many times, and during the journey North duly relayed to me his late master's full description of the noble Count. His appearance held no surprises. But what was surprising was that he was not alone upon the dais. At De La Gardie's side, and slightly behind him, stood a clean-shaven fellow of forty years or so, short and slight but starting to run to fat. Pale and long-faced, with high eyebrows and heavy eyelids framing large, penetrating blue eyes, his expression was haughty and disdainful. One shoulder was evidently higher than the other, and conjured up in my mind a disconcerting memory: a visit to the theatre with my brother a few months earlier for a performance of *The Tragedy of King Richard the Third*, with Betterton's posture as the murderous tyrant being not dissimilar to that of the man who stood before me now, studying me intently. He was plainly garbed in comparison with the opulent High Chancellor, wearing but an unadorned velvet tunic, although curiously, he wore white gloves. The room was warm, so I concluded that this choice of garment could have one of only two causes: simple affectation, or else the concealment of scars too terrible to expose. The man was either a fop or a warrior.

North and I approached the dais and genuflected but once: not as frequent nor as deep as the *congée* we would have offered a crowned head, nor as elaborate as that which a publicly accredited ambassador would have made, but a telling and honourable show of respect none-theless.

'Sir Matthew Quinton, Mister North,' said the High Chancellor. His French was flawless, as befitted a man whose grandfather was of the Languedoc. 'We bid you welcome in the name of His Majesty Karl the Eleventh, by the Grace of God King of the Swedes, Goths and Wends. May I present the Count Dohna,' said De La Gardie, gesturing toward the man at his side. The Count bowed his head only slightly. 'The noble count is a most valued advisor of mine, particularly in matters of diplomacy. He will remain in attendance during our discussions.'

I glanced sideways towards North, but his normally imperturbable expression was strangely altered. He was quizzical, even perplexed. It came to me then that he, this youngster who prided himself upon his omniscience – in emulation of his master Arlington – had never before heard of this Count Dohna. This should have been no surprise: at every court, new favourites rose and fell in the blink of the eye. But if the High Chancellor had a new advisor, the careful calculations that must have underpinned the planning for Conisbrough's embassy were sud-denly overset. Was this Dohna for France, for England, or for a strict neutrality? North evidently did not know. I did not know. The game was altered.

But protocol still had to be observed. 'My Lord Dohna,' I said, bow-ing deeply.

'We wish to express our most profound regret upon the unfortunate death of the most noble Lord Conisbrough,' said De La Gardie. 'I have ensured that Their Majesties the King and the Queen Regent have writ-ten to King Charles to express their condolences.'

'My Lord Conisbrough was a good friend to Sweden,' said Dohna, speaking for the first time. 'I knew him well, and mourn his loss.' The count's French was immaculate, his words spoken in a deep yet somewhat curious voice; Dohna had a slight but unplaceable accent that had not been present among the other Swedes of my acquaintance, such as Ter Horst and De La Gardie.

I sensed the discomfort of Lydford North, alongside me, and could easily surmise his thoughts. *If Dohna knew Conisbrough well, why did his late lordship not name him to me?*

It was time for His Britannic Majesty's confidential ambassador to assert himself. 'That being so, Excellencies,' I said boldly, 'on behalf of Charles, by the Grace of God King of England, Scotland, Ireland and France, I demand the arrest and extradition of the traitor John Bale, called Lord Bale, on suspicion of the murder of the said Lord Conisbrough, and for the undoubted fact of the murder of his late Majesty of blessed memory, King Charles the First.'

This was not the speech that North and I had agreed during our discussions on the journey: I was to present my sovereign lord's compliments upon the prodigious learning of the young King Karl (despite the fact the child was universally renowned to be a dolt), upon the manifest wisdom of his mother the Queen Regent (despite the fact she was universally acknowledged to be a monstrous shrew, as Erik Glete had confirmed), and upon the enlightened policies of the High Chancellor (despite the fact he was universally reviled for avarice and inconstancy). Yet surely a diplomatist, like a sea-captain awaiting a favourable wind, seized his opportunity when it presented itself?

I saw Lydford North cast me a sideways glance of approval that seemed to say, *perhaps Matthew Quinton will make an ambassador after all.*

Dohna leaned forward and whispered something in the ear of De La Gardie, who seemed momentarily flustered by my presumption and forthrightness. The High Chancellor listened, shook his head, then spoke in measured tones. 'We understand your position, Sir Matthew, but I pray you, also understand ours. Lord Bale has a certain... following, let us say, in Gothenburg, and that city itself is markedly fractious, as you have observed. For us to comply with your request would risk public disorder, if not worse.'

'Less than ten years ago, Gothenburg was our only window on the west,' said Dohna. 'The Danes held all the land on either side of it. The late King Karl conquered those lands, but many in them still hanker after Danish rule, and the Danish crown itself seeks the reversal of the humiliation it suffered. If Gothenburg, the key to the whole coast, was suddenly to descend into chaos, do you think King Frederik would hesitate to exploit our weakness?'

Dohna spoke impressively, with a quiet, incisive command. But I saw an opportunity in his words. 'That being so, excellencies,' I said, 'should Sweden not embrace wholeheartedly an alliance with the enemy of King Frederik?'

Dohna and De La Gardie glanced at each other. The High Chancellor waved his hand airily. 'Sweden has been engaged in wars for most of the last sixty years, Sir Matthew. I know this personally, for my father, the High Constable and Field Marshal of this realm, fought in most of them. It is true that we have been fortunate in these wars. God has bestowed his grace upon Sweden, granting us victories and conquests beyond the imagining of our forefathers. But –'

'But war is expensive, Sir Matthew,' said Dohna. I was bemused; any man who dared interrupt the effective ruler of a kingdom was either markedly impudent or markedly powerful. 'Our armies and navies, our fortresses and colonies, place a vast burden upon Sweden, which is not a wealthy land.'

De La Gardie was clearly not irritated by Dohna's intervention; far from it. He inclined his head amicably toward his advisor. 'As the noble Lord Dohna says. We have had peace now for five years, Sir Matthew. Far too short a period to mend the finances of the kingdom, but a veritable eternity of tranquillity for those of us who were born in the midst of war. So you see, for Sweden to abandon such a felicitous condition would require either a profound threat to this kingdom's safety, or else the existence of certain inducements, if one might call them that, offered by those who would have us draw our sword from the scabbard once again.'

So we had quickly arrived at the crux of it. And in that instant, a profound revelation came to me. At bottom, that which great men call 'diplomacy' is nothing more than an elevated version of what the rude multitude do every week upon market day: that is, the naming of prices, the consequent haggling, and the offer of money by the one side to the other.

'King Charles is prepared to offer the most generous terms,' I said, reciting the script in which Lydford North had versed me during our journey. 'A subsidy for three years of half a million Dutch dollars a year. A preferential exemption for Swedish shipping from the strictures of our Navigation Act. A grant of territory of the King of Sweden's choosing in the treaty eventually to be concluded with our current adversaries – Surinam, perhaps, or Curacoa, or else the rich territory in the Americas now named New York.'

De La Gardie closed his eyes and appeared to be in deep contemplation of the terms offered. But Dohna's eyes remained upon me, penetrating, unsettling. At length he smiled thinly. 'A subsidy of five hundred thousand dollars a year. Identical, in other words, to that which was paid to your erstwhile ally, the Prince-Bishop of Munster. Is Sweden worth the same as tiny Munster, Sir Matthew, or is this paltry sum all that King Charles can afford?' North essayed to speak, but Dohna raised a glove hand emphatically. De La Gardie opened his eyes and nodded approvingly to his companion. 'And an exemption from your Navigation Act. I do not question how beneficial that might prove to our Gothenburg merchants, but I do question your ability to make such an offer. Would not such an exemption to an act have to be sanctioned by the very institution that passed the act in the first place, namely your Parliament? And from what I know of it, Sir Matthew, I cannot believe that the members of your House of Commons will gladly allow access to

England's trade to those they term a crew of greasy Northmen when they deny such access even to their brethren, the Scots and Irish. Am I not correct in this, gentlemen?' In desperation I looked across to North, but for once, the so-confident young man seemed genuinely nonplussed. And still Dohna pressed on, mild, quietly spoken, but utterly relentless. 'You offer us colonies. But Sweden has had them, and found them wanting. Our New Sweden was greater than your pitiful New York, but we abandoned it as being – what is your English term? – not worth the candle. We possessed Cape Coast until but a few years past, but found we could not defend it against the Dutch. Just as the Dutch, in their turn, could not defend it against an expedition in which you played a part, did you not, Sir Matthew?'

I shifted uncomfortably upon my feet. This strangely unsettling Swedish milord was remarkably well informed. 'I had the honour to serve as second in command under Major Holmes –'

'Sir Robert,' said Count Dohna emphatically. 'You will not have heard, then, that your old commander was knighted by King Charles at the recent launch of the great ship, the *Defiance*?'

North evidently sensed my profound discomfort, for he rallied to my assistance. 'My Lord, the precise amount of the subsidy offered by His Britannic Majesty is open to negotiation, as is the nature of any territorial recompense that might be granted to the Three Crowns. As for the English Parliament... I assure you that such matters can be accommodated, My Lord Dohna. The House of Commons is full of ignorance and bluster, rather like the fourth estate of your Riksdag.'

High Chancellor De La Gardie had been passive, even amused, until that moment. Now he stirred himself. 'Mister – North, is it? I fear your comparison –'

'–is worthless,' said Dohna, interrupting his superior yet again and completing the High Chancellor's sentence as a forward wife completes her husband's. 'Our fourth estate is composed of the peasantry of Sweden, and they are honest and incorruptible to a man. I believe the same cannot be said of your House of Commons. But Sir Matthew, I understand that your good-brother, the eminent Sir Venner Garvey, serves as a member of that institution. Thus are you not amply qualified to pronounce upon the matter?'

Great God. Oh, great God almighty: send down thy fiery chariot and bear away your unworthy servant Matthew Quinton from this infernal place and this infernal all-knowing man. 'The House of Commons is a veritable congregation of sages,' I heard myself say, thus uttering perhaps the most monstrous lie I have ever voiced during my inordinately long life, 'Sir Venner being one of the foremost amongst them.'

Heaven alone knew where the words came from. Defending in the same breath my serpentine brother-in-law and the venal coterie of timeservers that pollute Westminster: thus was completed Sir Matthew Quinton's transformation into that which the world calls a 'politician'.

De La Gardie and Dohna looked at each other and smiled, evidently sharing some private jest.

'Well, indeed,' said the High Chancellor of Sweden. He stood, and I realised that the audience was about to be ended. This was my moment.

'There is another matter, Your Excellency,' I said hastily.

'Another?' said De La Gardie, settling back heavily into his chair of state.

'The matter of the prohibition of felling mast-trees,' I explained.

'Mast-trees?' laughed Dohna. 'Sir Matthew, you are the strangest ambassador I have ever encountered. Ambassadors do not concern themselves with *wood*.'

'I am an ambassador by default,' I said, 'but a sea-officer of my king by profession. And sea-officers most certainly concern themselves with wood, for else, my Lord Dohna, there would be no ships.'

'And there is the rub,' said Dohna, plainly amused by the exchange. 'This last dozen years, all that you English and the Dutch and French alike have wanted are ships. More and more ships of war, each larger than the last, and for all of them you require masts. Sweden is not immune from this craze, Sir Matthew, for we have built ships so we may say we have more than the Danish king. So we cut down our great trees, and then one morning, we awake to find that our forests are gone yet every dockyard in Europe is stocked to the brim with Swedish trees. Every dockyard, that is, apart from those of England, a nation which expends ships and masts alike with wanton profligacy and no regard for the future. So, Sir Matthew – is it Sweden's fault that England alone assumes that trees grow upon money?'

Finally, I was upon firm ground. This was the realm of a king's captain, and none in that vast empty room in a Swedish castle could deny me that part. 'My Lord Dohna,' I said, 'is it England's fault that Sweden assumes only French money grows upon trees?'

Dohna was silent at last. He stared at me, but his gaze was inscrutable: I could not tell if it bespoke respect or contempt. When he spoke, his words were not the ones I had expected: namely some sort of a riposte upon the subject of the mast trees. Very quietly, he said 'You are not like your brother, Sir Matthew. Not like him at all.'

I had no time to digest Count Dohna's unexpected revelation that he had known Charles. De La Gardie rose once again from his throne, and this time it was clear the audience was concluded.

'Sir Matthew Quinton,' he said formally, 'we note your representations on behalf of His Britannic Majesty King Charles. On behalf of His Majesty the King of the Swedes, Goths and Wends, I assure you that we shall consider the case you have presented. Further negotiations upon all of these matters will be taken forward at another level.' He gestured toward North, who bowed. De La Gardie stepped down from the dais and put a hand upon my shoulder. 'Now, Sir Matthew, you will accept our hospitality here at Lacko before you set out for Gothenburg once more?'

I glanced at North, who nodded. 'It would be an honour, Your Excellency,' I said.

Inwardly, I knew that the High Chancellor's notion of 'hospitality' probably meant at least three or four days of pointless junketing and further evasive audiences. North had assured me that such would be essential to show the respect and gratitude of King Charles and his ambassador for the munificence of our Swedish hosts, but I felt deeply uneasy about it; to delay my return to my duty at Gothenburg simply to dine sumptuously with a man who had no intention of satisfying my supplications went against the Quinton grain. But such was the essence of the diplomatists' art, North insisted, and thus I was resigned to my lot.

North and I performed a deep *congée*, and when we rose, I saw to my surprise that Dohna had vanished: only De La Gardie stood upon the dais. The Count had not walked past us to the outer doors, so there must have been some concealed doorway behind the High Chancellor's chair of state. But I only came to that conclusion later. At the time, I was very nearly convinced that Dohna was a wraith who had simply disappeared into thin air.

Chapter Nine

I lay upon a truly vast bed in a circular tower room overlooking the lake of Vanern, contemplating the lavish tapestries upon the wall and the silk hangings that adorned the bed. De La Gardie had not stinted on either the decoration of his guest quarters or on the hospitality he extended to his English guests. Musk, for one, had taken considerable advantage of the fine wines and *akavit* that flowed like water in the servants' hall, and was now snoring loudly upon a bolster in the substantial anteroom of my chamber. I did not find sleep so readily. Like a play being performed time after time, the next performance beginning the moment the previous one concludes, my mind repeated the audience with De La Gardie and Dohna. For some hours, until well past midnight at any rate, I was convinced that the fiasco of that meeting was entirely my fault. I had been too brazen, too importune. I had offended against the high self-regard in which these Swedes held themselves. There would be no alliance; England would face its dreadful array of enemies alone; and it would all be the fault of Sir Matthew Quinton.

But some time after midnight, with sleep still far away, other thoughts began to intrude. Between them, Lydford North and Henry, Lord Arlington, had dealt me what was indisputably a weak hand: Dohna's acid contempt for the terms offered was perfectly justified. Perhaps Conisbrough would have played the hand better – after all, he knew De

La Gardie for certain and perhaps Dohna, too, even if he had never mentioned him to North – but at bottom the hand would have remained the same, and it was difficult to conceive even of the persuasive Conisbrough being able to pass off a broken-down dray horse as a stallion fit to win a steeplechase. And the hand that was dealt was entirely the conception of the dealer, that being His Britannic Majesty Charles the Second. It was not the first time that our illustrious but wholly duplicitous monarch had sent me on a foolhardy mission, doomed to fail; and even if his role in the present matter was less direct, I had no doubt that I was dealing with the same handiwork.

That being so, I reflected as the castle bell struck one, perhaps there was a second saving grace for King Charles's unworthy ambassador. The terms had been rejected immediately and contemptuously: hardly the response I had expected, nor, clearly, had North, whose experience of the world of the diplomat was far greater than mine. (Perplexed by the presence of Count Dohna, North left me immediately after the audience to make enquiries about the man: but no courtier would talk, and no servant could be bribed. At Whitehall, of course, it would have been the opposite. North retired to his chamber in some dudgeon.) All of which led inexorably toward one conclusion: the fate of my embassy had been determined long before. The Swedes simply had no desire to listen to the overtures of the King of Great Britain. They had no intention of being brought into the war on his side, even if His Majesty offered them the perpetual cession of Norfolk. Either the proud and arrogant Swedes believed they could and should stay aloof from the fight, or else their neutrality – or, far worse, their outright adherence – had already been purchased by another.

I rose, made my way to the water bowl on the chest below the shuttered window, broke the thin layer of ice on the surface, and splashed some of the cold water onto my face. As I did so I heard footsteps upon the spiral staircase outside. The room was at the top of the tower; there was nothing above other than the roof and a starry sky. No one would pass by unintentionally, and it was unlikely that any would come this high by accident. As silently as I could, I drew my sword from its scabbard and made my way toward the door that opened directly onto the staircase. I recalled that Musk had turned the key in the lock before retiring, arguing – correctly – that the castle was likely to be teeming with those who wished us ill, that Lady Quinton would never forgive him if I was stabbed in my bed by a Dutch assassin, and so forth. I thought of the attempt upon my life the previous night, and chided myself for having been convinced I would be safe within the castle walls; as was so often the case, perhaps Phineas Musk was right and I was wrong.

The key was large, the lock mechanism slow, and to my mind the turning of the one in the other made sufficient noise to raise the dead. Finally I pulled open the handle, burst out with sword in hand onto the tiny landing in the spiral stair, and saw –

– nothing, and heard nothing. The stair, illuminated only by one small lantern set high on the wall above the landing, was empty. There was no sound of footsteps below.

I ran down the stairs, realising too late that the stone slabs were as cold as the winter outside and that I was barefoot. At the next landing, a long, dark corridor led off toward the centre of the palace. It seemed undisturbed, and surely I would have heard one of the many doors leading off it being closed in haste? Down, then, to the next landing, and another empty corridor. I knew that the floor below contained the main public rooms, where servants were still likely to be bustling about their business and some of the courtiers might still be abroad. The spy, if such he had been, was unlikely to have gone that way. I began to venture down the dark corridor, but again, every door seemed firmly closed. Half way down, though, was a side corridor, running at right angles to the main one. I moved slowly along its length. There were no lanterns here, no candles, but my eyes were now accustomed to the dark.

I edged slowly forward. I sensed that someone was close by –

The sword-thrust came out of the blackness. I reacted with the speed and instincts of youth. My blade came up just in time, and steel deflected steel. There was a doorway, and it contained a tall, cloaked figure who now stepped out into the corridor. His arm was extended, and the hand contained a sword of Toledo steel with an elaborately interwoven hilt: a weapon I had seen before. My assailant's blade-point circled my own menacingly.

'This is neutral soil, Sir Matthew,' said a familiar voice. A voice that added a fresh, deep chill to the bitter cold that pervaded the castle. A French voice. 'The High Chancellor will not take kindly to swordplay in his own home.'

'Then lower your blade, My Lord Montnoir,' I replied in his tongue. Now I could see his gaunt, forbidding face and the familiar silver eight-pointed star upon the left breast of his cloak. I had prayed never to see him again, but the God of the Quintons had clearly chosen to ignore the supplications of His humble servant. So I advanced, waving the tip of my own sword but making no aggressive move. If blood was to be spilled here, on what was indeed neutral soil, then Montnoir would be the aggressor, not I.

I first encountered Gaspard, Seigneur de Montnoir, during a voyage to the Gambia River some years earlier: a madcap expedition instigated by the avarice of my master, King Charles. Montnoir was a Knight of Malta, one of many Frenchmen who served that ancient order in its ceaseless crusade against the Mahometans of Barbary and the Levant. But that was only one manifestation of Montnoir's fanatical obsession with rooting out any belief that did not conform precisely with the theology of Tridentine Rome. I had become another: my thwarting of his schemes in Africa made him swear revenge against me, and he had already proved his intent – and the dark depths of his means – by using my own sister-in-law, the late Louise, Countess of Ravensden, as a weapon against me and my entire family, very nearly exposing to the world the kingdom-shattering secrets that we possessed. Montnoir held great influence in his native France; influence, indeed, over her mighty king Louis the Fourteenth, as my noble Gallic friend Roger, Comte d'Andelys, had warned me. But what, in the name of God and all the angels, was he doing here, a mere sword's length away from me, in the castle of the High Chancellor of Sweden?

The Knight of Malta kept his weapon raised, the blade close against mine. He backed up the corridor; away, I realised, from the larger thoroughfare, and any chance of discovery. The rooms in this quarter of the castle seemed entirely empty.

'And put myself at your mercy, Sir Matthew? I really think not.'

With that he lunged, his blade aimed at my chest. I parried and countered. We exchanged five initial exploratory blows, perhaps six, the clash of steel echoing through the dark, empty corridor. Montnoir's style seemed more Spanish than French, his sword arm held out directly from the shoulder, the point ever circling, favouring the downward cut. For my part I followed the trusty English methods of Swetnam, thrusting rather than cutting, feinting frequently; but Montnoir was equal to it all. Our blades struck each other again and again, but I could find no way through his defence, he none through mine. And the noise, contrasting with the silence all around us, seemed deafening. Surely the guard would be alerted, and the entire palace awakened –

All the while Montnoir maintained a fighting retreat, one or two paces forward, two or three back, keeping his distance. I was too engrossed in my swordsmanship to reflect upon the strangeness of this, or indeed upon the skeletal figure's very presence in this place, at this time: Montnoir's obvious tactic was to attack, ideally to kill or disable me, but if he could not do so then to get by me, out to the thoroughfare beyond. For it was clear to me as I advanced that this corridor led nowhere. A great door sealed its end.

'I commend you upon your skill, Sir Matthew,' said Montnoir. His speech was even; there was no trace at all of a shortness of breath from his exertions. 'It is rare to find an Englishman with such finesse.'

He feinted for my head before turning the attack into a sweeping cut into the abdomen. I parried again, this time only barely in time.

'As it is rare to find a Frenchman who fights like a Spaniard, My Lord.'

Montnoir was now very nearly backed up against the door. He had nowhere to run, whereas I had all the room for manoeuvre in the world, and could choose my point of attack –

The door opened, and Montnoir stepped backward, passing through it. I followed tentatively, my sword arm extended. There was a great dark space beyond. Yet not entirely dark; I could make out the wintery moon through a vast, stained glass window. As my eyes became accustomed to the cold light, I made out elaborately carved wooden screens and statues. There was a strong whiff of incense upon the air. A few paces ahead and still facing me, Montnoir was backing slowly toward a tall altar.

A chapel, then. And a chapel not to be expected in the castle of the Protestant Chancellor of the most militantly Protestant nation in Europe: it was Catholic.

'Would you still fight me in this holy place, Sir Matthew?' Montnoir taunted.

'You began this, Montnoir. You chose the ground.'

'Not so,' said a new voice, slightly behind me and to my right. 'I chose the ground.'

Count Dohna. But where had he come from? He could not have come through the door, for I was still close enough to it to be aware of anyone coming from that direction. He had not been in the chapel when I entered it, of that I was certain. I recalled his equally sudden disappearance from De La Gardie's great hall and wondered whether the High Chancellor had installed a network of secret passageways in his vast new palace.

Yet I had a far more immediate concern. If Dohna had a sword in his hand, my flank was exposed; and if he was allied to Montnoir, I faced odds of two against one.

'Lord Montnoir,' said Dohna patiently, placing one foot in front of the other in a curiously military pose, 'you are my guest – Sir Matthew, you are the guest of the High Chancellor. In either event, both of you have been invited onto the soil of Sweden. You will show respect to the land that hosts you, and you will show respect to the house of God. Drop your swords, sirs, or I summon the Chancellor's guards.'

Montnoir glanced across toward Dohna, his expression quizzical. I could have taken advantage of the diversion to attack, but that would have placed me entirely in the wrong; and as Dohna said, this was consecrated ground in a neutral land. I would be guilty of both a secular and a spiritual sin. Slowly, reluctantly, I lowered my sword until its tip was almost upon the chapel floor. Montnoir did the same. As we eyed each other warily, I took in the full import of Count Dohna's words: *Lord Montnoir, you are my guest.* So much for the speculation of North and myself upon the allegiance of the mysterious Count. Now there was no doubt of it. Dohna did the bidding of France, and if France's chosen agent to him and to this land was the unrelenting fanatic Montnoir, then John Bale undoubtedly had the right of it: there was indeed a dark force at work in Sweden.

'Now, sirs,' said Dohna levelly, 'how came you to swordplay in this, of all places?'

'The Lord Montnoir and I are acquainted of old,' I said. 'There are outstanding matters between us.'

I did not elaborate: Dohna did not need to know that Montnoir sought revenge upon me for denying him a legendary golden mountain in Africa (whether such truly existed or not was, it seemed, entirely immaterial to the Frenchman), and that one of his means of so doing had been to employ my own good-sister in a devilish conspiracy to dishonour both the house of Quinton and our sovereign lord King Charles.

'Then which of you sought out the other?'

'I sought him out, of course,' said Montnoir stiffly. 'Like so many of his race, this man is a manifest heretic and an enemy to France. I know why he has come for audience with the High Chancellor. He seeks to deflect this kingdom from the righteous course ordained for it.'

'That being alliance with France against England, Lord Montnoir?' I demanded.

The Knight of Malta seemed genuinely affronted by the remark. 'How typical of you English, that you see this world solely in terms of the petty combinations or squabbles of earthly princelings!' He nodded toward Dohna. 'Our purpose here is a far greater one, a more noble one, Sir Matthew, for before you is –'

'Enough, My Lord!' said Dohna emphatically. I had not imagined the cold, arrogant Montnoir being amenable to correction by any man, but he accepted Dohna's rebuke meekly. The Swede turned to me. 'Sir Matthew, on behalf of the High Chancellor and the monarch of the Three Crowns I crave your apology for the unforgivable conduct of the Lord Montnoir. I hope you believe me when I say that he has assaulted you thus without my knowledge or approbation. Quite the opposite, in fact.'

Dohna exuded an air of quiet authority, and his anger against my enemy seemed genuine enough. Inwardly, I was torn. Matthew Quinton the warrior and sea-captain was prepared to damn the Swede's apology as worthless, to challenge Montnoir to a duel to the death there and then (neutral ground or no), and to threaten Dohna and De La Gardie with war against the three crowns of King Charles Stuart. But Sir Matthew Quinton the ambassador knew full well that the threat of war was an empty one and that killing Montnoir on Swedish soil – assuming I was capable of so doing, for he was evidently a highly skilled opponent – would have placed me and the cause I served entirely in the wrong, whereas at that moment I had aggrieved right entirely upon my side.

'I shall need to take counsel,' I said in what I took to be true diplomatic fashion. With that, I bowed my head to Montnoir and Dohna in turn, turned upon my heel and walked from the chapel, not without half-expecting Montnoir to ignore Dohna's entreaties and take the opportunity to stab or shoot me in the back. But no such blow arrived, and as I walked briskly back toward my chamber, I heard the unmistake-able sounds of an argument breaking out between Dohna and Montnoir, the former being dominant.

* * *

Lydford North was summoned to my chamber by Musk. The young man listened intently as I related all that had transpired, his face by turns contemplative and frowning angrily.

'Thus it seems our embassy has been a folly of the first order, Mister North,' I said. 'Montnoir is already ensconced with De La Gardie and Dohna, no doubt bringing promises of subsidies from King Louis so vast that they will make King Charles's offer resemble an almshouse charity box. For Montnoir now to attack me is an affront against hon-our that cannot be tolerated. We must leave at daylight and return at once at Gothenburg.'

Inwardly, I was relieved that Montnoir had resolved my dilemma for me: he had provided the perfect excuse to abandon the days of empty banqueting and pointless audiences that might otherwise have lain before me.

'Oh joy unbounded,' said Musk, who evidently thought differently. 'A four day ride through Hell's own garden, then we turn straight round and make a four day ride back again. Musk's arse will be like a year-old side of beef, that it will. A side of beef frozen in ice.'

North, who always seemed perplexed by the latitude I permitted Musk, ignored him. 'I understand your anger, Sir Matthew, but I fear such a departure might be perceived by our Swedish hosts as intemper-ate – as an affront to *their* honour. It may be that our cause is a hopeless one, and perhaps it always was, even if the late Lord Conisbrough had undertaken the embassy in your stead.'

'Maybe more so, Mister North. Conisbrough would not have known Montnoir, even if he encountered him. Thus he would have been unlikely to expose the perfidy of the Swedes so quickly. Your embassy might have dragged on for months, providing false hope to our masters in Whitehall, when all the while Dohna and Montnoir ensured that Sweden secretly took the side of our enemies.'

North was thoughtful, his eyes seemingly fixed upon the shuttered window as though he were trying to see the stars beyond. 'There is another possibility, Sir Matthew.'

'Another?'

'Montnoir told you his business was greater than that of mere alliances between kingdoms. And, Sir Matthew, you say that you know this man to be a *dévot* of the most extreme sort, an implacable enemy to all who follow the reformed faith.' North turned and looked at me directly. 'Then could not a case be made for saying that this Montnoir or his agents might have killed Lord Conisbrough?'

The full enormity of North's suggestion took a moment to register. If, somehow, Montnoir had got wind of the secret embassy – and the French king's network of spies within the English court reached to the very highest levels, as I knew from experience – then surely it was entirely feasible that he should have sought to forestall it in the most brutally direct manner possible?

'So we're staying after all, then?' Musk asked hopefully.

'No, Musk,' I said. 'Whatever Montnoir is about is not my affair, even if he truly was My Lord Conisbrough's killer. I have played the part you demanded of me, Mister North, and I have failed in it. Honour and duty alike demand that I resume the part given me by His Royal Highness, the Lord High Admiral, as captain of the *Cressy*.'

North looked hard at me, but he knew full well he had no hold over me now. The belief that we might somehow bring Sweden into alliance with England had been dispelled for good and all by the discomforting revelation of Count Dohna's sway over the High Chancellor and by the presence of Montnoir, who was evidently engaged with Dohna upon some dark scheme, designed no doubt for the greater benefit of France and the Church of Rome.

'Very well, Sir Matthew,' said North reluctantly, 'if you will have it so. With your permission, though, I will remain here for some days more, perhaps longer. It may be that a limited understanding of some sort with this kingdom can still be achieved.'

To this day, I marvel at North's perseverance in the face of patently hopeless odds. But I have learned many times since that this is the lot of the diplomatist: to strive for accommodations and agreements long after all reasonable men have abandoned hope and the unreasonable have drawn their swords. Musk put it more succinctly: 'Determined bugger, that. Reckon he'll go far – perhaps secretary of state one day in the stead of old Cut-Nose Arlington, unless all those enemies do for him first.'

Our peremptory departure from the castle of Lacko took place two hours later, after sunrise. It followed a brief audience with the High Chancellor, this time *sans* the presence of Count Dohna. De La Gardie expressed outrage – perhaps feigned, perhaps not – at the profound offence committed against me by the Lord Montnoir. He implored me to stay, to enjoy his hospitality and to learn that Swedes knew how to make good wrongs done on their soil, but I remained adamant. I made a final plea for him to give credence to the terms offered by King Charles, to permit the deportation of the traitor Bale and to renew the felling of trees, but despite his seeming concern to mollify me, De La Gardie's replies on all points remained studiously evasive. His final words were to beg me to convey his undying respect to King Charles, to pray that our two nations would enjoy the felicity of peace and good understanding, and all the grand, empty phrases that I have heard a thousand times since from the mouths of sovereigns and statesmen galore.

To provide further proof of his regrets and respect alike, the High Chancellor provided a greatly enhanced escort of two dozen cavalry-men under a Major Elfving, a far more refined and garrulous creature than the lumpen Captain Larssen. He had fought at Nordlingen and Leipzig; moreover, he had been to England and even met Cromwell when serving in the escort to the ambassador sent by Sweden to our late and unlamented Lord Protector, so he possessed a smattering of English (thankfully of a more refined variety than that of General Erik Glete). Thus he provided good companionship upon the road, the same one we had taken from Gothenburg to Lacko so few days before, and he knew the country better than Larssen, which meant that he found us better inns and was able to purvey better victuals. I was grateful for this, for my Montnoir-disturbed sleep of the previous night was telling on me by dusk of the first day of the journey. Those who use the sea are accustomed to mere snatches of sleep, two hours here and three there, the pattern being dictated by the inexorable tyranny of the watches; for even a captain, the one man to whom the tolling of the ship's bell does not dictate, cannot permit himself the luxuries enjoyed by our slugabeds ashore, who remain beneath the covers for as many as five hours in summer or three-and-three in winter. Even so, by the evening of that first day out of Lacko I was mightily weary and glad to find a good bed in a good inn, untroubled by wolves, cutthroats or Frenchmen.

The following morning onwards, the weather began steadily to worsen. The wind had shifted from north-east to north-west and sometimes due west, and although that brought the promise of an imminent thaw and the release of the mast-ships, in the first instance it brought sharp flurries of snow, sometimes driving directly into our faces. Our progress was thus slower, and by the late afternoon of the fourth day of our journey we were still some forty English miles from Gothenburg, facing the prospect of at least another two days on the road. MacFerran was again positive that we were being followed, but on this occasion I was less certain and in any case less concerned. If any wished us ill they would surely have struck before now, so I was inclined to believe that the elusive men in the woods were perhaps nothing more than wolves, or at worst merely common robbers seeking an opportunity that had not come and would not.

We were two miles short of our inn for the night when the blizzard struck. It came on unexpectedly; the leaden grey clouds seemed no different to those that had been present throughout the journey. It also came on rapidly. From the first flakes to the full force of the snow was a matter of only minutes. Head down, chin tight into my chest, I endeavoured to stay in sight of the man in front of me, one of Elfving's soldiers, or at the very least to steer my horse by the hoof-prints in the snow of the steed in front. But the snow blew so hard that I often lost sight of the rider in front, and the prints were being covered as soon as they were made. I kept rubbing my forearm across my eyes, but it made little difference. The snow stung my flesh like so many tiny dagger-pricks. It was as though I was within a prison of pure white, with jets of snow pumping directly into my face: and after barely two or three minutes, I realised that I did not have the faintest idea of my direction. My horse, poor beast, struggled on determinedly, his own head bowed against the onslaught, but of other riders, or indeed of the road itself, there was no sign. Not wishing to stray too far from the road by accident, I turned, reined in and came to a stop, so that at least both the horse and I presented our backs to the blizzard. As I halted, I dimly made out a dark shape in the snow. Another rider. I had not strayed from the party after all, and whoever was behind me had made a better fist of keeping me in sight than I had with the man in front of me.

Too late, I saw the weapon in the rider's hand. His arm went up sharply and came at me through the snow, a black blur cutting through the white. Whatever was in his hand – sword, club, pistol – struck my temple. I was aware of blinding pain, of falling, of the white cushion of snow enveloping my body, before all was darkness.

Chapter Ten

I awoke slowly from a comforting dream of my Cornelia. But there was no comfort in this awakening. My head throbbed with a relentless pain, and I recalled the blow that had brought it. I opened my eyes with difficulty; my eyelids felt as though they were sinews tearing apart from a battle-wound. I saw the whitewashed walls and domed ceiling of a round, bare room. I raised my head a little from the rough bolster upon which I lay, but the effort caused me very nearly to scream in agony. After lying for a few minutes more I tried again, and despite the pain I managed to turn my head a little to take in more of my surroundings. There was a door at the far end of the room: closed, no doubt locked. A single small window was slightly to my left, high up, and the dreary light from it suggested that it was daylight; but what hour, God alone knew. Between the door and the window was a small fireplace, lit, giving out but a feeble warmth that did little to counter the bitter cold of the Swedish winter. There was something strangely familiar about the place, but it took me some little time to identify it. Finally, my senses recovered enough to grasp the truth, at once so elusive and yet so obvious. I could smell brine, and I could hear the familiar sounds of waves lapping upon a shore and the cry of seabirds. This was not Lacko; wherever it was, it was by the sea.

Keeping my head upright lessened the pain, and after a few minutes

I looked down. I was still in the clothes I had worn when I was taken, but one addition had been made during my slumber. I was now adorned with a manacle of iron, to which was attached a chain fastened to a bolt in the middle of the floor, some feet away.

A prison, then.

Slowly, painfully, I pulled myself up. There was pain in my side too, presumably from the fall from my horse. Finally, I managed to sit up on the side of the bed. Now I could see an opening covered by a grill in the floor, between the fireplace and the door. I knew it immediately; had seen its kind many times in the dungeons of England's venerable castles. A pit, into which prisoners with no hope of redemption could be cast down to die of starvation or despair. The fact that I remained above ground, in relatively comfortable circumstances, must mean that I still had a chance of remaining alive. But who was my captor, and if there was to be redemption for Matt Quinton, then who might be my redeemer?

I do not know how long I sat there, contemplating my situation, but at length a hatch in the door was pulled sharply aside and, through the small grill thus revealed, I saw a face. A female face: round, old and dirty. I called out – something to the effect that I was Sir Matthew Quinton, a knight of England, and that the wrath of King Charles and his infinite legions would rain down upon her head if she did not release me at once. Whether the crone understood a single word of it, I very much doubt. After a minute or two the hatch was shut and I was left alone once more.

Perhaps an hour passed; or it might have been two.

Finally the door opened, and the crone reappeared. She pushed a tray across the floor until it was just within my reach, but she herself took care to remain just beyond the furthest point I could reach. Without a word, she left. The heavy lock on the door closed once again.

I stretched out and pulled the tray to me. It contained but a cup of brackish water and a small crust of mouldy bread. Even so, I ate and drank greedily, for I knew not when a better meal might come: or indeed, whether another meal of any sort would ever appear again.

My repast done with, I lay back upon my pallet. My thoughts raced this way and that. I wondered what my friends were doing. Searching for me, no doubt, but this was an unfamiliar land, any trail was sure to have been covered by snow, and at some point Kit Farrell would have to fulfil the higher duty that now behoved him as acting captain of the *Cressy*, namely to take the ship and the mast fleet home to England. I thought upon Cornelia, and the grief my disappearance would cause her –

The grill opened once again, the crone looked in on me briefly, then I was left once more to my troubled imaginings. At some point I must have lapsed into sleep, for when I awoke the cell was even darker and far colder. I brought my knees up to my chest for warmth, but still my teeth chattered and my fingers became steadily number. I remained in that posture for I know not how long; then the grill opened once again, although it was now too dark for me to see the face framed in it. But after a few minutes the door opened. The crone shuffled in and flung a thin, ancient blanket across the room. I snatched at it eagerly and covered myself. It seemed clear that whatever other fate my captor intended for me, I would not freeze to death.

Dawn came; or at least, a thin grey light appeared through the tiny window of the cell stop. I stood and walked about as much as my chain would permit, hoping thereby to keep my blood flowing. I began to pray that the crone would return, if only to bring a banquet equal to that of the previous evening and to take away my slop bucket, but the hours passed by and there was no sign of her. With a heavy heart I sat down once again upon the pallet and tried to occupy my mind by recalling lists. The Kings of England, with their dates, beginning with Brutus and thus on to Lear, Alfred, Canute and all the rest. The Earls of Ravensden, beginning with the first Earl's elevation to the rank after Agincourt. But these occupied too little time. On, then, to the list of the Navy in England – the First Rates, *Sovereign, Royal Prince, Royal Charles...*

I was halfway through the catalogue of the Fifth Rates, just beyond my old command the *Jupiter*, when the door opened. I realised at once that it was not my familiar mute gaoler. The figure framed in the doorway was taller, and thinner. At first it was too dark for me to make out his face, but I knew him at once. He wore the same all-enveloping black cloak that I had seen before, both on the River Gambia and in the castle of Lacko.

He stepped into the room. 'Good evening, Sir Matthew,' he said in his precise, emotionless French.

I stood and met the black eyes of my old foe. I even essayed a slight bow of the head. 'My Lord Montnoir,' I replied.

* * *

Montnoir stared at me appraisingly, as though judging a sale animal at a fair. Then he raised his hands in a posture of prayer, looked up to the heavens and said, 'Thanks be to God, the blessed virgin and all the Saints, for delivering you into my hand, Sir Matthew Quinton. The ways of the Lord are mysterious, but is not the fact you are now in my power proof of the righteousness of my faith? Our paths have been destined to cross, and yours has been destined to end here, in this place.'

'As I see it, a snowstorm and your agents delivered me into your hands. God seemed to have precious little to do with it.'

'There speaks an inveterate heretic, oblivious to the truths laid so manifestly before him. But the manner of your delivery to me is of little consequence. What matters, Sir Matthew, is that you are here in this place, and none know where you are. The famously royalist captain of an English man-of-war disappears in the vicinity of Gothenburg, a town full of Dutchmen with whose land his own is at war, and rebel Englishmen hell-bent on vengeance against all cavaliers. The home of a regicide who would surely think nothing of murdering a knight, having already killed a king.' Montnoir was contemptuous. 'Who can be surprised by such a disappearance? You are already dead to the world, Quinton.'

'You have seized the King of England's captain upon neutral soil, Montnoir. You can have no power over me here in Sweden,' I said, feigning more conviction than I felt. Could Montnoir really be in Sweden solely to lure me into his power? If he wished me dead or his prisoner, surely he could have effected either outcome far more easily in England –

'Do you see any other power before you, Sir Matthew? Here, in this room, I am judge, jury – yes, and executioner, if I wish it.'

He was quoting back to me words I had once spoken to him, on a sun-baked parade ground in Africa.

'If you wish to kill me, be swift about it, my Lord. I fear I may catch a chill if I stay longer in such draughty lodgings.'

'English humour,' said Montnoir. 'Always make light of matters, always make a jest. More proof, if it were needed, of how mean and worthless a people you are – of why your pitiful island will never amount to anything in the world.' Montnoir walked away, toward the window. With his back to me he said, 'But in one sense, you are right. I did indeed order your death upon your journey from Gothenburg, but my agents proved singularly incompetent. I sought to accomplish the same end with my own sword in the castle of Lacko, but was thwarted by – by the intervention of another. Yet the Lord moves in mysterious ways, and those failures gave me time to pray and to understand that there might be another way, a better way, of dealing with you. But do not be mistaken. There is ample cause to pass sentence of death upon you, Sir Matthew Quinton, and I have already done so in the name of the righteous God of Heaven.' Gaspard de Montnoir as God's viceroy: the sheer arrogance of the man appalled me, but did not surprise. Yet I still lived, and his words suggested he did not intend to kill me at once. He continued: 'Your crimes are manifest and manifold. You are an undoubted heretic, so my oath to the Grand Master of the Order of Jerusalem, Rhodes and Malta impels me to place your sinful body upon a pyre and burn it in cleansing fire. Such ought to prove an ample remedy for the chills and draughts that assail you, Sir Matthew.'

'Be careful, my Lord,' I said, 'your words are very near to our English humour.' Behind my bluster, though, I was remembering a scene from my childhood: my uncle Tristram frightening me beyond measure with his descriptions of the fates of Archbishop Cranmer and the other blessed martyrs burned in Queen Mary's time. Tris was an excellent storyteller, but now I had cause to wish he had not been quite so vivid. For I could almost feel the flames licking my flesh, burning it slowly from the bone.

Montnoir ignored my jest. Turning back toward me, he said 'But you are guilty of a secular crime too, Sir Matthew. The murder of your own good-sister, the noble Lady Louise, late Countess of Ravensden. Thus you are doubly dammed, and I have double cause to condemn you to death, here and now.'

I could feel my heart beating faster. 'She killed herself, Montnoir. She flung herself from a castle tower.'

'Did she fall, or was she pushed? Is that not also an example of your English humour, Sir Matthew? There were no witnesses other than members of your own family, who sought to be rid of her.'

Montnoir's words were striking home with more effect than he realised. Ever since the death of my inconvenient sister-in-law during the previous summer, I had been troubled by guilt: both guilt over the manner of her dying, and guilt over feelings about her that at that time I could not even begin to acknowledge.

'She was a traitor to England,' I protested, albeit with a catch in my throat, 'an agent of France – of *you*, Montnoir –'

'Quite so,' said the Knight of Malta, 'an agent of mine, and no traitor, for it is not possible to be a traitor to a heretical cause. Thus again I have double cause against you, Sir Matthew. You are guilty of the murder of an innocent woman, and of obstructing the designs of my master, the most Christian King. Yes, you deserve to die, beyond all hope of redemption.' He was perfectly still: the epitome of the harbinger of death. 'And before you are placed upon the pyre, your sins make you deserving of some of the other delights of this place. This is an old castle, and the adjacent cellars contain many instruments employed upon the recalcitrant in earlier times. Why, there are implements here that were unknown even to the holy Inquisition, which I had the honour of attending for some months after the peace of the Pyrenees. But fear not, Sir Matthew – whatever pains you endure in these dungeons will be spirited away by the cleansing fire. A brief moment of bliss before you face an eternity of agony, first in Purgatory and thereafter in hell.'

With that, he turned upon his heel and left. I did not doubt the truth of his words: Montnoir wished me dead, had ample cause in his own eyes, and by his possession of this Castle – presumably through the good offices of the duplicitous Dohna, or perhaps even De La Gardie himself – he plainly had the means to bring about my end. I sat upon my pallet, imagined Montnoir presenting my burned ashes to Cornelia, and shuddered.

* * *

I found but little sleep that night. What little I had was disturbed by dreams of fires and burning flesh, or else by an image that was not a dream but a vivid memory: the sight of my good-sister falling through air, her eyes fixed upon me right up to the very moment that her body shattered upon the ground.

Long before dawn, the door of the cell opened again, and once more the forbidding presence of the Seigneur de Montnoir stood before me, his pale face seeming to float, disembodied, against the blackness of his garb and the cell walls.

'Do you have trouble sleeping, my Lord?' I asked, summoning more impudence than I truly felt.

He ignored me. Instead he came very close until his face was barely inches from mine. I could easily have reached up and placed my hands upon his throat, but I had no doubt that beneath his cloak his hand would be resting upon his sword hilt, ready to run me through if I dared even to lift a finger against him.

'A heretic's death,' he whispered, 'alone, here in a Swedish castle. No one will know where or how you died, none will know even that you have no burial place and that instead your ashes are blown by the bitter Swedish winds. Should that really be a fate for a Quinton, Sir Matthew?'

'I had not imagined you would concern yourself with my family's honour, Montnoir.'

The Frenchman affected not to hear me. 'Yet you are an entire dynasty of heretics and enemies of France,' he said. 'Your grandfather was a mere pirate who fought against God's own righteous crusade, the armada of King Philip. He and his father before him did more than most to put to unworthy death the blessed martyr Mary of Scotland at the behest of that unnatural bastard and heretic Elizabeth Tudor. You Quintons have troubled the true church for generations. You should pay the price for their sins too, Sir Matthew.'

'Your knowledge of my family's history is commendable, my Lord.'

'More than you know. For instance, I know that a form of mitigation for your sins flows within you. I speak of your grandmother's blood.'

Unexpected, this. Louise-Marie de Monconseil-Bragellone had married the much older eighth Earl of Ravensden but retained her Catholic faith, a fact that had caused much difficulty between them. My grandmother had also played a decidedly ambivalent part in my childhood, with she and my mother, the two Dowager Countesses of Ravensden, warring over the faith in which I should be brought up. But surely Montnoir could not know that –

'My grandmother, my Lord?' I said, essaying a riposte. 'True, it is thanks to her that I can speak with you in your own tongue–'

'She was a true servant of holy Church,' Montnoir interrupted, 'as all of her family had been. Do you know the history of your French ancestors as well as you know that of the Quinton heretics, Sir Matthew? No?

You should learn it. You would be amazed.' He moved a little further away, and I realised that despite the coldness of the cell, I had been sweating. 'And thus it seems to me a man with the blood of the house of Monconseil-Bragellone might deserve a better fate than to be cremated alive in the courtyard of a Swedish castle.'

I could barely comprehend what Montnoir was saying. Only hours before, he was threatening me with imminent and certain death, yet now he seemed to be laying some sort of alternative before me. Exhausted, hungry, and increasingly impatient of the Frenchman's diatribe, I snapped 'For God's sake, Montnoir, enough of this! You seek my death. Then do it swiftly, man, and spare me any more of your sophistry!'

'You mistake me, Sir Matthew,' said Montnoir lightly. 'In truth, I do not seek your death. Or rather, not your immediate death – unless you give me no alternative. Instead, I seek your soul.' I stared at him, speechless. 'Your grandmother instructed you in the true faith,' he said. 'She sought to have you brought up as a Catholic. Is that not so, Sir Matthew?'

How would he know that? Now, of course, I see that Montnoir did not need to know, nor even for the late Countess Louise to tell him what she had gleaned of my family's history: it might have been no more than a well educated guess. Having failed to bring up her own sons as servants of Rome, as the Catholic creed demanded (but which Earl Matthew would not have permitted in a million centuries), the Countess Louise-Marie chose her younger grandson as the likeliest candidate to enable her to fulfil her duty to her faith. But then, cold, disorientated in a dungeon and still in some pain from my fall, Montnoir's words disturbed me more than I care to remember.

The Frenchman took my appalled silence for assent. 'God's will has placed you in my power, Sir Matthew, and now God's will decrees that you will fulfil your destiny. You have a choice. You can choose the fate of a heretic and murderer, or else you can join with me to fight at my side.' He began to pace the cell floor. 'Perhaps you do not know that before the vile apostasy which heretics term the Reformation, English knights were ever among the most stalwart of my Order. Sir William Weston captained the ship that carried the Grand Master from Rhodes when it fell to the heathens. Sir Oliver Starkey fought alongside Grand Master La Vallette in the heroic defence of Malta against Sultan Suleiman's great siege. The English province of the Order still exists, Sir Matthew, albeit dormant. It needs only one valiant knight to restore it to life.' My confused thoughts could not take this in. What in the Devil's name was the man about? 'The Order also needs the swords and the skills of brave seamen, Sir Matthew. The Mahometan heathens are at the gates of Candia, and if it falls, where will be next for them? Rome or Vienna? Paris or London?'

My friend Roger d'Andelys had once told me that some in France believed Montnoir to be descended from the old prophet Nostradamus, and they might have taken his words to me as proof: for Candia, Venice's great fortress on Crete, did indeed fall some three years later, after a siege of a quarter-century, and within another fourteen years the Turks would be at the very gates of Vienna. 'I can see us, Sir Matthew, you and I, sailing together upon the Middle Sea, extirpating the heathens wherever we encounter them. Such a valiant destiny would absolve you of both your past heresy and your part in the death of the Countess of Ravensden. Join me, Sir Matthew. Return to the faith that your cousins in France hold dear to this day. Put aside the insignificant and doomed schism of a mere century. Return to the true church that countless generations of Quintons served and loved.'

Montnoir's proposition beggared belief. I felt my stomach turn, though whether from the enormity of it or from simple hunger, I knew not. One moment he was conjuring up for me a vision of burning at the stake, my hair in flames and my flesh blackening; the next, he was offering me the prospect of crusading alongside him, clad alike in the cloak and eight-pointed star of a Knight of Malta. I wondered briefly whether the Frenchman was jesting, but the grim-visaged Montnoir never jested.

The sheer incongruity of it all made me laugh, and laughter, in turn, made me defiant.

'I am a Knight already, Lord Montnoir – a Knight of the King of England, and there could be no high honour for an Englishman. What is more, I am a confirmed member of the holy Church of England, by law established. We abjure the Pope and the false idolatries of Rome. No, my Lord – I will not join you, however much you threaten me with the rack or the bonfire.'

Montnoir did not appear taken aback by my rejection of his blandishments; indeed, he seemed to expect it.

'Your faith is based upon sand, Sir Matthew. Your King is but an idle whoring fellow, a feeble mouse next to the great lion that is my master, King Louis. And your precious Church of England? Why, your church rests on nothing more than the delusions of the heretic Luther and the lust of your demented King Henry. Whereas I stand upon the rock of Peter, along with the Blessed Virgin and all the saints. A millennium and a half of truth and authority.' Montnoir leaned forward, and I saw that his eyes were ablaze. 'Come, Sir Matthew, recall what your grandmother taught you. Say with me the Latin credo and the Ave Maria.'

I knew the words well enough; had said them often enough. I still recalled the guilty pleasure that those words had given me, for they were a secret that I shared with my grandmother. A secret that was bound to – and eventually did – enrage my mother. But I would not resurrect those memories now to indulge the sinister figure that stood before me. I shook my head vigorously.

Once again Montnoir leaned closer to me, his long thin face barely inches from mine.

'You will convert, Sir Matthew,' he said. 'I see it in your eyes. Your grandmother planted a seed that has never quite died within your heart. You merely require a guide to take you back to it and then forward to your destiny. I shall be that guide, Sir Matthew. Or else I shall be the man who puts the brand to the faggots.'

Chapter Eleven

Thus it began.

There was no more food, no sleep and barely any water. Instead, there was Montnoir. Always, relentlessly, Montnoir, for hours on end, until I lost track of day and night. He began with Scripture: Matthew Chapter Sixteen, John Chapter Six, and countless other of the texts from which the Roman Church claimed its authority. He veritably bombarded me with the early Church fathers from Tertullian to Athanasius and Saint Augustine. Then he ranged from theology (the supposed truths of transubstantiation, the nature of apostolic succession, and so forth), through history (the iniquities of King Henry VIII, Queen Elizabeth and their bishops), and finally, always finally, to my family and myself, to my grandmother and the death of the Countess Louise. I had heard of the Jesuits, and in due course I would meet several of them, but I never encountered a more formidable advocate for the Roman Church than Gaspard, Seigneur De Montnoir. He challenged every assumption about religion that I had ever possessed: his soft, ceaseless French monotone pulled down the entire edifice of Anglican faith and exalted in its place that which he termed the eternal glory of Rome.

In truth, I was ill-prepared to resist the onslaught. My faith was that of most Englishmen: I attended church dutifully every Sunday, sang the hymns, mouthed the prayers, and let my mind wander during the sermon. I could recite some of the more familiar psalms and give chapter and verse for some of the Bible's best-known passages, but beyond that, I was lost. For me, as for most of my compatriots, church was principally an opportunity to catch up on the week's news with one's neighbours, and for young men and young women to ogle each other. My uncle Tristram, a formidable intellect and brilliant debater, would perhaps have given Montnoir short shrift, but he was sceptical in religion, and although he had been diligent in teaching his nephew history, the classics, philosophy and the sciences, his own impatience with theology had translated into a reluctance to immerse me in it. Even my mother would have had little difficulty countering Montnoir's arguments: she was deeply devout and knew much of the Bible off by heart, but she had singularly failed to transmit such further to her second son. Thus all in all I was as unprepared for Montnoir's formidable intellectual siege as were the Trojans when the Greeks emerged from the wooden horse.

'Let us consider the sacrament of confession, so heinously rejected by the heretic Luther and your apostate Church of England. I shall lay before you the doctrine as it is expounded in scripture, in the gospels of John and Matthew, whose name you bear and should honour, the epistle to the Corinthians and elsewhere. I shall lay before you the unchallengeable pronouncements of the early elders, Irenaeus, Cyprian, John Chryostom and many others. I shall lay before you the eternal truths that were mingled with the lifeblood of your dear grandmother.' Montnoir kept his face close to mine, his dark, hostile eyes fixed relentlessly on my own. I could smell him; for an ascetic holy warrior, the Knight of Malta seemed not to have stinted on the finer perfumes. Montnoir held no Bible in his hand and referred to no printed tract. Every argument and every passage of scripture that he flung at me was conjured up from the depths of his formidable memory. 'So, then – Saint John, Chapter the Twentieth, the twenty-first to twenty-third verses. "Then said Jesus to them again, Peace be unto you: as my Father hath sent me, even so send I you. And when he had said this, he breathed on them, and saith unto them, Receive ye the Holy Ghost: Whose soever sins ye remit, they are remitted unto them; and whose soever sins ye retain, they are retained." Now, Sir Matthew, I put it to you that you stand in certain need of the absolution that follows confession – absolution of the sins of heresy and murder...'

Slowly, I realise that I was no longer certain what was true and what was not. My head reeled. I felt sick, and several times was on the point of spewing. Montnoir's argument was so plausible, so firmly founded upon Scripture, that I began to find it ever more convincing. Even in that moment, when I was so weak and my mind so clouded, I half realised what was happening: that Montnoir was reawakening feelings I had known before. His case was more densely argued and couched in more sophisticated language, but it was essentially the same one that the magnificent and imperious Louise-Marie, Dowager Countess of Ravensden, had deployed upon her impressionable grandson when he was but nine or ten, and had then periodically redeployed at intervals in the years before her death, contrary to all the remonstrations of her son Tristram and her daughter-in-law, my mother. Thus Montnoir's words often struck unconscious chords that he could not have anticipated, and took me back to a time when I was a young boy, fatherless and lonely amid the great ruins of Ravensden Abbey. A young boy intrigued by, and strongly attracted to, the apparent eternal certainties of the faith that his grandmother espoused. More than once Montnoir's face seemed to disappear, to be replaced by that of the old Countess, and more than once I was on the point of falling to my knees and reciting with tears of joy the words that Montnoir was so desperate to hear from my lips, the words I had uttered often enough as a child and which surely could hardly hurt now: *Ave Maria, gratia plena...*

Yet each time, somehow, I held myself back. Just as I was about to yield, my grandfather, the formidable Earl Matthew, would appear before my confused, racing mind, scowling reprovingly at his wife's shade and growling: *'Steady, lad. Stay true'.*

At one point, indeed, I rallied feebly against my tormentor. Montnoir was railing against the Church of England, and hitting home. 'Consider the church that your King has put in place since his restoration, Sir Matthew. It is the church of the late Archbishop Laud – altars and altar rails, bells and incense, genuflection and the sign of the cross. Why, it even has saints! The late King Charles, a saint and martyr! Come, Sir Matthew, you must see that the difference between this so-called Anglicanism and the true church of Rome is but paper thin. Is it so very difficult to cut the paper, to move from the one to the other as your grandmother wished you? Would you really condemn your immortal soul to millennia of Purgatory and hell, simply so that you may utter your creed in English instead of Latin?'

I was desperately hungry and tired, yet somehow I murmured 'We Anglicans do not admit of Purgatory, Montnoir. And I was never much fond of Latin.'

Montnoir remained implacable. 'Purgatory is the fate that awaits you if you do not repent, Sir Matthew. Purgatory, and then eternal damnation, for you and all those you hold dear. For your wife Cornelia, indeed. Purgatory and hell have special circles set aside for the Dutch. At once heretics against God and rebels against their divinely anointed monarch – yes, the Dutch face damnation, every man, woman and child of them!'

'If that is so, Lord Montnoir,' I said wearily, 'why does your King Louis ally with them in the present war?'

It was merely a chance remark, a mere reflex prompted by my anger at his mention of my dear wife, but Montnoir recoiled as though he had been physically struck.

'The Most Christian King does not always follow the path that God has ordained for him,' said Montnoir. There was a harshness in his voice that had not been present before. 'Some of those about him, about his court, advise him badly, and persuade him to pursue policies that are not in the interests of holy mother Church. Thus he makes alliance with an apostate republic when he should join with Spain, the Emperor and the Pope to extirpate Protestantism from Europe. Then, reunited and invincible, Christendom should turn East in crusade against the heathen hordes!' Montnoir's eyes blazed. '*That* is the true destiny of Louis de Bourbon! And yet the heretical Huguenots are permitted to worship freely, when his Majesty's every waking moment ought to be devoted to purging them from his realm!'

I had never seen the Knight of Malta so passionate, so enraged. Montnoir had talked dispassionately of what he termed the heresies of the English and the Dutch, and of the threat posed by those he termed the Mahometan heathens. Why, then, did the subject of the Huguenots in France animate him so? Unless –

I recalled an argument that Montnoir had brought against me, hours earlier – the story of Saul of Tarsus on the road to Damascus. I thought, too, upon something my French friend Roger, comte d'Andelys, had once told me about Montnoir's origins: of where his ancestral lands lay. At once, all was clear.

'You were a convert,' I said. 'You are a man of Guyenne, and that has ever been a stronghold of the Huguenots. That is why you detest them, and the whole of Protestantism. You have turned against your own, Montnoir – against what you once were.'

Montnoir's mouth fell open. He stared at me as though he were truly seeing me for the first time.

'How can you know that?' he gasped.

'As you persist in reminding me, Lord Montnoir, my grandmother was French. I have friends among the French. Thus I am not entirely ignorant of the history and geography of your country.'

Montnoir seemed about to reply, but thought better of it. Instead he turned abruptly and left the cell, leaving me blessedly alone. I put my head down upon my pallet and was asleep in an instant.

* * *

I do not know if it was five minutes or five hours later when the crone's shaking woke me. Montnoir stood behind her, the mask of cold contempt upon his face fully restored.

'You are obdurate, Sir Matthew,' said Montnoir, 'far more obdurate than I had anticipated.' He sighed, and seemed genuinely saddened. 'So be it. You resist the eternal truth, and you shall pay the price. It is evident that I have wasted my breath upon you, Quinton. You deserve the slowest, most painful death that can be inflicted on a man. Subjection to the instruments in the adjacent cellars, then consignment to the pit yonder, to be eaten alive by the rats.' He nodded toward the nearby grill in the floor. 'But to my regret, I am constrained by time and circumstance. Nevertheless, I do not require time or instruments of metal to inflict sufficient agonies upon you. I have observed many times that inflicting pain upon a man's loved ones, or the threat of inflicting it, often has a more powerful effect than merely crushing fingers or breaking limbs. Take your dear Cornelia, for instance –'

The very mention of her name was sufficient. Summoning what strength remained to me, I flung myself from the pallet and ran, head down, for Montnoir. But he stepped backwards smartly, and the manacle bit into my ankle like a man trap. I fell into the dirt that covered the cold stone floor, face down, my outstretched arms reaching impotently toward the feet of the Knight of Malta.

'You demon, Montnoir! You hell-spawned bastard!'

'Oh have no fear, Sir Matthew, I have no intention of maiming or killing her. Not yet, at any rate. But it occurs to me that the one thing sure to add to your death agony will be to perish in the knowledge that your wife will believe you betrayed her. With your own brother's wife, at that.'

I got to my knees, and saw the blood was flowing freely over the iron manacle from a great gash my ankle. 'It is a lie, Montnoir,' I gasped through the pain, 'I never loved the lady Louise.'

'That is of no account. Merely planting the suspicion will torment your wife long after you are dead.'

Montnoir's words came closer to the bone than he could know: in the aftermath of the Countess Louise's death, it had taken me several weeks to assuage Cornelia's suspicions that I might have had feelings for her.

'You will burn in hell, Montnoir,' I whispered angrily as I got unsteadily to my feet.

'I think not, Sir Matthew. Hell is reserved for the likes of you. And you shall be there soon enough. I have been giving the matter some thought, and have decided that although I cannot dispose of you as slowly as I would wish, mere burning is not an adequate punishment for such a gross reprobate as you, a heretic and a murderer. For you' – he stabbed a finger angrily toward me – 'you are far worse than those heretics who wallow in ignorance because they have never witnessed the eternal truth of the church of Rome. You, Quinton, were shown that truth by your grandmother, and yet you chose to reject it. Such wilful heresy deserves the severest punishment, and you shall have it. The Castle stables contain four horses, and the courtyard is amply wide enough for them. Thus at dawn, Sir Matthew Quinton, you will suffer the fate of Ravaillac. That will be especially appropriate, for your precious grandmother was there that day. She witnessed it. Indeed, she played a part in bringing those events to pass. I suspect that she will not have told you that. No? I thought not. So think of her, Sir Matthew, as you endure that which she witnessed.'

Montnoir left, and the cell door closed heavily behind him. I tore off part of a shirt sleeve and wrapped it around my bleeding ankle. Yet why was I attempting to heal myself, only to face the fate that the Frenchman had described to me: the fate of Ravaillac, murderer of Henry the Fourth, King of France, in the year 1610?

I knew the story well: at that time, who did not? The assassin was subjected to the most terrible death imaginable. First his right hand, with which he had driven the dagger into the royal breast, was plunged into a cauldron of fire and brimstone. Then the flesh was slowly pulled from his chest, arms, thighs and legs with red-hot pincers. Boiling oil, resin, wax, sulphur and brimstone were poured upon the wounds, and molten lead upon his navel. Finally, four horses were fastened to his limbs and set off in different directions. It was said that Ravaillac lived through all of this, enduring for hours, at last succumbing only when the Paris mob literally tore his body apart. Some of the more ghoulish peasant women were said to have greedily devoured pieces of his flesh. And it seemed that my grandmother had witnessed all of it; indeed, if Montnoir was to be believed, she had played some sort of part in bringing it about. I had thought my family had secrets enough, yet now here was another, and one that seemed about to come full circle in the most dreadful way imaginable. The Countess Louise-Marie would never know that her grandson had suffered the same fate as the assassin Ravaillac, but I had little doubt that by one means or another, Montnoir would ensure that both my mother and my wife learned exactly how Sir Matthew Quinton perished. It was this, more even than the horror that lay before me, that consumed my thoughts as day turned into night.

* * *

I did not sleep. Finally the room lightened a little as another grey Swedish dawn broke. I steeled myself for the door to open, for the walk to the courtyard, for the unimaginable horror of what was to follow. But no one came. Had Montnoir experienced a change of heart and decided to resume his campaign to convert me to Rome? Was he conjuring up an even more terrible refinement of my execution? Or was it merely taking him time to put in place all the dreadful elements of Ravaillac's end?

I do not know how many hours passed. Then, at last, I heard footsteps in the corridor outside. Heavy footsteps. A man's. An executioner's.

Slowly, the door of the cell opened. It took me a moment, perhaps several moments, to realise that the person framed within the door was not an executioner, and he was not Montnoir. This man was shorter, and bulkier by far. He wore no cloak, and had no hair.

It was Phineas Musk.

'I give you joy of your birthday, Sir Matthew,' he said.

Chapter Twelve

Musk led me up through empty, bare-walled and freezing cold chambers, each door jamb adorned with the initials GASR or CSR for King Gustavus Adolphus or his daughter Christina. He maintained a constant reassuring chatter. The *Cressy* was in good order, the mast fleet was inviolate, the ice was beginning to melt and break. No letter had yet gone for England, informing my wife of my abduction. I mumbled gratitude to Musk and God alike, but I could take in barely anything and could frame no more than a barely coherent word or two at a time as I stumbled along in his wake. I think I thanked him feebly for his wishes upon my birthday, although it seemed from his telling – for I had entirely lost track of the calendar – that it was but the twentieth-eighth day of February; admittedly, the nearest to a birthday that a leapling knows in three years out of every four. I was still half-convinced my liberation was but a waking dream, or even a dream proper, from which I would soon awake to be confronted once again by my tormentor Montnoir, or to be dragged to the place of execution in the courtyard of this great castle where the unbearable death-agony would begin.

I had a thousand questions to which I wished to give voice but could not. Above all, though, there was the one that weighed most heavily upon me: the one I now summoned up all my thoughts and strength to ask.

'Musk,' I said at last, 'where is Montnoir?'

'Gone. But another can tell you better than I.'

At last Musk led me up a broad staircase, stretching up toward a grand Doric wooden portal. Looking down, I saw that many of the steps bore names and inscriptions: gravestones, then, presumably appropriated from some churchyard or dissolved abbey. The doorway led into a great hall, of a similar size to that of De La Gardie at Lacko but lower and more plainly decorated. The wall to the left contained two great windows divided by a fireplace, upon which a great pile of logs blazed fiercely. There were a few paintings, one of which I recognised as the great Gustavus Adolphus, two or three of other kings or generals and one of a woman, but I paid little attention to them. At the far end was a dais bearing a chair of state, again all much plainer than the High Chancellor's extravagances, upon which sat an evidently careworn man. His head lifted toward us as we entered, and I recognised the face of Count Dohna. He was attired more simply than at our last meeting, wearing a plain jacket of black velvet, but although the hall was tolerably warm his hands were still gloved.

'Sir Matthew,' he said, rising, walking toward me and bowing his head, 'I trust you will accept my most profound apologies, and those of the High Chancellor. Your detention was reprehensible – an affront against the honour of the Three Crowns. The Lord Montnoir, a man in whom we reposed a certain confidence, has abused our hospitality.'

I had been profoundly shaken by my recent experience: I could still see Montnoir's face, and hear his words. For the nightmare to have been ended by the unlikely combination of Phineas Musk and Count Dohna, and for the Count to be apologising for my detention by his ally, had my head spinning.

'You did not know I was being detained here?' My voice was yet barely more than a whisper.

'I did not. I was still at Lacko in conference with the High Chancellor, and afterwards engaged elsewhere. As Montnoir knew very well. He and his French retainers, the men who followed and seized you, had free rein here for days, and would have still, had it not been for your bold Englishmen.' Dohna sighed. 'The man's presumption has been boundless and unforgiveable, Sir Matthew. It was bad enough to attack you at Lacko (for which affront the High Chancellor had already ordered him to leave the kingdom), but then to seize you, an ambassador of the British king, upon the soil of Sweden, and to incarcerate you here at Vasterholm –' Dohna's anger seemed genuine enough, and the information that De La Gardie had summarily expelled Montnoir was more than welcome. Perhaps now Lydford North's sojourn at Lacko would not be entirely unproductive after all. 'This is my castle, you see, so the dishonour is the greater,' said Dohna. 'Or at least, Vasterholm falls under my administration on behalf of – of another, who will be most displeased at the news of what has happened here. And you have it at a disadvantage, Sir Matthew.'

'I?' My thoughts still reeled from incarceration, the anticipation of a heretical death, and unexpected release. 'Forgive me, My Lord, how can I –'

'Didn't think only Musk would show up to get you out, did you, Sir Matthew?' growled the old man. 'I know I've performed miracles for the House of Quinton, but I'd have had to out-do the raising of Lazarus this time.' He nodded toward the windows along the west side of the hall. I took a couple of paces forward and looked out. There, beyond the snowy shore of the castle island, was the sea: we were probably somewhere in the archipelago south and west of Gothenburg, judging by the number of other islands in sight, with the mainland to the east. And in the midst of the sea lay the *Cressy*, at anchor, her larboard broadside run out, my men plainly visible along the ship's rail. 'Lieutenant Farrell's compliments and apologies, sir,' said Musk. 'He reckons he might not have accorded the full honours due to the Landtshere Ter Horst and the castle of New Elfsborg when he sailed in haste.'

'Now that Montnoir's Frenchmen have gone, this place has no

garrison left to it other than a dozen or so servants,' said Dohna. 'The walls are high and ancient. Your broadside would reduce Vasterholm to rubble within hours, Sir Matthew. Thus I am now your prisoner, I think.'

Still confused by all that had happened and was happening, I neglected to ask two essential questions: first, why such a brazenly hostile act by the *Cressy* would not instantly bring on war between the Three Crowns of Sweden and the three crowns of the British Isles; second, and far more importantly, *how had Musk and Kit Farrell discovered where I was?*

A young page boy entered the hall bearing a large silver plate laden with bread, cheese and salt beef, along with a goblet of wine. He held it out to me, bowing his head silently.

'Pray, Sir Matthew,' said Dohna, 'take some refreshment after your ordeal.'

Hunger and thirst elbowed decorum aside. I grasped eagerly at the meat and took a long draught of the wine.

As I ate and drank, order slowly returned to my senses. I had so many questions for both Dohna and Musk; but Musk was eternal and would be there to answer my questions tomorrow and the day after that (or to evade them, which was more likely), whereas this enigmatic Swede was a very different matter. I had been convinced this man was an enemy, a close ally of Montnoir, yet now he played the part of my friend. With sincerity or not? I needed to know. Thus I addressed myself to the High Chancellor of Sweden's confidential advisor.

'Whose castle is this, My Lord?' I demanded. 'Whom do you serve?'

Dohna looked at me quizzically. 'I was told you were an intelligent man, Sir Matthew,' he said, a certain disappointment evident in his deep voice. 'Nephew to Doctor Tristram Quinton, whose fame as a scientist bestrides Europe. Tell me – whom do you think I serve?'

Montnoir was at large, God knew what condition the mast-fleet was in, there was still John Bale to deal with, and yet this thin, quietly-spoken man wished to play games of the mind. With difficulty I resisted the urge to order Musk to signal the *Cressy* to fire a warning shot into the walls of this ancient castle. But ever since my uncle Tristram had introduced me to such intellectual conundrums, I was unable to resist them.

'This is not a castle of the king's,' I said slowly, 'else it would be properly garrisoned. And you, My Lord Dohna... You would not permit yourself to be seen in public among the throng of the High Chancellor's court at Lacko. Instead, you co-operated with Montnoir, the agent of France and above all of –' Revelation, when it came, struck as a thunderbolt. 'Of course! Of Rome. You are an agent of Queen Christina, My Lord. This is her castle. You and Montnoir are working together to inveigle De La Gardie into promoting the causes of France and the Catholic faith in Sweden.'

Lord Dohna smiled, nodded, and even made a little mocking clap with his gloved hands. 'Bravo, Sir Matthew Quinton. You have much of your uncle in you after all. Yes, you are right. I serve, and am steward of this castle in the name of Her Majesty Christina, Queen of the Swedes, Goths and Wends.'

'Sometime Queen, My Lord.'

Dohna shook his head. 'Perhaps so, Sir Matthew. Lawyers are divided upon the matter, I believe. An act of abdication takes away the power, certainly, but does it ever take away the dignity? Does it ever take away the absolute power inherent in her very being, the power bestowed upon her by God at the moments of her accession and coronation, and which she continues to wield over her own, wheresoever she may be? Her Majesty thinks not. And after all, Sir Matthew, did not your King Charles insist that you bow the knee to him and address him as Majesty during all those long years in exile?'

'His Majesty was still king by right, My Lord, even though he did not possess that which was rightfully his. He did not voluntarily renounce his title, it was forcibly torn from him.'

Dohna nodded thoughtfully. 'It would be stimulating to debate this further with you, Sir Matthew. But we have more pressing matters to attend to, I fear. Agent of King Louis or no, Montnoir must pay for the indignities to which he has submitted you. He must be prevented from leaving the realm, which means we must move quickly.'

'Do you know where he is?'

'I believe so. The High Chancellor's order gave him a week to leave the kingdom and put at his disposal a small Dutch fluyt, lying at Wilde on the mainland to the south of here. His obvious course will be to take her and make for Denmark, firm friend to the Dutch and thus to her French allies.'

Through the window I could see the winter sun, and thus had my bearing, while the swallow-tail Swedish pennant flying from the ramparts gave me the direction of the wind.

'A south-westerly,' I said, and looked across to my ship. 'Montnoir's ship will have the weather gage. It will be difficult for the *Cressy* to beat up into the wind to prevent his escape.'

Dohna nodded. 'For your ship, perhaps. But that is not the only course open to us, Sir Matthew. Sweden will redeem herself in your eyes. Sweden will make reparation for the wrong done to you.'

With that he called over the lad who had brought the victuals and spoke rapidly to him in Swedish. The lad left, returning after some minutes with paper, pen, ink, wax and a small writing tray. Dohna returned to the dais, sat, and hastily scribbled a note, sealing it in wax. He gave the paper to the lad, who bowed and left at a brisk pace. I had no idea what the Swede was about, and could not bring myself to trust a man who had seemed until so recently to be the ally of the Seigneur de Montnoir. But despite the food and drink, I was still weak, desperately tired, and more than a little confused; and Count Dohna had a strange, persuasive authority about him.

'Now, Sir Matthew, you must wash, and we must find you fresh clothes – though finding in this castle raiment suitable for a man of your height may not be easy.'

'Surely we have no time for such things, My Lord?'

Dohna smiled. 'Time enough. And the time we take over this will make you fitter for the saddle, I think. You are well enough to contemplate a brief canter, Sir Matthew?'

'Well enough indeed, My Lord Dohna.'

* * *

A little over an hour later, duly cleansed and changed into the plain garb of a particularly lofty servant who had once done duty in the castle's bakehouse, I was rather less convinced of the confident assurance I had given Dohna. My legs, sore from incarceration and the flesh-tearing manacle, and my side, still painful from the fall when I was taken, protested at the violent motion of the horse beneath me as it galloped along the snow-covered road that led north from the causeway linking the castle-island of Vasterholm to the mainland. Count Dohna's notion of a 'brief canter' was somewhat different to mine: he drove his own steed into an ever more thunderous and frenetic gallop, with a complete disregard for the treacherous nature of the ground beneath its hoofs. Whatever else Dohna might be, he was an astonishingly competent horseman. Either that or an astonishingly insane one.

I had little idea why we were riding north when Montnoir was meant to be to the south, but Dohna seemed confident in his strategy, whatever it might be. Before leaving Vasterholm I had implemented a strategy of my own, although I knew it had but little prospect of success: I ordered Musk back to the *Cressy*, there to pass on my command to Lieutenant Kit Farrell to get the ship out into the open sea, as far to the south and west as possible, by the most direct course Jeary could devise. But I knew it was a forlorn hope; the wind was too contrary, and in a smaller ship Montnoir could follow channels through this perilous archipelago that the *Cressy* simply dared not follow.

We had been on the road for perhaps half an hour, and my horse was already tiring noticeably. Conversely, I was strengthening: the bitterly cold air and the stimulation of exercise were reviving both my body and my mind. And as my thoughts became clearer, so my doubts about the sincerity of Count Dohna increased.

Finally Dohna turned off, taking a track through some trees. I followed, although my sense of anxiety was growing. The path gradually sloped downwards, and finally emerged from the trees into a small bay with a snow-covered beach. Rocky headlands extended out into the sea on either side of the bay.

Dohna dismounted at the water's edge, and I did the same, albeit warily. I was now very conscious of the fact that I was in an empty, wholly isolated place with a man who had been until recently the ally of Gaspard de Montnoir. What if Dohna still was that man, and had merely lured me away from Musk and my ship to a place where he could more easily deliver me back to my enemy, or else simply kill me? After all, I had only his word that he had rejected the wiles of the Knight of Malta; only his word that he was any of the things he said he was. Although I wore a sword, I still felt weak from my confinement. I did not know how good a swordsman Dohna might be, but if he wielded a blade as well as he rode a horse, he was probably a formidable one. Perhaps I had been delivered from the fate of Ravaillac merely to die here, on an empty strand, at the hands of a treacherous Swede.

The Count said nothing. He did not even look at me. Instead he stood at the water's edge, looking out to sea. It occurred to me in that moment that it simply did not matter how good Dohna was with a sword. The letter that his servant had carried away from Vasterholm might have been a summons to an entire regiment of murderers to come to this place, at this time. A deserted beach, far from the road, surrounded entirely by forest. I looked around, more and more convinced that behind every tree lurked a French assassin.

'My Lord,' I asked with some trepidation, 'why have we come here?'

I feared the answer would come in the form of a blade to the heart. But Count Dohna continued to stare intently out to sea. It was as if he were far away.

'Listen, Sir Matthew,' he said, very quietly. 'Can you not hear it? The sound that will make you trust me?'

Stranger still. I listened, but could hear only the lapping of wave upon rock, the cry of the birds, the whistling of the wind – but yes, something else, too. A familiar sound, yet one that eluded me at first.

I recognised the sound of oars swivelling in rowlocks only a moment before the bow of the *Fortuna* appeared from behind the headland.

Chapter Thirteen

After being ferried out in the galley's longboat, Dohna and I stepped onto the deck of the *Fortuna*. The minute figure of General Erik Glete stood at the head of an impressive file of musketeers, all young enough to be his grandsons, all in half-armour and all stiffly at attention. He brought up his own sword to salute Dohna and myself.

'My Lord Dohna,' he said proudly, 'welcome back aboard the *Fortuna*. It has been too many long years.' The little man seemed almost in a transport of delight: tears were running down his grizzled old face. 'Sir Matthew,' he said by way of afterthought, bowing his head perfunctorily to me.

As the larboard bank of oars deployed to push us away from the shore, I reflected that despite Glete's bluster, he was something of a pragmatist after all. He, who boasted that he took orders only from High Admirals, kings and God, seemed perfectly content to take them from Dohna; presumably he justified it on the grounds that Dohna represented De La Gardie, who represented the child-king Karl, but I would not have thought Glete capable of such sophisticated casuistry, especially given his contempt for the High Chancellor. On the other hand, Dohna's presence must also have reminded him of happier times, when a true Vasa sat upon the thrones of the Three Crowns and when both the *Fortuna* and her captain were not simply disregarded relics of a lost epoch. Now, suddenly, Sweden's last galley and her strange little general had a purpose again, thanks entirely to Count Dohna. As we moved out into the archipelago, the oarsmen steadily increasing their pace, the two men stood by the starboard rail, talking to each other in Swedish and in low tones.

As the two Swedes reminisced, I stood by the larboard rail and contemplated our situation. Low, snow-covered isles closed ever more tightly around us. The *Fortuna* was moving south-west, directly into the breeze in a way that no ship could ever manage, and even the galley's progress was severely slowed. Glete did not have his oarsmen rowing at anything like their maximum effort, which in any case could only be sustained for short periods. No doubt the general wished to conserve his men's energies for a final burst in pursuit of Montnoir's ship, if we ever got that close to it. But for a man who had commanded nimble men of war that could make ten miles or more in every hour, the *Fortuna*'s progress was funereally slow.

Glete might have sensed my impatience, for eventually he came over to stand by me.

'He's got a good start on us, Sir Matthew. But the old *Fortuna* still has a few tricks up her sleeve.' We were now in a channel between two islands, rather larger bodies of land than the countless rocks and islets studied the sea like jewels. 'That's Donso to larboard and Styrso to starboard,' said the old general. 'The people out here are sturdy, but the stupidest buggers you'll ever meet. Never marry off the islands. They're all each other's cousins, or closer still.'

The channel ahead seemed to be narrowing rapidly. Moreover, the strait between the two islands appeared obstructed by a cluster of rocks and islets. I would not have contemplated taking even a yawl through such a perilously small gap, but Glete seemed intent on steering the *Fortuna*, which surely had a substantial draught, directly for the tiny space.

My face must have betrayed my alarm. 'Nothing to be concerned over, Sir Matthew. Brought her through here countless times. Probably not in ten years, though. But I doubt the channel will have changed much.'

Glete's pilot, up in the bows, seemed to have a different opinion. He was clearly agitated, constantly looking back at the general and ordering a man to sound every four or five minutes.

The *Fortuna* drew ever nearer to the strait. Had I been captain, I would have been at anchor already, sending out my boats to sound rather than doing it from my own hull, and then getting them to tow us gently through if the water proved deep enough. But Erik Glete had no time for such feeble seamen's niceties. The galley moved relentlessly forward toward the eye of the needle.

And then the little general did something that even to this day, I still find difficult to credit. He barked orders in Swedish, and the drum that kept time for the oarsmen below shortened the interval between beats. The oars began to cut the water more rapidly. The *Fortuna* picked up speed.

There were rocks all around us now, and the islands of Donso and Styrso seemed to be closing like a vice onto our vessel. The gap ahead was narrower than ever, and if there were any rocks hidden beneath the surface, they would tear the galley's flimsy hull to pieces at this speed. Yet still the drum kept up its relentless beat, and still the oars cut the waters. I prayed with the fervour that only a man who has already been shipwrecked once can express.

We were at the channel. It was just wide enough for the hull, but surely not for the extended oars – they would snap like matchwood upon the gleaming icy rocks on either side, and without them, at this speed, the *Fortuna* would ride up onto the shore and be shattered –

But, in the blink of an eye, we were through. The rocks and islets receded behind us, and ahead lay open sea: far ahead, a distant solitary sail.

Glete went forward to exult over his timorous pilot, and Count Dohna joined me at the larboard rail. 'What do you think, Sir Matthew? Montnoir's fluyt, is it not? He has still to clear the southern point of Wrango, and in this wind, he will not find that easy. We shall have him.'

'God willing, my Lord.'

'You are pale, Sir Matthew, and shivering. I trust you are not catching a chill? Or still suffering from your detention?'

'In truth, my Lord, I think General Glete's notion of seamanship is the cause.'

'Ah. Yes, I recall I felt much the same the first time he brought me this way. Pride is the general's great weakness, Sir Matthew – pride in this craft and its crew.'

The beat of the drum remained steady: Glete was pressing his men hard. We were in more open water now, but a myriad of islands still lay all around. The fluyt was dead ahead, wearing and tacking to try and work into the wind and get out into the open sea that lay beyond the island of Wrango. In the open sea and with a following wind, even such a cumbersome vessel might hope to outrun a galley. But among the islands and with the wind against her, the fluyt had not a hope. To emphasise the point, Glete ordered a shot across her bows from one of his chase-cannon. The little general evidently drilled his gun-crews well: a small fountain of water a few dozen feet ahead of the fluyt's bow gave due warning to her skipper that if the *Fortuna*'s captain so chose, his ship would swiftly be reduced to mere flotsam upon the brine. The fluyt's great sail was loosed and she hove to.

Glete despatched one of his young ensigns and a dozen men to search the vessel and bring back the Seigneur de Montnoir. Time passed. No man emerged from below decks on the fluyt. Finally the ensign appeared at the rail and made a universal gesture that needed no translation by the old general. There was no sign of the quarry: the Knight of Malta was not aboard.

The skipper of the fluyt was brought over to the *Fortuna*. He was a big man, bearded and with dirty straggling brown hair, and he towered over Erik Glete. This mattered not a jot to the general, who proceeded to berate the skipper in furious Swedish. One needed no mastery of the language to comprehend that the man was being singularly uncooperative; his responses consisted principally of grunts and the occasional murmured sentence.

'A Hallander oaf,' said Glete for my benefit. 'Still loyal to Denmark, a full twenty years after we took it off them. Won't say a damn word worth the hearing, but I'd say the bag of gold *Louis d'or* my men found in his cabin speaks loudly enough.'

Just then Count Dohna came back on deck, having been below to answer a call of nature. The Halland skipper frowned, then abruptly hid his face in his hands and shook his head vigorously. Dohna stepped over and spoke so quietly to him in Swedish that no others aboard the galley could hear his words. At length, the skipper lowered his hands and spoke. His reply was far more voluble than anything he had said to Glete. I could make out none of it, other than one word that I recognised. A place name: Uppsala.

Dohna raised a gloved hand and the skipper fell silent again. The Count spoke once more, this time receiving a lengthy and gabbled reply from a man who now seemed to be unable to get words out of his mouth quickly enough. Finally Count Dohna turned to Glete and myself: 'It seems Montnoir employed this man and his ship as decoys. The Frenchman anticipated pursuit, and chose instead to cross to Denmark in a fishing craft. I do not doubt that he paid her skipper equally well. A remarkably resourceful man, our Lord Montnoir.'

Glete looked out to larboard, toward a distant island distinguished by an unusual double lighthouse. 'There's an entire fleet of them to southward, over by Nidingen,' he said. 'He could be anywhere amongst them, or already slipping out of the fleet and making for Danish water.'

'Then he is gone,' I said. 'With such an advantage, neither *Fortuna* nor *Cressy* have a hope of catching him.' Kit Farrell and the *Cressy* would be beating far out to the west to avoid the treacherous rocks of the archipelago before trying to come back up into the teeth of the breeze; a tiny craft such as the one Montnoir would be aboard could sail much closer to the wind and thus outrun a Fourth Rate easily.

'Indeed,' said Dohna. 'That being the case, General, we should return to land.'

'As you say, My Lord. And the skipper? A confessed traitor? To be confined below, then turned over to the courts?'

'I think not, General. This man might have been deluded by King Louis' coin and a lingering loyalty to Denmark, but he is a sturdy fellow – formerly a merchant of Varberg, indeed, before he fell on hard times in the late war, and a representative of Halland's fourth estate in the *Rijksdag* when it first came under the Three Crowns. I would have such a man proclaim to his fellows Sweden's beneficence rather than be an example of its vengeful wrath.'

Glete raised urgent and loud objections to this, but Dohna's reply was brief and all too evidently curt. The old general bowed his head stiffly in the Teutonic manner and reluctantly ordered the release of the skipper.

* * *

With the south-westerly still blowing strongly, the *Fortuna* was able to hoist sail for the voyage back to the galley dock west of Gothenburg. The rowers emerged onto the upper deck and took the air before indulging in the substantial victuals that Glete ordered to be broken open for them. He intended to remain on deck, he said, putting his cabin at the disposal of Count Dohna and myself. It was smaller than the space available to me as captain of the *Cressy*: smaller and much lower, which fact caused no little difficulty to an English knight who stood more than a foot taller than the tiny general who commanded the vessel. But it was decorated as fantastically as any captain's cabin of an English first rate, the planking overhead being adorned with a gaudy portrayal of the deeds of Magog, grandson of Noah, from whom the Goths and then the Swedes descended. Or so Count Dohna claimed.

I was still hungry after my incarceration and set to the plates of salt-fish that Glete's servants provided with some vigour. Dohna ate only sparingly, picking up only the occasional morsel with his gloved hand, and at first he said little. I still harboured doubts about the enigmatic count. He seemed to have proved his allegiance by setting the *Fortuna* to pursue Montnoir's decoy ship; but the Frenchman's escape made me wonder whether the whole episode might not have been a charade devised by Dohna to distract me while Montnoir fled Sweden by another means. Perhaps it was but a ruse to delude me into placing my entire confidence in him, prior to some future betrayal that he and Montnoir had hatched before the latter's flight. It was, I decided, time finally to confront the Count Dohna.

'So, my Lord,' I said, finishing a glass of acceptable and most welcome Rhenish wine, 'how came you to do the bidding of such a serpent as Montnoir?'

The large round eyes flashed angrily. 'I do no man's bidding, Sir Matthew. Montnoir deceived me, just as he deceived the High Chancellor.' Dohna looked away. 'But in one sense, perhaps you are correct. I did not realise just how dangerous a man the Seigneur de Montnoir is. I thought I had the serpent by the tail, but all the time his teeth were buried in my flesh.'

'You will tell of it?'

He looked back at me and fixed me once again with that unsettling, penetrating stare of his. After what seemed like an eternity, he said 'Yes, Sir Matthew, indeed I will. You see, I would not have you remember me as either a devilish villain or a foolish dupe. For you must certainly think me one or the other, do you not?'

I sensed that Dohna appreciated plain speaking. 'One or the other, my Lord.'

He smiled. 'As would I, were I in your place. Very well. You know that I serve Christina. I was one of those who accompanied the Queen to Rome, following her abdication. She retained sovereign rights over her own court, so we were our own little country, invulnerable to the laws of whichever land we were in. Her abdication settlement bestowed upon her extensive estates to enable her to maintain that dignity. Of late, however, Her Majesty has become increasingly convinced that the High Chancellor is depriving her of a portion of the revenues that are rightfully hers by the terms of her instrument of abdication. As the steward of her castles and estates here in the west, I was sent back to find evidence of De La Gardie's delinquency.'

'The High Chancellor seems to look upon you as an ally rather than an enemy, My Lord.'

Dohna smiled. 'The Queen has always exerted a – let us say, a powerful influence upon Count Magnus.' So maybe Lord Conisbrough was right; perhaps the curious queen (who was, my uncle said, perhaps a hermaphrodite, or else a follower of the rites of Lesbos) had found love with a man after all. 'But before I left Rome, a second and far more secret element was added to my mission.'

'Namely to further the schemes of Lord Montnoir,' I said.

Dohna nodded. 'He came to Rome with full accreditation from King Louis, deploying the force of argument that only the gold and power of France can provide. He insinuated that De La Gardie and the Queen Regent were increasingly unfriendly toward the Most Christian's cause – indeed, that they planned to join England in her war against France. Queen Christina had seen enough of the dire effects of endless war upon her kingdom while she reigned,' said Dohna sadly, 'and was easily convinced that it was her duty to prevent further needless loss of Swedish life. Thus I was sent to assist Lord Montnoir in frustrating the High Chancellor's schemes and ensuring that Sweden was not committed to a new war.'

Hence, of course, the reason why Lydford North had been unaware of De La Gardie's new advisor: Dohna, closeted with Christina in Rome, would not have figured in Arlington's lists and assessments of the men of power in the kingdom of the Three Crowns.

'I know Montnoir of old,' I said, 'and I find it difficult to conceive of him – or his king, in truth – having such an altruistic concern for the preservation of peace.'

Dohna grimaced. 'So it proved,' he said. 'Once we were in Sweden, it soon became clear to me that Montnoir had another plan – whether of his own devising, or that of his master King Louis, I am still not certain. It was true that he wished to prevent an alliance between your king and ours, which was the position he took publicly with the High Chancellor after I introduced him secretly to De La Gardie at Lacko. But we had no inkling of the lengths to which Montnoir would go to achieve that objective, namely his killing of poor Lord Conisbrough and his abduction of yourself, Sir Matthew. But then, of course, I believe he also had very personal reasons for wishing to have you in his power.' I nodded. These were plainly difficult words for Count Dohna to utter; in effect, he was confessing that he had been duped, and such an admission is never easy for any man. 'But Montnoir also had a greater goal in mind. A far greater goal, which only became clear to me when we had actually arrived in this country. He envisaged the restoration of Christina to the throne, if necessary by means of a French army, and the forced reconversion of Sweden to Rome.'

The revelation should have been shocking, but somehow, when I thought of the Seigneur de Montnoir, it was not. King Charles the Second himself had once told me that Montnoir was the sort of man whose dearest wish was to see Protestants herded onto bonfires, and I also recalled the Knight of Malta's own words to me when he had me in his power. In Montnoir's twisted notion of reuniting Christendom for a final apocalyptic crusade against Islam, what could be more natural than his seeking to turn to his cause Christendom's most formidable military power?

'The restoration of Christina and a forced conversion of an entire nation? With respect, My Lord, that seems ambitious even for Montnoir.'

'I am not sure that Montnoir's ambition knows any bounds, Sir Matthew. His self-belief certainly does not. And yet he has a curiously simplistic view of the world. In France, of course, what King Louis says becomes law, and I think Montnoir believes kingdoms which permit the existence of institutions representing the people – your Parliament, say, or our *Riksdag* – have them only because of their monarch's craven unwillingness to exercise the unbridled power that Louis wields without restraint. In the case of your own king, he attributes the continued existence of Parliament entirely to Charles Stuart's laziness.' I thought for the first time that perhaps I did not entirely disagree with Gaspard de Montnoir on every point. 'Montnoir cannot conceive of constitutions as being anything other than unnecessary inconveniences, and he as good as told me once that all the restored Christina would have to do would be to issue a decree declaring Sweden to be Catholic and it would be so. Especially if the decree was implemented by fifty thousand of Marshal Turenne's best men, that is.'

'But you are a Catholic, My Lord,' I said, seeking to assure myself that my reading of the man Dohna was correct. 'Surely a Catholic Sweden would be welcome to you?'

'A Sweden that becomes Catholic by persuasion, by a willing recognition of the eternal truths of the Holy and Apostolic Church – yes, of course, Sir Matthew! But honest Swedish burghers and peasants forced to convert at the point of French pikes? Never! When I was –' Dohna stopped himself, thinking better of whatever words he had been about to utter. 'Swedes might be ill-educated and boorish, but they are honest, and they are stubborn. A simple people made for a simple religion. They hold to their faith with a conviction and tenacity that the Queen respects. She would never wish to see her people forced to adopt the faith that she chose out of love and truth. Sweden is tolerant, and Christina is tolerant – she detests bigotry, Sir Matthew, whatever its origin. She may think her people mistaken in their religion, but she respects their right to believe as their consciences dictate.' Dohna was now speaking with some passion. 'And she would certainly never permit her dear country, the land that her father and her own generals built into one of the most potent on earth, to be reduced to a mere puppet of France.'

'You know her mind well,' I said.

'I trust that I do. Remember that I have known her since we were children, Sir Matthew. I was one of those of her own age brought up with her to provide friends for a fatherless child.' Dohna's words struck a chord, for Queen Christina and I would have been the same age when we both lost our fathers in battle. 'And that being so, I knew what she would have wished me to do once Montnoir's true ambition became apparent. Besides, there was no time to send to Rome for her instructions and to await their return.'

'Then I am grateful to both you and the Queen for rejecting the way of Lord Montnoir.'

'I will convey your gratitude to Her Majesty. But tell me, Sir Matthew,' said Dohna, 'now that Montnoir is beyond the reach of either of us, do you intend instead to pursue the regicide Bale?'

'John Bale's presence in Gothenburg is an abomination, My Lord,' I said with righteous indignation. 'It is a slur upon Sweden, which shelters him, and frankly upon the High Chancellor and the Queen Regent, who permit this abomination in the name of the young king.'

Dohna's large, penetrating blue eyes narrowed. 'And by implication, Sir Matthew, a slur upon myself, who has not advised the High Chancellor to act to the contrary?'

'I cast no aspersions, My Lord,' I said, but I do not doubt that my voice betrayed my true feelings. 'But I fear that even if you and the Chancellor were to reconsider, Landtshere Ter Horst's antipathy and the citizens of Gothenburg themselves will stymie any attempt to get him back to England. As you yourself made all too clear at Lacko.'

Dohna looked out, over the side of the galley, toward the distant snow-capped shore of the mainland. 'I remember the Queen's reaction when news came to Stockholm of the beheading of your King Charles,' he said. 'I was with the Queen when she first heard the news,' he said sadly. 'Along with the likes of De La Gardie, of course. None of us had ever seen her so upset, Sir Matthew. She retired to her chamber for two days, and would not eat or drink. That her fellow monarch, one of God's anointed, should be done away with in such a manner, was truly unspeakable. Although the murdered king was your sovereign and not mine, you can only have been a child when he was beheaded – you cannot conceive of the horror and rage that the other crowned heads of Europe felt. Even our violent neighbour the Tsar Alexis was outraged.'

'My uncle told me something of the reaction among the other kings and princes,' I said. 'Even as the merest child, I resented the fact that they seemed to have issued countless proclamations denouncing the enormity of the crime, yet none raised a finger to help our martyred monarch's son and lawful successor, his present Majesty.' My anger grew apace within me. 'Tell me this, then, My Lord Dohna. Perhaps you can enlighten me a little, as you were there. You witnessed how Christina received the news of King Charles's murder, as you say. Did she retire to her chamber and not eat or drink for two days truly out of anger at the enormity of the crime committed against my king, or out of fear that perhaps her own head might be the next upon the block?'

Dohna seemed genuinely perplexed, even shocked, by my question: the first time I had seen that poised and confident man seemingly at a loss for words. At length, and very slowly, he said 'Now that is a thought, Sir Matthew Quinton. Do you know, in all these long years I have never considered it in that way? Perhaps that was indeed in the Queen's mind – I have very little doubt it was in that of Tsar Alexis, but then, beheading is regarded as one of the milder fates for sovereigns of Muscovy.'

I was in no mood to contemplate the response of a ruler we English then regarded as a wild tyrant in a barbaric land far away, of which we knew or cared but little. My anger still welled up against Sweden, and John Bale, and a Queen who had done nothing to avenge my King's death. 'Whether she cried her tears out of sympathy or fear, Lord

Dohna, did not Queen Christina swiftly dry them, recognise the Commonwealth and receive Cromwell's ambassador?'

The large eyes flashed angrily. 'Politics, Sir Matthew. A vile but necessary evil that sometimes forces monarchs to act against their better judgements. The Queen did her utmost for your cause, as your brother well knows.' *My brother* – 'Perhaps I shall be able to prove that to you, too. A double proof, indeed. Proof of what Christina did, those long years ago, and proof that Sweden is indeed a kingdom where honour prevails.' Dohna called over Erik Glete and spoke rapidly to him in Swedish. The enigmatic Count was more animated than I had seen him before, again with one foot in front of the other in martial stance, his arms waving as he emphasised a point. I recognised very few words in the entire discourse: several times, though, Lord Dohna uttered the names 'Ter Horst' and 'Bale'. The minute general listened intently, but appeared shocked at what he was hearing. He asked several questions, but each time, Dohna seemed abruptly to dismiss his concerns. Finally Glete raised his hand to his helmet's visor in the age-old gesture of salute, turned, and went below to his cabin.

At last Count Dohna turned back to me. 'I spoke too peremptorily of Gothenburg, during your audience at Lacko. Now I can see a way of ensuring that Gothenburg does not erupt if justice is allowed to prevail.' Gothenburg? Justice prevailing? The man was speaking in riddles. And then, quite abruptly, he was not. 'You want the regicide Bale,' he said. The exuberance that had been in his eyes and voice when he spoke to Glete was gone, replaced in a moment by the same arrogance and determination that had been evident at Lacko. 'Very well, Sir Matthew. You and England shall have him.'

Chapter Fourteen

The *Fortuna*'s boat landed Count Dohna at the jetty of Vasterholm Castle and proceeded to Gothenburg, putting me ashore at the dock below the ruins of the Old Elfsborg Castle. Glete despatched a young officer to escort me to Gothenburg as far as the inn of the Sign of the Pelican, where I could safely await the return of the *Cressy*. Lukins greeted me like a long-lost son and provided a lavish repast of stewed venison washed down with Rostock beer, the first proper meal I had seen in days. I set about it with vigour, only to be disturbed after a few mouthfuls by the arrival of Phineas Musk and Lydford North. The latter was effusive, giving me joy of my liberation and declaring that he had ridden post-haste from Lacko upon learning of my capture; albeit not before he had given the High Chancellor a lecture on the gross affront to the honour of King Charles that had been committed by my abduction upon Swedish soil. De La Gardie was most abashed, North said, and he had left Lacko with assurances ringing in his ears. The treaty terms we offered would be reconsidered, the embargo on cutting mast-trees would be reviewed, and so on and so forth: but North, this strangely old young man, did not believe a word of it, and was indeed half-convinced that De La Gardie was complicit in my detention. He listened avidly as I gave him a full account of Montnoir's machinations, of the seemingly genuine remorse of Lord Dohna, and of our fruitless sea-chase after the errant Knight of Malta. Above all, though, he responded to the news of Dohna's assurance about John Bale with a momentary reversion to the enthusiastic youth he must have been so very recently. He very nearly sprang from his stool and thumped his fist upon the table.

'By God, Sir Matthew, we have him! We have the traitor!' But as he settled back down, a cloud passed over his face and the mask of the calculating diplomatist – or assassin, perhaps – returned. 'But you are certain we can trust this Count Dohna? And what means does he propose for taking Bale? Are the Swedes to arrest him themselves?'

'No, Mister North. We are to devise and execute the means of taking him. Count Dohna assures me that the Swedes – Ter Horst, in other words – will not interfere. But he did not specify how he would assure that. As for trusting him, well, perhaps that is for you to judge. This is your world, Mister North, not mine. But if we are to take Bale, do we have a choice?'

North did not reply. Instead, Musk spoke up; and his words were among the least expected, and the least welcome, I have heard in the course of my perversely long life. 'Seems to me we've got the choice not to take him at all, Sir Matthew. Especially as you should be grateful to him. Especially as he was the one who told us where you were.'

I sensed my mouth was open as I gawped at Musk. I closed it rapidly and in that performed better than Lydford North, who continued to stare at my clerk in frank astonishment.

'Seen panic many times,' said Musk. 'You should have seen how the Parliament-men in London beshat themselves when the King's army reached Turnham Green back in the year Forty-Two. But that was as nothing to the panic among our party coming back from Lacko when we realised you were gone after the snowstorm cleared. That Swedish major despatched men in all directions, but it was MacFerran who got the first inkling of what had happened. Good lad, that, despite being a stinking Scots ball-scratcher.' Coming from Phineas Musk, this praise for one of our Caledonian brethren was rare indeed. 'Even with the fresh snow, he found the blood where you fell and signs of riders making off for the south-west. We followed in that direction, but it was impossible, that it was. Snowfall after snowfall, we had, until not even MacFerran could find a trail. Besides, the Major reckoned they must be too far ahead for us to stand any chance of catching them. So back we came to Gothenburg. Lieutenant Farrell was beside himself – stormed off to see Ter Horst at once, who was all hand wringing and tears but did bugger all. A good three days this went on, with us trying to find even the smallest clue to your whereabouts. The crew were getting mighty fractious, too. They were convinced Bale's men or the Dutch must have done away with you – there was a running fight down the side of the Great Canal with a crew of lousy Dutchmen, another with some of the Scots from that privateer –'

'Musk!' I said sharply. 'In God's name, man, get to the heart of the matter! Bale. What was his part in it?'

'That was the thing, Sir Matthew. Evening of the third day, which must have been the fifth since you were taken, Mister Farrell got an anonymous note telling him to go to a Dutch inn over on the other side of the town from this place. I went with him and as stout a band of Cressys as could be assembled. There he was, large as life, lording it from a settle in the corner. And he says just one thing to Mister Farrell and me. "There is a castle upon an island to the south of this place. The Swedes call it Vasterholm. That is where Sir Matthew is being held, if he still lives." As God's my judge, those were his exact words.'

North and I exchanged astonished glances. 'How would Bale know that?' I demanded. 'And why should he offer this help unsolicited when he knows full well what we seek to do with him?'

'Mister Farrell and I asked each other much the same questions,' said Musk. 'But a man can't look a gift horse in the mouth, even if it is a foul king-killing sort of a horse. The Lieutenant took advice of some of the loyal old men of these parts and decided to sail the *Cressy* down there on the next day's tide, as the wind stood fair. Meanwhile I was sent overland with a good strong party – three dozen men, no less. And while we were in position around the end of the castle causeway, waiting for the ship to come down to us, along comes a small party of five horsemen riding hell-for-leather for the castle. So we detained them, and it proved to be that Lord Dohna and his attendants. He was agitated, that he was, but said he could put all to rights if only we'd draw away from the causeway. That we did, and an hour later we saw Montnoir and a dozen of his Frenchies ride out. We loosed off a few shots, but that Count had ordered us too far back to have any chance of doing them harm. So then we made our way into the castle and secured it while the *Cressy* anchored opposite it in case Montnoir or this Dohna had any tricks up their sleeves.'

So much was not right. I had an explanation of Dohna's motives and actions from his own mouth, but whether his words could be trusted was another matter entirely. Yet if the noble Swedish Count's deeds were mysterious, they were as nothing to those of John Bale. Somehow he had discovered where I was and had offered that information gratis to my friends; and if that was so, he, the regicide and arch-enemy of all I stood for, had undoubtedly helped to save my life from a slow, tormented death at the hands of the Seigneur de Montnoir.

'Cunning,' said Lydford North. 'Very cunning. I had not thought Bale capable of such a Machiavellian stratagem.'

'Mister North?'

'Whatever he might be, Sir Matthew, Bale has no love for the papists. He would certainly have no love for the likes of Lord Montnoir, even if in the present war the French happen to be allied to Bale's friends, the Dutch. So giving us your whereabouts and thwarting Montnoir's intentions is hardly counter to his inclinations, especially as saving your life might serve him well.'

'How so?'

'Why, is it not obvious, Sir Matthew? If he comes before an English court, what can a man who signed the death warrant of England's king possibly offer in mitigation? By saving the life of an English hero, might he not improve the prospect of sparing his own life from the gallows?'

Musk snorted derisively. 'As if the King will let him escape the noose just for that!' As an afterthought, he hastily added 'Begging your pardon, Sir Matthew.'

'Bale knows he is a dead man walking,' said North, 'and in my experience such men will clutch at any straw.' I was not entirely convinced by North's certain explanation, but kept my peace. 'Our duty is clear, Sir Matthew. As soon as your ship returns and we have her men available to us, we must form a plan to seize the person of John Bale and return him to England.'

Strangely, this prospect now seemed to me altogether less attractive, inevitable and just than it had done only days before.

* * *

The *Cressy* returned to her anchoring place in the Road of Gothenburg that night, and late in the morning North, Musk and I were rowed out to her. Kit Farrell greeted me with a side party and a proper salute from himself when I stepped onto her deck, but he seemed somewhat hesitant and nervous. I soon understood the reason why. As I entered the familiar surroundings of my cabin, I realised that it contained a most unfamiliar inhabitant: the Maiden Ter Horst. She was clad modestly in grey skirts and a manly jacket, and she bowed at my entrance.

'You have had her aboard, Lieutenant?' I demanded.

'She proved greatly useful to us in our voyage to Vasterholm, Sir Matthew. She knows the islands and the castle well, and between them, Ali Reis and Jeary command enough Swedish to be able to translate her advice.'

'That may be so,' I said, struggling to restrain my feelings, 'but you are aware of the Duke of York's many injunctions against keeping women aboard ship?'

Kit was unexpectedly defiant. 'By my observation, Sir Matthew, those injunctions seem more honoured in the breach than in the observance.' Kit Farrell quoting Shakespeare; the times were strange indeed. 'Women are commonly aboard ship in coastal waters by the immemorial custom of the navy. And does not Captain Jennens have his wife aboard every one of his commands, all of the time?'

'He doesn't trust what she might get up to ashore while he's afloat,' said Musk, who was evidently enjoying our argument hugely.

'Women are permitted aboard ship in *England's* coastal waters, Mister Farrell. As for Captain Jennens...' I did not complete my sentence, for I knew I was upon dangerous ground; Will Jennens might be a strange and contrary man, but I knew full well that he was not alone in flouting our Lord High Admiral's commands against officers having women aboard ship. Indeed, my Cornelia had used very much the same arguments with me in her efforts (as yet futile, albeit repelled only with difficulty) to persuade me to do what other captains did and install her in my cabin, perhaps under a man's name as a 'captain's servant' so I could then pocket her pay, as several of my fellow captains were known to do. I even knew of a gentleman captain who had entered his dog in the ship's books as an able seaman named Bromley.

Perhaps sensing the weakness of my position, Kit stood his ground as I had never known him to before. 'But of course, Sir Matthew, Captain Jennens is a gentleman. Might there perhaps be one law for him, and one for the plain tarpaulin?'

And so we came to it. The royal preference for gentleman captains, like Will Jennens and myself, was widely criticised in the coffee houses, in scurrilous pamphlets and in many a steerage and forecastle, where those masters, boatswains and gunners who saw their paths to command blocked by feckless sprigs of gentility were said to mutter darkly into their cups. I had never imagined Kit Farrell to be of such a metal, and could only imagine that too much discourse with the mast-ship skippers had poisoned his mind. Yet I could not deny the uncomfortable truth of what he said. In their dealings with their sea-officers, the royal brothers Charles and James undoubtedly did enforce one law upon the well-born, another for the rest.

'Very well, Lieutenant, I shall take the matter no further on this occasion,' I said stiffly, aware of Musk's and North's eyes open me. The latter's expression was openly contemptuous, conveying the very clear message that he, Lydford North, would have exerted a very different discipline over this upstart tarpaulin. 'But you will please arrange for the Maiden Ter Horst to be landed at the earliest convenience. Naturally I shall require the use of my own cabin again, and I take it you would agree that a lieutenant's cabin in the steerage is hardly an appropriate lodging for a lady.'

Whether the Landtshere's daughter was either a maiden or a lady seemed to me a point worthy of debate. I had no doubt that the acting captain of the *Cressy* had accommodated her in my cabin, and I doubted whether they had spent their entire time learning each other's languages and discussing the geography of the archipelago. As it was, Kit took the dismissal of his mistress with good grace, or at least with a polite nod of the head. But I sensed something between us had changed, perhaps for ever.

Once the lovers had said their farewells, Kit, North and I settled to the business of plotting the arrest and deportation of John Bale. Inevitably, Phineas Musk inveigled himself into the meeting by claiming that none of my young servants could be trusted to serve on us while we discussed such weighty matters; besides, Musk possessed information about Bale that none of the rest of us had. We did not know for certain where the regicide lived, whereas at least Musk had been to the inn which had to be the prime candidate for his abode.

'A quarter full of Dutchmen and other such low creatures,' said Musk, 'the other side of the Great Canal, over toward what they call the Karl the Ninth bastion. Should have seen the number of evil eyes we got. But for our numbers and the weapons we had in our hands, there'd have been a battle to outdo the Lowestoft fight there and then.'

'The King Johan Inn,' said Kit, still evidently somewhat abashed following our discourse of the Maiden Ter Horst. 'That's what the place is called. Larger than this, with a warren of outbuildings at the back in a walled yard. Easy to defend but hard to attack, Sir Matthew, especially with the surrounding streets full of our enemies.'

North examined a map of Gothenburg that had been among Lord Conisbrough's papers.

'And even if we can seize him from the inn,' he said, 'we need to get him out of the city. A walled city with just four gates, all guarded. Do Lord Dohna's assurances mean the guards will allow us free passage? It is a mighty risk, Sir Matthew.'

The thin smile upon North's face conveyed his thoughts amply. If getting the living John Bale out of Gothenburg alive was likely to prove so difficult, there was of course an alternative: the one which Lydford North had probably favoured all along.

I stood and walked to the stern windows. The tide had swung the ship so that I was looking toward the river of Gothenburg; although I could not see the city itself, I could see the smoke rising from its chimneys. The great blocks of ice coming downstream demonstrated that a thaw was well under way. Very soon, probably within only a day or two, the mast ships would be free. The ice in the Great Canal of Gothenburg was already well broken, and during my sojourn in the city on the previous day, a few optimistic skippers were already making ready for sea –

A thought came to me. At first it seemed no more than a mad inkling, but the more I considered it, the more plausible it seemed.

'There might be a way,' I said. 'If we can but get him out of the inn, I think I know how we can get him out of the city.'

* * *

Accompanied by a particularly churlish Phineas Musk, early the next morning I made a very conspicuous visit to the mast ships. It was now possible for the *Cressy*'s longboat to row a large part of the way up to the fleet, and it did so in some state, the King of England's ensign streaming from its staff so there could be no mistaking what we were about. My reception by the skippers was somewhat friendlier than before; not even they could quarrel with a man who had been imprisoned by one of England's most inveterate enemies. Gosling reported that the repairs to the *John and Abigail* were complete, that the fleet was taking in victuals, that the ice encasing it was rapidly thinning and breaking, so that within a matter of days the ships ought to be ready to sail upon a conjunction of wind and tide. I ordered the ship masters to fall down in convoy as soon as they were ready and to join the *Cressy* in the anchorage above New Elfsborg. That done, I returned to the longboat and made my way to my next destination: the single most essential element of the intended abduction of John, Lord Bale.

During our subsequent dinner at the Sign of the Pelican, Musk made clear his feelings upon the matter. 'Mad. To make the whole scheme depend upon such a sort of people – I tell you, Sir Matthew, your grandfather will be turning in his grave.'

'The man who stole a treasure from within the castle of Vera Cruz and abducted the wife of the Viceroy of New Spain? I rather think not, Musk.'

In the middle of the afternoon, Musk and I left the inn and strolled, outwardly without a care in the world, through the melting slush of Gothenburg's streets. Near the Dom Church we encountered, seemingly by chance, a rowdy leave party of Cressys led by John Tremar; I remonstrated publicly with them, urging them to uphold the honour of England, and our ways parted. Musk and I made our way east until we were almost in the shadow of the Gustavus Magnus bastion, then cut sharply down into an alley way into a yard behind a clutch of metalworkers' shops. There, we waited. When the distant bell of the Dom Church finally struck three, two other parties joined us in the yard: Lydford North, Kit Farrell and six Cressys from the west, Julian Carvell and six others from the north.

'He's inside?' I demanded.

'He was a quarter hour ago, Sir Matthew,' said North, as excited as a small boy playing at knights in armour. 'Your man has been watching the inn all day.'

'And Lanherne's men?'

'Will be in position at the rear, Sir Matthew,' growled Carvell.

'Very well,' I said. 'May God be with us all.'

I led the way along a side alley, halting at the very end of it. There, down and across the road, was the front door of the King Johan Inn. A small crowd of men stood in front of it, drinking and smoking on their clay pipes, talking loudly in Dutch; but such innocent pastimes could not disguise the fact that they were evidently an armed guard for the man within.

They, and we, heard the shouts in the same instant. Drunken shouts, coming toward the inn from the direction of the Great Canal. English voices. Above all, Cornish voices. 'God save King Charles!' they cried. 'Death to all traitors! Cromwell be fucked! Dutch butterboxes, burn in hell!'

The raucous mob of Cressys staggered into sight. Tremar, leading the band with inebriated vigour, pointed derisively toward the men outside the inn, gesturing obscenely with his fingers. A bluff old boatswain's mate named Stratton dropped his breeches and showed the Dutchmen his arse.

As the Cressys edged menacingly along the street, the guards of the King Johan inn drew blades and advanced to meet them. Attracted by the commotion, other men emerged from the inn: I recognised a number of them as being among the party that had escorted Bale at Conisbrough's funeral. They spoke in English, chiefly in the accents of London and Essex, those hotbeds of rebellion and fanatical forms of religion. But the Cressys' taunts affected them equally, and they joined their Dutch allies to form an impressive phalanx that easily outnumbered Tremar's drunken contingent. Nevertheless, the Cressys stood their ground and continued to goad, to gesticulate and to denounce the manhood of their opponents. Finally the Dutchmen and our English traitors could stand it no longer. They broke into a charge, at which the Cressys turned and ran. With their bloodlust enraged, the enemy pursued them out of the street.

I drew my sword, turned and nodded. Then I ran out into the street, making straight for the front door of the King Johan Inn. An elderly woman, who had come out to see what all the noise was about, led out a great cry, stepped back through the door and attempted to close that stout wooden barrier against us. Kit, Carvell and I reached the door in the same moment and charged it with our shoulders before the locks could be drawn shut within. A pistol fired and I heard a sound barely inches from my temple. Turning, I saw that the ball had embedded itself in the door, but I had no time to contemplate my fortunate escape. A blade came from nowhere and struck mine. I retaliated with a thrust of my own and edged further into the inn, my men pouring through the door behind me. There were barely half a dozen men before us, one of whom was trying frantically to reload the pistol he had fired at me. Musk, at my side, stretched out his arm, levelled his own weapon, and fired. The enemy's right eye vanished and his body spun round, slumping against the wall behind and sliding down it, leaving a stream of blood, brain and eye to mark its downward passage. Kit wielded a clumsy old cutlass to sterling effect, hacking down into the shoulder of the man opposite him and almost taking the whole arm off with that one blow. Witnessing the carnage around him, my own assailant backed away uncertainly. He was no swordsman, that much was certain. I feinted right, drawing his blade away, then thrust left, directly for the heart, and felt my sword cut through his thick shirt to dig deep into his chest. As the body fell away from by blade, I caught a glimpse of Lydford North's face. The young man might fancy himself a cold, ruthless assassin, but it was clear that slaughter upon this scale was beyond his experience, and deeply shocking to him. For one unlooked-for moment, I recalled the first time I ever killed a man: at the Battle of the Dunes in the year Fifty-Eight, when I was still but a boy. So I knew how North felt, but on the other hand, I had seen enough of fighting, battles and death to see that this skirmish in the King Johan Inn was as child's play to much of what I had witnessed – and inflicted – since that day on the sands before Dunkirk.

A door at the back of the inn burst open and we all turned, weapons gripped tightly, ready to confront a new foe. But I recognised the square, crop-headed features of Martin Lanherne, who saluted formally before reporting in his gruff tones, 'Yard and kitchens secure, Sir Matthew. Three of 'em dead. Not a scratch on one of us.'

'Very good, Mister Lanherne.' I turned to the rest of our men. 'Upstairs, men!'

There were two good rooms and four small ones on the first floor, all empty apart from a whore or two and a fat naked Dutchman who surrendered at once. The second floor was a low-ceilinged maze. We stormed along the landing, bursting open doors, overturning beds and spilling pisspots. It was Musk who discovered what we had come for: there, in a bare room toward the front of the building, stood John Bale.

He was unarmed, and apparently quite calm.

'Sir Matthew,' he said. 'I rejoice to see you so well, and give you joy of your freedom.'

His presence and his words distracted me: I was almost unaware of Lydford North, at my shoulder, levelling a pistol at the regicide. I spun on my heel and brought up my sword, striking North's weapon in the moment of firing. The ball went through the ceiling, bringing down a small cloud of plaster and dust.

'*No!*' I cried. 'This man will face a proper trial, in a proper court.'

North's face was twisted in hatred, whether of me or of Bale I could not be certain. But it was the regicide who answered me.

'A proper trial, in a proper court? You really believe that?' He took up his sword, which lay undrawn upon the mattress, and presented it hilt-first toward me. 'But it matters not. I am your prisoner.' As I took his sword and Julian Carvell stepped forward with rope to bind him, Bale looked at me intently. He seemed curiously passive and distant. 'Although I will be intrigued to see how you propose to get me out of Gothenburg, Sir Matthew.'

Chapter Fifteen

We bundled John Bale out of the King Johan Inn and along a street that ran north and west, parallel to the Great Canal. Dutchmen and Swedes alike taunted us, but we formed a tight and formidable phalanx, Cressys brandishing weapons in all directions, and none dared challenge us. Bale's regiment of Dutch and fanatic guards was nowhere to be seen, probably still being led a merry dance through the streets of Gothenburg by Tremar and the rest of his sham-drunkards. Of the Landtshere's guards, too, there was as yet no sign; it would take time for word of what had happened to get to Ter Horst's residence, more time for him to despatch his orders, yet more time for his officers to form a troop strong enough to confront us. If they were to confront us at all: I still had in mind Count Dohna's ambiguous assurances, but had no inkling of what they might mean or whether they were to be trusted.

Meanwhile Lydford North stayed well away from me, while keeping close to our prisoner. He had said nothing since I prevented him summarily executing Bale at the inn; I did not know whether he felt I had denied justice or denied him the rewards that would undoubtedly be bestowed by our sovereign lord upon the man who put to death one of the murderers of His Majesty's father. Perhaps there was an admixture of the two. For my part I was determined to keep John Bale alive: not necessarily to place him before a court of law in England, but to ask him the question that struck at the very heart of the business and at the regicide's curious compliance with his capture. The question to which I found Lydford North's answer unsatisfactory. Why, in the name of God, had the king-killer John, Lord Bale of Baslow, effectively saved the life of Sir Matthew Quinton, son to a fallen Cavalier hero, brother to the present King of England's confidential friend?

Such were my thoughts as I half-walked, half-ran through the streets of Gothenburg, my sword drawn and brandished from time to time to cow some particularly recalcitrant-looking shopkeeper or artisan. As we came out onto the quayside of the Great Canal opposite the German church, the press of people increased. A woman screamed at the sight of our weapons; now there were angry shouts in Swedish, German and Dutch, and a mob began to form. I heard a man call out Bale's name, and another shouted in English, 'Bastards! Villains! Cavalier scum!' We had the advantage of being formidably armed, but the mob had weight of numbers on its side and was forming around us, pressing us back toward the canal. If we could not escape the throng swiftly, within only a minute or two the advantage would pass from us to them.

But our destination was in sight now, and very close. Unmoored in the middle of the canal, poles pushing her away from the vessels along the quay and warp-lines pulling her toward the canal's sea gate, was the Scots privateer, the *Nonsuch* of Kinghorn. From her staff flew the ensign of the Kingdom of Scotland. Upon her tiny quarterdeck stood the barrel-shaped, one-legged figure of Captain Andrew Wood, with whom I had come to an understanding that morning, when I attended him after my visit to the mast-ships.

'Ye're in a little bother there, Sir Matthew!' he shouted in his barely intelligible brogue. 'The Sassenachs need a helping hand from the Scots, methinks. 'Twas ever thus.'

With that, a tarpaulin that had been covering the larboard rail of the *Nonsuch* was pulled away and the barrels of six immaculately polished six-pounders protruded outward, threatening the mob upon the quayside.

In the same moment some two or three dozen men appeared at the ship's rail, brandishing muskets, grenadoes and half-pikes. Privateers were ever heavily manned, the better to enable them to man prize-crews, and the *Nonsuch* was no exception.

A gangplank was flung from the *Nonsuch* onto the deck of an empty hoy moored immediately behind us, and the Cressys steadily retreated across it to safety aboard the Scots privateer, North manhandling Bale while Kit and Musk stood by him to ensure that Arlington's protégé did not slit the regicide's throat. I remained at the head of the party on the quayside, waving my sword threateningly at the angry mob. Finally I, too, edged backward across the deck of the hoy, along the gangplank and onto the *Nonsuch*.

I turned to our host. 'My thanks, Captain Wood.'

'Weesh, Sir Matthew, 'tis the least I can do for a fellow subject o' the King o' Scots.'

Wood was a taciturn fellow, but he had a curious side to him. At our meeting in the morning he had displayed none of the hostility to the English that characterised many of his nation, nor had he balked at the prospect I laid before him: indeed, he had been positively enthusiastic to play a part in bringing to justice a member of that court which had ordered the execution of a Dunfermline-born King of Scots without actually consulting the Scots themselves. I had half-expected Wood to demand some exorbitant payment for aiding us, and was prepared to agree to whatever he demanded, but he simply and honourably stated that he would be proud to do his duty in this matter. As we parted, the privateer also proclaimed to me that he was a great-great-grandson of one Sir Andrew Wood, admiral to James the Fourth, King of Scots, and (so he proudly claimed) the scourge of the English at sea. Whether the story was true or not, Wood was clearly an excellent seaman with an easy command of his large crew, which sailed by virtue of a Letter of Marque from the Lord High Admiral of Scotland, the feckless Duke of Richmond and Lennox. But even the finest seaman on earth would have fretted and raged at the sluggardly pace of our passage down the Great Canal of Gothenburg. There was nothing to be done: the wind was bow on, and although that would aid a swift passage down to the *Cressy* once we were out of the sea-gate, for the present it stymied any prospect of using the sails to aid the pushing and warping that provided our only momentum.

Kit Farrell suddenly pointed over the starboard quarter. 'The Landtshere has stirred himself, Sir Matthew,' he said.

Indeed he had. At least a hundred soldiers were running along the quayside from the town square, with others joining them from the streets that ran down to the German Church from the Crown House. True, the *Nonsuch* had cannon, and the Swedes would never be able to bring up such weapons before we were out of the canal and clear into the river. Moreover, I did not doubt that the privateer's captain would have loaded his guns with grapeshot or canister; but actually firing upon the King of Sweden's army was a very different proposition to the mock-show of cowing an angry mob, and both Wood and I knew it. So much for Count Dohna's reassurances: all just so much empty bluster. He had done nothing to aid our flight – though to be fair, he had certainly not had time to get a message to the High Chancellor at Lacko and receive a reply authorising whatever course of action he contemplated. So now all depended on us getting out of the canal before Ter Horst's troops could cut us off –

And upon a second factor.

Ahead of us, row-boats were scurrying around the canal mouth, securing lines and pulling into position the great boom of chains and log-piles that normally sealed the entrance to the canal by night. I had calculated that if we seized Bale quickly enough, before the Swedes had time to raise the alarm, and if Wood could get the *Nonsuch* out into the main channel of the canal adjacent to the sea-gate in time, we could escape into the open river before the canal could be sealed. But the Swedes had reacted more quickly than I anticipated, and it would now be a very close thing. Too close, by God.

The soldiers were forming files of three upon the northern quay-side, alongside the starboard quarter of the *Nonsuch*: the order of battle for rotating fire. And the Swedes, who had swept all before them from Munich to the Arctic, defeating some of the mightiest armies of the age, knew this method of fighting better than any other force in Europe. True, the *Nonsuch's* guns could have slaughtered them where they stood, but that would undoubtedly have brought on war between England and Sweden. Whereas if Ter Horst's ranks fired upon us, they were entirely within their rights to do so, in lawful defence of their own native earth.

Like all of us aboard the privateer, I looked frantically from the mus-keteers to the closing boom and back again. Perhaps we would just make it through –

But then a Swedish officer, as bold as any man I ever saw, calmly strode to the warping bollard and raised his heavy cavalryman's sword. He was barely feet away from our bow. Lanherne and several of the Scots raised muskets and levelled them: at such a range, they could not miss. But I looked at Captain Wood, and he looked back at me. Almost with one voice, we gave the same command: 'Hold fire!' And with that, the Swedish officer hacked down into the warping cable and, with three cuts, severed it.

The *Nonsuch* lost what little headway she had, and the boom closed into position. The canal was sealed. We were caught.

'Near, Sir Matthew,' said Wood. 'Damnably near.'

He nodded to one of his men, who struck the Scottish colours. With that, I turned my sword and offered the hilt toward the Swedish officer who had cut the warping cable.

* * *

We were marched, disarmed and under escort, to Ter Horst's residence on the Gustavus Adolphus square. Once again we filed into the Landt-shere's lavish audience chamber, lined with his acolytes, among whom John Bale was given pride of place; indeed, we were positioned very close to Ter Horst's daughter, who seemed barely able to restrain her tears at the sight of Kit Farrell. But the regicide seemed curiously detached. Surely he should have revelled in his fortunate release, but he seemed almost embarrassed by the entire business.

Before us stood a very different Ter Horst to the superficially courteous one who had appeared before us previously. The Landtshere raged with righteous indignation, whether feigned or not it was impossible to say. I suspected that inwardly, he was greatly enjoying this opportunity to humble the proud English.

'An affront to the honour of Sweden!' he raged in French for my benefit. 'Gross and horrid crimes, committed here upon her very soil! Seizing the person of Lord Bale, to whom we had granted our particular protection! Threatening the citizenry and garrison of Gothenburg with armed violence – why, even with loaded cannon!' The man was red-faced; I contemplated the odds of him being struck by a paralytic stroke.

'These are capital crimes, Sir Matthew Quinton. Capital crimes, do you hear me? You and your men are nothing more than pirates, but then, that is what you English have always been. Your cried-up Drake, and your own grandfather – what were they all, but mere pirates?'

Captain Wood, standing alongside me (indeed, chained to me) was unimpressed.

'What's yon blaigeard blathering on about?' he demanded.

'He is accusing you of being an English pirate, Captain,' I said.

'Jesus and Mary, better men than he have called me a pirate and I'll answer to that, but *English?*'

Ter Horst stared angrily at us for having the impertinence to interrupt his torrent of bile. 'You will pay for all these affronts, Quinton – you and all of your fellow pirates. We will take you – yes, all of you! – to Stockholm, there to face trial before the Riksdag itself! Invasion! War upon Sweden's soil! Treachery! You will hang, or your head will be cut from your shoulders as it so rightly was in the case of your late king! Your King Charles will not save you, Quinton, not if he wishes to avoid war with the

Three Crowns! You are doomed, sir, for he will not want to face the very armies that humbled the Emperor, and the Spanish, and the Poles –'

I affected a great yawn. 'Really, My Lord Ter Horst? And how do you propose to get your so-mighty armies to England? Will you hope that the entire North Sea freezes over so you can merely walk across, as your late King did when he invaded Denmark? You might be waiting for quite some time, My Lord.'

Musk and some of the other Cressys behind me sniggered. Ter Horst looked at me in astonishment: he was evidently not accustomed to being interrupted, and he was certainly not accustomed to irreverent English wit. I thought for a moment that he was going to step forward and strike me, but as it was, he stepped away and began haranguing the audience of burghers and army officers in Swedish, no doubt repeating for their benefit his tirade against all the gross and manifest iniquities of the English since the days of King Lud.

But as he did so, a curious thing happened. The door behind him – the very one through which John Bale had entered, the first time I had been in this room – opened and admitted a familiar figure: the tiny frame of General Erik Glete, as magnificent as such a tiny creature could be, attired in a breastplate, a black-and-gold burgonet helmet and a large blue cloak. A file of a dozen or so of his own men, whom I recognised from the deck of the *Fortuna*, stepped quietly into the hall behind him.

He listened for some moments to Ter Horst's harangue, then belched ostentatiously. 'Shut your fucking pompous mouth, you great Dutch shit-sack,' he bawled in immaculate barrack-room French.

Ter Horst spun around in astonishment. He unleashed a torrent of vitriol upon the little general: true, it was in Swedish, but vitriol in any tongue is not difficult to identify. Glete, in turn, gave as good as he got. The two men edged nearer to each other until Ter Horst, who was not a tall man, towered over the general, yet still Glete held his ground. I understood not a word of it other than occasional mentions of the name 'De La Gardie' and frequent uses of the words *kung* and *drottning*, but the audience of Swedes were evidently stunned by what they were hearing. Finally Glete drew out a folded document bearing a large wax seal and handed it to Ter Horst. The Landtshere opened it, read the words upon it, re-read them, and let the paper fall to the floor. The blood drained from his face; it was as though he had been stuck in the gut by a pike. Glete stooped, picked up the paper and read it aloud in Swedish. There were gasps among the audience, followed by much whispering. Magdalena Ter Horst, already emotional at the sight of her lover, wailed hysterically, but Kit, chained to the rest of us, was unable to go over to comfort her.

Glete barked an order, and the soldiers who had been guarding us from the quayside shuffled uncomfortably, looking at each other nervously. Glete's own men moved across the hall and took up position by our guards. Glete repeated the same words, and this time keys were brought out, locks opened and chains released. We were free; and as proof of our freedom, a Swedish sergeant brought in a bundle containing our swords. Erik Glete recognised mine (the extravagant hilt of my grandfather's weapon was unmistakeable), took it up and handed it to me.

'Sir Matthew,' he said in French so that Ter Horst could understand, 'I believe this is yours. You will require it, sir, to do battle with the Dutch, those devious and implacable foes of England and Sweden alike.'

'What has happened here, General?' I asked in English.

Glete shrugged. 'Let us say there has been a transition in the affairs of this city, Sir Matthew,' he replied, still in French for Ter Horst's benefit as well as my own. 'From the old Landtshere of Gothenburg to the new. By royal command and commission, and with the assent of the High Chancellor of the Swedes, Goths and Wends.'

And with that, Lieutenant-General Erik Glete, Landtshere of Gothenburg, grinned fiercely.

Chapter Sixteen

A saker upon our forecastle fired, and our foretopsail was loosed: the signal for the fleet to get under way. A team of Cressys pushed upon our jeer capstan to bring up our bower anchor. Away to the north-east, sails were loosed upon the mast-ships: slowly and shabbily, as is ever the way aboard merchants' hulls which bear as few men as possible to save their owners the expense of a proper crew. By contrast, the Cressys – volunteers almost to a man – were now something of a crack crew. As Jeary, Lanherne and the other officers bellowed orders through voice-trumpets, they responded instantly and crisply. The fall of the mainsail was immaculate, and it was sheeted home with speed and precision, the other sails and their crews not far short of that mark. The steady, cold breeze from the north-west caught the great sheets of canvas, which cracked and billowed. Slowly, the *Cressy* began to move upon the ocean once again, the mast fleet following raggedly in our wake: at its head, Gosling in the *Thomas and Mary*; bringing up the rear, the *Delight*, the most heavily laden of the mast-ships. We saluted the castle of New Elfs-borg with eleven, and I offered up a silent prayer of thanksgiving that at last Matthew Quinton was putting behind him those infernal hell-holes, Gothenburg and the Kingdom of the Swedes, Goths and Wends.

In truth, of course, I was doing nothing of the sort, for the most potent legacy of my time in Sweden was below decks, chained to the mizzen on the orlop deck. After our release by Erik Glete and the invisible good offices of the Count Dohna, we had escorted John Bale back to the *Cressy*. North was all for incarcerating him at once in the darkest recesses of the hold, and I suspected that Arlington's protégé was still furious at my denying him the opportunity to place a pistol ball in Bale's skull at the King Johan Inn. At my insistence, though, our prisoner was sat down in my great cabin, his hands and feet securely tied and with the heavily armed Ali Reis and John Tremar training loaded muskets at him. I had two questions to ask the regicide, and the first was that to which every true and loyal Englishmen demanded an answer.

'Why did you sign the King's death warrant?'

North snorted; no doubt he anticipated the usual fanatic tirade upon Charles Stuart's alleged misdeeds, or else upon the so-called iniquity of the institution of kingship. But Bale said nothing of the sort. He fixed me with a firm stare and took some moments to answer.

'Do you know, Sir Matthew,' he said finally, 'for at least the last ten years I have asked myself that same question in almost every waking moment?'

North stepped forward and punched him hard upon the left cheek. '*Liar!*' he screamed. 'Do not pretend that you repent of the crime, Bale! That falsehood will never win you favour in a court –'

'Mister North,' I said sternly, 'you will favour me by not striking the prisoner here in my cabin or aboard my ship!'

North shot me a furious glance but moved away reluctantly to stand by the stern windows.

'But there you have my answer,' said Bale. 'The blind enthusiasm of youth. I was twenty-one when I signed the warrant, Sir Matthew. I was fourteen when the civil wars began. My eldest brother was killed at Edgehill, the next at the first Newbury fight. My home was burned by Prince Rupert's men; the first girl I ever loved was raped and killed by one of his dragoons. I was afired by my belief in God's righteous cause, convinced that He had made me an instrument of His divine justice, so as soon as I was old enough I went off to fight. But when I inherited my father's title and went to the House of Lords, what did I find? The timeservers were discussing new terms to be offered to Charles Stuart! To the man who had inflicted nought but blood upon the land for long years on end!' A furious North stepped toward the prisoner once again, but I raised a hand sharply. 'So I listened eagerly to those who proposed another course – to General Cromwell and those like him who denounced the King as a man of blood. And when the moment came to sign, to place my name first upon the warrant – ah, the pride that I felt! I truly believed we were giving birth to a new England, a land free of tyrants, a land where the will of the people would prevail.' He shook his head. 'If only I had known then that I was signing my own death warrant as surely as that of the King.'

North could bear no more. 'Lies! Damnable, impudent lies! But they will not save you, John Bale! Nothing can save you! Sir Matthew, you may persist with this travesty if you wish. I will have no more of it.'

He stormed past me and left the cabin. 'A dangerous young man,' said Bale. 'He reminds me greatly of myself at that age.'

'The regicides remained inveterate to a man,' I said, ignoring his comparison of himself with Lydford North. 'You were all proud of what you did. Why is it that you alone claim to have repented, John Bale?'

'I was the most senior of them, as a peer of England, but I was also by some considerable measure the youngest, too. They were firm in their opinions, but mine were as yet barely formed. And as I grew older, I came to see things were not as I thought them to be. Oliver Cromwell, a man whom I had believed to be a vehicle of godly reformation for England, took upon himself more power than even the dead king had ever possessed. Great God, Sir Matthew, he was even offered the crown itself, and very nearly took it. So what had it all been for, if I had brought down a tyrant only to set up a far greater one? To behead King Charles only to put King Oliver in his stead? At much the same time I married Conisbrough's daughter and my son was born. Marriage and fatherhood change a man's perspective mightily. You have found that yourself?'

'I am married,' I said, 'but we have not yet been blessed with the joy of children.'

I had no idea why I was confiding in this creature, who had committed the most heinous crime of all.

'I trust you will come to know such joy. But that is how I come to my present condition, Sir Matthew. If I could have had my life over again, I would never have dipped my quill in the ink pot and applied it to the parchment. Four letters – my name. Four letters that damn me, my wife and my son.'

I was taken aback by his apparent honesty; I knew the devil would be equally plausible, but as he spoke, there seemed to be less and less of the diabolic about John Bale. Time, then, to ask him my second question.

'Was that why you told my men where Montnoir was holding me? Did you seek to mitigate your crime by saving my life?'

'Sir Matthew, nothing can mitigate my crime. In that, young North is undoubtedly correct, although I think both you and I know it's just as well. I will die a traitor's death, and I am prepared for it. No, I saved your life because you were a fellow Englishman in peril at the hands of a Frenchman and a papist. I have many friends in Gothenburg – men opposed to the High Chancellor, able to glean intelligence from all kinds of quarters. So I knew of your Lord Montnoir and his designs, Sir Matthew. Of what he proposed to do in Queen Christina's name. Even if you and I disagree upon the ideal form of government for England, I think we would both agree that a Catholic Sweden is something that all true English Protestants should oppose with all their might.'

'I am grateful to you for my release,' I said, although a part of me still found it galling to make such a gesture to a king-killer.

'And I to you for saving me from North's pistol shot when I surrendered,' he said.

'Surrendered? I have two men with wounds testifying to how hard we had to fight to capture you!'

'I did not wield the sword against them. I wished to surrender myself to you, but my men would not permit it. To them, I was a symbol – they believed I had to live and be free as a sign that Charles Stuart will never prevail, that what they call the cause of the godly will triumph once again,' said Bale. 'But I came to think differently. With Conisbrough dead, I knew my life here was not worth the candle. Sooner or later, a man like your Master North – or a Swede bought with Charles Stuart's coin – was bound to put a pistol to my head or drive a knife into my ribs. In truth, I have been a dead man walking since I put my signature to that accursed piece of paper. How the hot-headed follies and enthusiasms of our extreme youth can condemn us, as surely as my act that day condemned the late king! I am tired of concealment, Sir Matthew, and above all, I have a mighty urge to see my wife and son before I die. That is all the repayment I ask of you. Intercede with the King to permit them one interview with me before the executioner does his work.'

I thought of my King, that infuriating, inconstant crowned enigma. The one cause to which he was constant – indeed, fanatically so – was the relentless pursuit and destruction of his father's murderers. I doubted whether I could convince him to permit the indulgence that John Bale had requested; but perhaps my brother, the Earl of Ravensden, one of his most intimate friends, could succeed if I could not. I chided myself for even thinking such thoughts, for why should I pander to this regi-cide? But then, I undoubtedly owed this regicide my life.

'I can guarantee nothing,' I said, and ordered Ali Reis and Tremar to take John Bale below.

* * *

The fleet moved south-south-west through the archipelago at a painfully slow rate. The *Cressy* had constantly to shorten sail to accommodate the speed of the slowest mast-ship, although there seemed to be considerable competition for that dubious honour. Several, notably the *Delight*, tended to fall away sharply to leeward, compelling their inadequate crews to struggle to adjust sail sufficiently for them to be able to beat back up to the body of the fleet. It was soon plain to me that even with so little distance to travel, we would not make the isle of Wingo, and thus the exit from the archipelago, before nightfall; far from it. The flood tide was nearly begun, and I knew from the outward voyage how powerfully the current ran in those waters. Rather than risk losing one or more of the mast-ships by attempting to steer through shoal water and a host of islands by night, against the tide, we would need to lay up and proceed again in the morning. As this realisation grew within me, I paced ever more impatiently upon my quarterdeck. Every hour of delay increased our danger. It was already more than likely that intelligence of our sailing had been despatched across the few miles of water that separated us from Denmark, and if our enemies had ships ready for sea, which they were surely bound to do, the wind was in their favour. The westerly was nearly ideal for ships sailing from Frederikshavn or Kristiansand, whereas we would have to tack into it; and having seen such clear evidence of the ineptitude of the mast-ships in an easy beam reach, I dreaded the thought of them attempting to beat up into a steady gale.

Reluctantly, I ordered the hoisting of a blue flag at the mizzen peak, the agreed signal for the convoy to drop anchor. We did so in the lee of a small island that the charts named as Buschar, the *Cressy* lying to windward of the mast-fleet. As our bower anchor was loosed and the maintopsail was furled, the lookout barked a report that the *Fortuna* was in sight. This time Erik Glete approached at a leisurely pace, his craft approaching out of the dying light in the south-west, the Swedish pennant streaming from her ensign staff. One of his bow guns fired a salute of three; I had one of our larboard sakers return the same. The proud old galley came alongside, and both the little general and Count Dohna came aboard.

'Had to give you a proper farewell to Sweden, Quinton,' said the new Landtshere of Gothenburg as Kit, North and I entertained our visitors in my cabin. 'My Lord Dohna insisted upon it.'

'Quite so,' said Dohna. 'But there is something I wish you to see, Sir Matthew. In private.'

We drew apart from the others and went to stand by the stern windows of my cabin. Dohna gestured to one of his young attendants, who came over and presented him with a leather case. From it the Count drew two sheets of paper. He gave them to me and said, 'Here is the proof I promised you – the proof of what was done in this place by your brother and others so many long years ago.'

The top sheet was a receipt, and it was written in English.

> *Item, of cannon: twelve.*
> *Item, of cannonballs: one thousand, two hundred.*
> *Item, of muskets: six thousand.*
> *Item, of swords: four thousand.*
> *Item, of pikes: five thousand.*
> *Item, of suits of cavalry armour: two thousand.*
> *Item, of drums: fifty.*
> *Received in the Crown House of Gothenburg, this nineteenth day of March in the first year of the reign of Charles the Second, King of England, Scotland, Ireland and France, and the sixteenth year of the reign of Christina, Queen of the Swedes, Goths and Wends, Sixteen Hundred and Forty-Nine.*

Signatories of the first party:	*Signatories of the second party:*
Montrose, Captain General	*Oxenstierna, High Chancellor*
Brentford	*De La Gardie*
Ravensden	*Conisbrough*

The fact that Lord Conisbrough had signed upon the Swedish side, or the shock of seeing my brother's familiar handwriting upon such a document in such a place, seemed less remarkable to me at the time than the information upon the second sheet, which lay beneath the receipt. It was exactly the same inventory, but this time it was written in French, dated from Uppsala eleven days before the receipt; in other words, it was the original order to issue the specified items to the Cavalier leaders. It was signed by exactly the same florid hand that had written the rest of the document. And there was the rub. It seemed simply inconceivable to me that the signatory would not have employed a clerk, or even High Chancellor Oxenstierna himself, to itemise the likes of cannonballs and drums. For the signature, alongside a wax seal bearing three crowns, read: *Christina R.*

I looked up and met Dohna's gaze. 'This is the equipage of an entire army,' I said in amazement. 'And the Queen made it a personal order, to the extent of writing out the entire inventory herself?'

'So it was,' the count replied. 'The equipage of the army that would win back the throne for your King Charles. Remember I told you how deeply the Queen felt about it, Sir Matthew.'

As I studied the two documents, I recall how my mother had railed against the duplicity of the crowned heads of Europe, who claimed to have been outraged by the execution of one of their own yet then did not lift a finger to help his son's cause. It was clear now with that she was mistaken: one monarch had taken up the gauntlet on behalf of the young, exiled King Charles, and that was the one monarch who was not a man.

'Queen Christina provided the arsenal that could have defeated Cromwell and won back the kingdom,' I said admiringly. 'If only, My Lord Dohna.'

Dohna nodded. 'Indeed, Sir Matthew. If only. The Queen's generosity could have and should have won back your kingdom, but for the petty hatreds and staggering incompetence alike that then prevailed among your king's supporters.' The noble Swede's features were animated now; it was though a dam had been broken, and the enigmatic Lord Dohna's true thoughts were pouring through in a torrent. 'Take Lord Montrose, for instance. The best, the most valiant of men. I met him, you see, along with your brother, during those fateful months in the year Forty-Nine. Sweet Mother Mary, there were legends and heroes galore stalking Europe in that year of all years, when the war of thirty years had just ended – Field Marshals, Generals, all of them with dozens of battles to their name, yet whom did they all respect? Montrose. To fight the campaigns he fought, against the odds he faced... And yet what became of him, Sir Matthew? Betrayed, executed and chopped into pieces by those who claimed, like him, to be fighting for your King Charles the Second. Christina would have done better to arm the idiots and lunatics that infest the alleys of Gamla Stan in Stockholm than to provide such an equipage to the treacherous crew of incompetents that made up your so-called Cavalier party at that time. I can still recall how the good men – the likes of your brother and Lord Conisbrough – fretted and raged against the vicious factions in your exiled court. Her Majesty told me much later that she realised the mistake she had committed in that March of 1649. You English royalists did not need weapons, Sir Matthew – you had plenty enough of your own. Instead, she should have sent you just three of our Swedish generals, fresh from thirty years of battle against the best generals in this world. They would have hit heads together, rooted out your chaff, put paid to your factions and given you victory in three months. After all, Sir Matthew, what was your Cromwell, your proud, strutting Lord Protector, other than a mere farmer but ten years before?'

I detested the memory of Cromwell: in one sense he, like Bale, was but one of the fifty-nine king-killers, but he was so much more than that, for his rule as Lord Protector of England had both denied the rightful king his inheritance and very nearly brought the House of Quinton to ruin. But Cromwell was yet an Englishman, from the same soil as myself (give or take the very few miles that lay between Ravensden Abbey and

Huntingdon), and for all the Cavalier spirit that lurked within me, I secretly cheered the chilling dread of old England that his success in arms had driven like a dagger into the heart of every foreigner. Every foreigner, it seemed, except the Count Dohna.

My honour prevented me from defending Noll Cromwell; thus I blustered, and endeavoured to change the subject.

'A mere farmer, as you say. But tell me, my Lord – do you think there might be at least some prospect of the High Chancellor reconsidering his position over the treaty that was proposed?'

'I think England should not be sanguine,' said Dohna. 'I know de la Gardie. He will be outraged against Montnoir for the crimes he has committed in this kingdom, but he is intelligent enough to see that Montnoir is not France. And as I said to you at Lacko, Sir Matthew, the inducements offered by your king are feeble – hardly enough to make the three crowns abandon the rare state of peace it now enjoys.'

'And the cutting of trees, my Lord?'

Dohna smiled. 'Ah, your precious wood again. In truth, I cannot see the High Chancellor abandoning an embargo he imposed so very recently. And no man can deny that forests need to recover from the despoiling of recent times. But Sweden is a large country, Sir Matthew. There are few troops to patrol it. Most of the army is garrisoned across the Baltic, holding down our new empire. And I shall be returning to Rome within a few days.' The enigmatic Count shrugged. 'In my absence, it is not unlikely that evil men will seek to circumvent the embargo by cutting down trees on the Queen's estates and then, let us say, shipping them to England from one of the Queen's more secluded harbours, where they are unlikely to trouble the High Chancellor's customs officers. Perhaps in ships flying false neutral colours – those of Spain are said to be particularly immune to searches. Why, it would not surprise me if those evil men were even now seeking out some of your English merchants in Gothenburg to seal contracts to that effect.'

I nodded as the true meaning of Dohna's words dawned on me. 'England would be eternally grateful for such a blessing, my Lord.'

'A blessing, Sir Matthew? A manifest crime against Sweden? The high Chancellor would be appalled to hear you speak so, as would her Majesty Queen Christina.'

I bowed my head slightly. 'As you say, my Lord Dohna.'

Glete turned away from his conversation with Kit Farrell and Lydford North. 'My Lord,' he said, 'we had best be away to make best use of the flood tide.'

Dohna nodded, and we escorted our guests back to the entry ladder on the starboard side of the *Cressy*.

Dohna turned to me one last time. He signalled to his serving-boy, who ran forward with what seemed to be a small package. The lad handed it to his master, who in turn held it out toward me in his gloved hand. 'A token of my respect, Sir Matthew,' said Count Dohna, 'and thanks for the service you have rendered Sweden.'

He pressed the object into my hand. It was evidently a book; I could feel the worn leather binding, and my thumb traced the outline of an ingrained armorial. But the curious, long face and large penetrating eyes of Count Dohna still held my attention, and I did not look in detail at the imprint.

'Service to Sweden, My Lord?' I said. 'I fear I have rendered precious little.'

'Do not be so certain of that.' Dohna smiled. 'The mysteries of the world are manifold, Sir Matthew. And yet for every mystery, there is an answer. So it is. So it has always been. Adieu, my friend, and may God guide and defend you in your perilous voyage to come.'

I did not quite know what to make of such an ambiguous speech. 'Adieu, My Lord,' I said hesitantly, 'and my gratitude for your gift.'

With that, Count Dohna stepped over the side of the *Cressy* and went down onto the deck of the *Fortuna*. I handed the book to young Kellett, instructing him to place it in my sea-chest, and thought no more of it.

The galley cast off, and the last I saw of her was heading north-east, back toward Gothenburg. The oars cut the still icy water with their accustomed precision. At the stern rail stood General Erik Glete, waving his sword about his head like a madman possessed, and the Count Dohna, as still as a statue, his eyes evidently intent upon the fast-receding shape of the *Cressy*.

* * *

At dawn I ordered a gun to be fired and the fleet weighed upon the ebb, at first making clumsy progress west-by-south before tacking north-by-west. By noon, though, we had progressed no more than a dozen miles or so, the *Delight* in particular wallowing dreadfully and the *Cressy* having constantly to shorten sail to accommodate her inadequacies. Truly, there are few experiences more galling to a sea-captain than command of a convoy: knowing that one's own ship can veritably race across the oceans, yet having constantly to fall back and dawdle so that the last sluggard under one's charge can manage to keep up, if only barely. And this was the Sound, one of the busiest sealanes in the world; far busier now than it had been in our outward voyage, as the first tentative signs of spring brought forth not only snowdrops but sails, an abundance of them. Large Eastland fluyts, outward bound, crossed our path, staying well away from us, while small fishing craft and coasters plied hither and thither. None of these concerned me, not even an odd little ship three or four miles in our lee which flew the unusual flag of the great Commonwealth of Poland-Lithuania. As the *Cressy*'s bell rang for one of the afternoon, my concern was fixed entirely upon two sails, at first no more than specks upon the western horizon, now clearly identifiable as ships bearing down rapidly upon the wind. Large ships. One, the more southerly, very large indeed.

I fixed my telescope upon this larger ship as it drew nearer. There was no mistaking it: the botched repair of the beakhead, the odd alignment of the gunports beneath the poop, the eccentric stepping of the mizzen.

'Our old friend, gentlemen,' I said to the company upon the *Cressy*'s quarterdeck, 'Captain Rohde and the *Oldenborg*.'

'Come to escort us out of the Sound,' said Musk sarcastically. 'That's good of him.'

'We have had no word of a declaration of war,' said Kit. 'But I'd say she has a distinctly warlike air about her, Sir Matthew.'

'A distinctly warlike air indeed, Mister Farrell.'

'Perhaps he intends only to affright us,' said Musk. 'Doing a good job of it, by my reckoning.'

I could now see the men upon the upper deck of the *Oldenborg*. Her guns were manned, and pike-points glinted in the sunlight. And yet, what if Musk was right? What if Rohde sought only to alarm us, as Erik Glete and the *Fortuna* had done so successfully in the anchorage at New Elfsborg? Perhaps he sought to provoke us into firing first – a second outrage by the perfidious English would surely give the hesitant King Frederik an even stronger excuse to declare war –

'Her consort,' said Seth Jeary, peering intently through his own eye-piece, 'is a Dutchman, though she flies Danish colours. Presumably one of the frigates that the States-General has loaned to King Frederik as an inducement for him to enter the war. Cut for thirty-eight guns, by the looks of her, but she seems to bear only thirty-six.'

'A blessing,' I said with feigned merriment. 'Two guns fewer – that will make all the difference, gentlemen.'

In truth, we all knew that two guns made almost no difference to the odds against us. The enemy ships had twice as many guns, could fire double our weight of shot, probably carried at least two hundred more men than we did. If the Danes were intent upon battle, declaration of war or no, then by any rational calculation the *Cressy* ought to be doomed, and with it the mast-fleet. Every man on the quarterdeck – no, every man on my ship – could see that as plainly as I. But was that indeed the Danes' intent?

A flurry of movement at the maintop of the *Oldenborg* put the matter beyond all doubt.

'Sir Matthew,' said Kit, 'they are hoisting a flag at the main.'

Had the Danes given us the honour of being despatched by a full admiral, then? Perhaps even their famous commander Niels Juel? To die at his capable hand would at least be an honour –

I was immediately disabused, for the colours that broke out at the maintopmast head of the *Oldenborg* were not the white and red of Denmark. They were the fleur-de-lis upon a white ground of the Most Christian King of France. Any ship that flew those colours was at war with England and an enemy of the *Cressy*; and in those waters, there could be only one Frenchman for whom such colours had been hoisted.

'Him,' said Musk wearily. 'Will we never be rid of that foul death's head?'

I knew not how Montnoir had been able to appropriate two Danish men-of-war, including one of her greatest, but immediately chided myself for wondering at it: if the Knight of Malta had been convinced that he could singlehandedly bring about Sweden's reconversion to Rome, then persuading King Frederik to grant him two ships would have been a mere detail. But the Frenchman's arrogant presumption deserved a response, and I vowed he would have it.

I called for Kellett and told him to go below to Lydford North, requesting him to come to the quarterdeck at once. The lad complied eagerly, and Arlington's protégé duly emerged onto the deck, evidently in bad grace at having been diverted from yet another interrogation of John Bale (if a one-sided litany of abuse can be distinguished in such a way).

'You summoned me, Sir Matthew?' he said brusquely.

I pointed toward our oncoming assailants. 'Behold our difficulty, Mister North,' I said.

For once the confidence drained from the face of Lydford North, leaving in its place a markedly affrighted young man. 'I – Sir Matthew, I do not see what I can – how I can –'

'Observe the flag upon the mainmast of the *Oldenborg*, Mister North.

The larger ship. The one to larboard – to the left,'

'The colours of France. Upon a Danish man-of-war. She bears a French admiral, perchance?'

'No, Mister North. She bears the Seigneur de Montnoir, my recent abductor, a Knight of Malta once accredited by King Louis as an ambassador. Presumably he claims a right to that flag by virtue of that rank, for ambassadors are entitled to fly their nation's colour at the main as though they were a monarch or an admiral, are they not, Mister North?'

'I believe My Lord Arlington once told me something to that effect, Sir Matthew.'

'Well then, Mister North – in your opinion, would Lord Arlington and His Majesty the King object if an ambassador of theirs, albeit merely a confidential one without full accreditation, matched the impudence of yonder puffed-up Frenchman by bearing their own colours into battle?'

North frowned. 'Sir Matthew – you seek my opinion upon *the hoisting of a flag*?'

'You are a diplomatist, Mister North,' I said reprovingly. 'Is there a higher matter of honour than the hoisting of our country's flag?'

The young man looked at me with a peculiar expression that might even have been tinged with respect. 'No, Sir Matthew,' he said slowly, 'there is not. You have served as an ambassador of the King of Great Britain at the risk of your own life, and I will gladly vouch to His Majesty that you have earned the right to bear his flag.'

'Very well, then.' I turned to the company upon the quarterdeck. 'Mister Lanherne! Break out the Union at the main!'

Suitably, the hoisting of the colour was undertaken by MacFerran, one of the few Scots in the ship's company and one of my closest followers since my fateful commission in the *Jupiter*. As the strange confection of red, blue and white, so unlike any other flag conceived by man, unfurled from the masthead, a proud cheer broke out among the Cressys upon the deck. With that, I ordered our trumpets to sound and our decks cleared for battle.

Chapter Seventeen

As the *Cressy* echoed to the sound of partitions being taken down, gun port lids swinging open and guns being run out, Kellett approached me with an unexpected report. I thought hard before I responded to it, but we had ample time, perhaps an hour still, before we engaged, and Lydford North was at the larboard rail, seemingly absorbed by Musk's bloodthirsty description of exactly what horrors he could expect to experience in a sea-battle. All of that being so, some strange compulsion made me accede to the request that Kellett had brought me.

I went below, elbowing my way past Cressys intent on nothing but readying their ship for battle. I returned nods and makeshift salutes galore, as well as acknowledging growls of 'God be with you, Sir Matthew'. As I did so, I wondered how many of these men would live to see another dawn. They were a good crew, a veteran crew, many of whom had been with me since my time in the *Jupiter*. Yet some were surely destined to die in the next few hours, in a battle against a land with which England was not at war; a battle seemingly brought on at the behest of one fanatical Frenchman, obsessed with vengeance against me. Indeed, I thought, perhaps I was one of those so destined. If that was to be the case I ought to be penning a last letter to my Cornelia, not embarking on this peculiar pilgrimage to the very depths of the ship's hull.

The orlop stank of the bilges and the waste of countless seamen who had failed to reach the heads in the bow. It was the lowest of the decks in both senses of the term, and even bending nearly double still put me in constant danger of colliding with each and every beam. It was also the darkest place on the ship, below the waterline, lit only dimly by one lantern. Even so, the light was sufficient for me to see the unkempt form of John Bale, sitting upon a rough seaman's mattress lying on the deck. Both his hands and his ankles were manacled, this at North's insistence; and fresh gashes and bruises upon the regicide's face bore witness to the fact that there were not the only painful indignities Arlington's creature had heaped upon Bale. Despite the enormity of what he had done, I, who myself had been chained so recently, could not help but feel some sympathy for the man's plight.

He looked up as I approached. 'You face battle, Sir Matthew. The boy who fetched your Mister North took great delight in telling me. Two ships, one of them far greater than this?'

There was little point in dissembling. 'They are not insuperable odds,' I said.

'But nonetheless, they are against us?'

'Us': I bridled at the presumption of the man in placing himself upon the same side as myself and all the other loyal Cressys. But then I understood – or thought I understood – Bale's concern.

'This will be the safest place on the ship,' I said sharply, 'and if we succumb to the odds, well, then – you will not be the only man to die this day, John Bale. Drowning down here will be a quicker and cleaner death than that which awaits many of us above. A quicker and cleaner death than you deserve, despite the service you rendered me by telling my men where Montnoir was holding me.'

'That may be,' he said levelly. 'Do I not then deserve an opportunity to atone for the manifest sin I committed, Sir Matthew?'

'Atonement for you can come only from God.'

'If that is so, and I truly believe you have the right of it, then why not put the matter in the hands of God?' His eyes fixed intently upon mine.

'I fought, Sir Matthew. I rode with Cromwell at Preston and at Worcester. I can wield a sword with the best, and I can aim a musket. You will need every man you can get in the fight to come. So let God judge me. Either I perish in battle, and His will be done, or I live to face the king's judge and executioner. In either case, justice is served upon John Bale. But if it is to be the former, at least my son will know his father died redeemed, fighting for the country he loved.'

The impudence and enormity of his demand took my breath away. 'You would have me release you, and give you a weapon?'

'Just so, Sir Matthew.'

Every Cavalier instinct in my body raged against it. I could almost see my mother's face, red with fury and forbidding. I could visualise the terrible wrath of my king. Yet there was another voice, too: a still, small voice, that spoke to me in very different words.

The distant sound of the *Cressy*'s trumpets, so shrill their notes carried all the way down from the poop to this fastness, brought me back to the moment.

'I shall think upon it,' I said, and turned upon my heel.

I returned to the quarterdeck to see that the *Oldenborg* and her consort had separated. The smaller frigate, now identified as the Dutch-loaned *Faisant*, was sailing large to the south-east upon the wind. Her intent was obvious: she would cut well astern of us, then turn north again close-hauled to fall upon the mast-fleet. Rohde, or Montnoir, or whoever truly commanded the Danish squadron, knew their business. It would be an easy matter for us to fall away down the wind and prevent the frigate reaching the fleet; but that would leave the mast-ships exposed to the full force of the *Oldenborg*, which could set a course for the headmost vessels and be upon them in precious little time. Whereas if we held our course to block the approach of the greater ship, the lesser would have free rein to wreak what havoc she could. That being so, there was only one thing I could do; or at any rate, only one thing I could do with honour.

'Mister Farrell, Mister Jeary!' I cried. The two officers approached and touched their hats in salute. Inevitably, Phineas Musk shuffled nearer so as to be within earshot. 'Do not the great Classical authors tell us that for a general to divide his force is the most unutterable folly?'

'Perhaps they do, Sir Matthew,' said Kit, thoughtfully: I, who had taught him how to read only a few years since, knew full well that he had never encountered a Classical author in his life.

'Indeed they do, Lieutenant. Thus it appears to me that the only way of preventing one or other of the Danes falling upon our charges is for us to batter the other so mercilessly that his second has no choice but to come to his aid. Divide and conquer, gentlemen. Our enemy has obliged us by dividing, and now we shall conquer.'

'Which ship, Sir Matthew?' asked Jeary, although he knew the answer as well as I did.

'I do not imagine Captain Rohde would go to the assistance of a mere hired Dutchman,' I said. 'The Lord Montnoir certainly would not.' I nodded toward the proud bulk of the *Oldenborg*. 'There is our foe, gentlemen. She flies the flag of France, and have not Englishmen in war always found humbling those colours an irresistible prospect? Mister Jeary, a course directly for her, if you please.'

* * *

The *Cressy* wore ship and came round onto the same tack as the *Oldenborg*, steering north-east toward the headmost of the mast-ships. The distance between us closed rapidly. The starboard rail of the enemy ship was lined with men chanting ferociously: *Danmark! Danmark!* These were descendants of the Vikings, I reminded myself, and they would not be awed by the sight of English colours. I levelled at my telescope upon her quarterdeck, and there was Captain Rohde, his own eyepiece fixed upon me. Beside him stood the unmistakeable slender figure of the Seigneur de Montnoir.

Phineas Musk appeared from below with my breastplate, pistols and sword. By rights, the task of attiring the captain of the *Cressy* for battle should have fallen to one of my young attendants, but I could readily imagine how easily Musk would have brushed them aside. 'God knows what inspired me to volunteer for this voyage,' he said as he fastened my baldric and scabbard. 'Little pay. Weather cold enough to freeze a man's piece off. I could have stayed before an open fire in London town.'

'Come now, Musk, surely you would not have wished to miss our great victory over the Danes and, let us pray, the end of our mortal foe, Lord Montnoir?'

'Victory, defeat – they both look damnably similar after a while. Not my words, your grandfather's, and he'd seen more of war than the Horsemen of the Apocalypse. As for the end of that infernal Frog, I'd rather have read about it.'

I smiled; and that, of course, was Musk's purpose. He was no coward, but he had a way of knowing how to cheer Sir Matthew Quinton: for otherwise I might have been prone to think too much upon the prospects for the coming battle and of the terrible condition that would befall Cornelia, Lady Quinton, if her husband fell.

Lydford North and Reverend Eade, the *Cressy*'s chaplain, came onto the quarterdeck to join the growing throng that also included Kit Farrell, Seth Jeary and two of his mates. North looked uncomfortable in a breastplate acquired from the armourer's store, and his eyes met mine only fleetingly before he withdrew to the rail to study the *Oldenborg*. Lord Arlington's protégé was evidently brave enough when pointing his pistol at a regicide, but like so many of our young cavalier blades, he had never experienced a proper battle before. Would Lydford North prove to be nought but a craven and a coward? I did not know, and no doubt neither did he.

The chaplain recited the prayers before battle, but I do not know how many of those manning the guns in the waist heard him. I doubt whether all of us on the quarterdeck did. Eade was a mumbler at the best of times, and now he was very nearly struck dumb with fear. Once again I wished that Francis Gale was with us instead, for even those aboard the enemy ship would have heard his thunderous delivery of the prayerbook litany; and having delivered it, Francis would then wield a cutlass as ferociously as any man in the crew –

The *Oldenborg* opened fire, her upper deck guns belching flame and smoke. The two ships were still perhaps five hundred yards apart.

'Impatient, to fire at such a range,' said Seth Jeary calmly. Most of the Dane's shot fell short; a ball or two hit the hull, high up, but with most of the force expended, they had little effect against stout English oak.

'Like the Dutch,' I said. 'Firing on the uproll, for our rigging, making best use of his lighter shot – I reckon he has nothing above twenty-four pounders.' Kit nodded. 'And with his advantage over us in the size of his complement, I do not doubt that he will also seek to emulate the Dutch by boarding us if he can. That being so, Mister Farrell, you know your duty.'

Kit saluted and went below.

I moved to the quarterdeck rail and called down to the *Cressy's* master gunner, who was in the waist of the ship checking the condition of our larboard eight-pounders and their crews. 'Mister Blackburn! All is ready, as we discussed?'

'Awaiting your command, Sir Matthew!'

'Very good. Today we avenge the good men the Danes killed at Bergen, Mister Blackburn, so pray ensure that every gun aims true!'

The gunner saluted and returned to his duty. As he did so, the *Oldenborg* fired again. Her gun crews were finding their range and their aim now. Most of her shots struck home: two holes were rent in the mainsail, another in the fore, and three or four shrouds snapped. I calculated the range between us. Three hundred yards – a good English fighting distance. I drew my sword. Gunner Blackburn's eyes were upon me. I waited for the downroll and slashed my blade downward.

Blackburn bellowed through his voice trumpet, the gun captains repeated the command, and in an instant the larboard broadside of the *Cressy* roared out, the bass roar of the great demi-cannon intermingled with the tenors of the culverins, eight-pounders and sakers. I was accustomed to the apocalyptic cacophony and the great shuddering of a ship's hull that accompanied it, but Eade and North were not. Both men looked about them in sheer terror and belatedly covered their ears.

As the smoke rolled away, I studied the *Oldenborg* intently. Several hits in her hull, some of which had penetrated: one had shattered the planking directly alongside a gunport, and as I watched, a man with the side of his chest torn away fell through the hole into the water below, where his gushing blood stained the sea.

The Dane returned fire, his shot again whistling through our rigging. And once more the *Cressy* responded. It was clear already that the interval between our broadsides was shorter than our adversary's; most of my men had fought the previous summer and had been well drilled by John Blackburn. But now the tactic I had concocted with my master gunner came into full play. While the heavy guns on our two lower decks continued to fire on the downroll, double-shotted with round shot to batter the Dane's hull, the lighter weapons upon the upper deck fired on the uproll also, laden with case-shot, bar-shot and bags of bullets. Great holes appeared in the *Oldenborg*'s canvas; a large splinter sheared off her mizzen yard, and two men upon the yard fell dead to the deck.

If we continued to fight an artillery duel side-by-side, the *Oldenborg*'s greater size and overall weight of broadside would count for nought. The *Cressy*, her veteran gun crews and above all the heavy thirty-two pound balls of the demi-cannon smashing into the Dane's hull low down would win, and win quickly. Which meant if Captain Jan-Ulrik Rohde was as good an officer as I took him to be, there were two things he could do to tilt the odds back in his favour: close with us for boarding, relying on his larger crew to overwhelm the Cressys, and recall the *Faisant* from her attack on the mast fleet. And as he proceeded to do them, I offered up thanks to Almighty God – even though if he brought them off, they might prove our undoing.

The Dane had the weather gage, and now her great bows turned toward our own. Rohde's men were massing forward, upon his forecastle. And at the foremast head, a plain blue flag broke out. I was not privy to the intricacies of the Danish signal book, but there was no doubting what it was: a recall command.

I looked over toward the mast-fleet, in our lee to the east of us. As usual the *Delight* was adrift of the rest and well astern of her nearest neighbour. The *Faisant*, sensing an easy prize to commence her day's work, was bearing down on her with a will. Perhaps I had misjudged matters: she might bear the Danish flag, but the *Faisant*'s crew were all Dutchmen who might feel no great compunction to come to the assistance of a Dane – and perhaps even less to that of a Frenchman, their most unlikely allies in this war. If the Dutch captain preferred above honour the opportunity to win himself a healthy sum of prize money, then there was nothing I could do to prevent it.

A fresh broadside from the *Oldenborg* briefly curtailed such bleak thoughts. She was closing the distance between us, but only slowly.

'Prevent her crossing our hawse for as long as you can, Mister Jeary!' I shouted. The master nodded grimly and barked fresh orders to the helmsman at the whipstaff below and to the men adjusting the sails from the yards.

The *Cressy*'s double broadsides thundered out once more, the lower batteries upon the downroll, the uppermost upon the uproll. I ran from the larboard rail to the starboard. Through the smoke I caught sight once again of the mast-fleet and the *Faisant*. Thanks be to God, the Dutch ship had answered the command flag aboard the *Oldenborg*. She was changing tack in order to bear directly for the *Cressy*, as I had prayed she would. But it was clear that her captain's change of heart was not born entirely of a belated recognition of where his duty lay. Another ship had interposed itself between the *Faisant* and the mast-fleet and was now following close in the Dutchman's wake, darting in to fire off a few guns, then backing her sails to fall behind again before the frigate's far more powerful broadside could do her much damage. The little vessel had lowered the red-white-red flag of Poland-Lithuania that she had sported previously, and now flew an altogether more familiar ensign. As the Scots colours streamed out from the ensign staff of the *Nonsuch* of Kinghorn, I wondered briefly how, if he fell this day, Captain Andrew Wood would explain to the shade of his illustrious ancestor his decision to come to the aid of a Sassenach.

Off to larboard the bows of the *Oldenborg* crept nearer to our own, despite Jeary's best efforts to keep the distance between us. Her broadside was more ragged now, ours more determined, but still Rohde kept his men massed in the bows, no doubt hoping and praying that he would shortly be able to cross our hawse – to secure onto our bows, allowing his greater weight of manpower to pour across onto the *Cressy* and overwhelm our crew.

I drew my pistols; very soon we would be within range where they could do good service. As I did so Kellett ran up from below and almost flung himself up the stair to the quarterdeck.

'Murder below, Sir Matthew! Mister North – Mister Musk –'

Without hesitation, I followed him down.

* * *

As I reached the orlop our broadside roared out once again. It was the first time I had experienced a man-of-war's gunfire from its lowest deck. It seemed as though the entire ship would break apart, such was the force and the noise. Frames and beams seemed to scream in protest. The sound of the demi-cannon firing and recoiling on the main deck barely inches above my head seemed like the opening of the gates of hell.

But it was not the only manifestation of hell in the low, dark stinking space of the orlop deck. As my eyes adjusted to the dim light, I could see two men struggling behind the chained shape of John Bale, who was struggling against the chains securing him to the mizzen mast.

'North has a blade, Sir Matthew!' the regicide cried. 'He came down to kill me while you were all occupied with the battle, but Musk interposed himself –'

I saw the glint of Lydford North's dagger. Musk had a tight grip on him, but North was a much younger man. Tentatively I raised my pistol, but they were too close together and it was too dark.

'North!' I shouted. 'Drop your blade, man! As captain of this ship, I demand it!'

North ignored me, but my sudden intervention seemed to distract Musk. North's blade slipped downward, and Phineas Musk fell heavily to the deck.

An unspeakable feeling of sorrow and rage swept over me. Musk – dear, infuriating, loyal Phineas Musk – had been struck down –

'Very well, Sir Matthew,' cried Lydford North, 'the honour can be yours! Fire your pistol, sir, despatch the regicide and avenge your king!'

I stood dumbfounded, Kellett cowering behind me. Competing emotions raged within me. Phineas Musk lay there, wounded – and, perhaps, killed - by as loyal a cavalier as I was. And there sat John Bale, the embodiment of every anathema known to the cavalier cause, very much alive. I had but to fire in order to carry out my promise to my mother, and my duty to king and country –

'Damn you, Quinton, *fire*!' North screamed. He stepped forward, the blade in his hand. A blade discoloured by the blood of Phineas Musk. 'Very well, as you prevaricate, *I* shall be the instrument! *Vivat Rex*!'

Lydford North lunged forward, his blade aimed for John Bale's head. I pressed my trigger. The pan ignited. As the puff of smoke before me cleared, I saw that the ball had struck home. North gripped his chest with his hands, but he could not stop the blood that oozed steadily over his fingers. He looked at me wide-eyed, his expression a tangle of astonishment and pure hatred. Then he fell backward onto the deck, and Lydford North was no more.

I ran to the recumbent figure of Phineas Musk and raised his head. Blood was seeping from his side onto the deck, but was it a death wound?

In the darkness of the orlop, it was impossible to tell.

'Said that North would make enemies,' Musk whispered. 'Didn't reckon you'd be the one who'd do for him, though.'

'Kellett!' I cried. 'Run and fetch two men to carry Mister Musk to the surgeon's cockpit –'

My words were cut off by a thunderous crash that almost flung me to the other side of the deck. It was not a broadside: the sound and the way in which the hull shuddered were entirely different. So it could only be one thing. The *Oldenborg* had crossed our hawse. Her bows were entangled with ours. Her men were about to board.

I stood, for my duty now was to return to the upper deck and marshal our men to repel the onslaught. But as I did so, John Bale looked up at me.

'Now you have saved my life, Sir Matthew, as I saved yours. Are we not then brothers in arms, at the last?'

I stared at him, and prayed to the Blessed Saint, Martyr and King, Charles Stuart, to forgive me for what I was about to do.

'Kellett,' I commanded, 'free the prisoner. See that he has whatever weapons he desires.' I looked down at John Bale once more. 'Let us see if you can kill Danes as well as you can kill kings, Lord Bale.'

Chapter Eighteen

On the upper deck, it was as I expected it to be. Danes were swarming across onto our beakhead. Kit Farrell and the men he had massed upon our forecastle were giving them a hot reception, and thus far none of the enemy had gained a foothold upon our deck itself. Meanwhile Gunner Blackburn was maintaining our fire, although we no longer needed to worry about the roll of the ship. The ships were not side-by-side, the *Oldenborg* having come into our bow at an oblique angle, and Blackburn had moved some of the upper deck guns back from their ports, angling them at their maximum elevation in order to continue to fire into the rigging of the Danish ship. Meanwhile, our lower batteries continued to hammer the hull of the *Oldenborg* relentlessly. Indeed, it was no longer possible for the Danes to man their lower batteries, which had fallen silent. But Captain Rohde knew his trade. He had moved his men either to the boarding party in the bow, or into the tops to fire down a hail of musket and pistol shot onto our deck, or else to man his upper deck battery, which was firing murderous volleys of grape- and chain-shot. Fortunately, his higher hull meant that Rohde could not depress his muzzles far enough to fire properly across our deck, for just a few such broadsides would have slaughtered every man above decks on the *Cressy* within minutes. But his cannonade was playing havoc with our rigging, and the men he had in the tops were causing harm enough. All of our sails were torn to pieces, the maintopmast was swaying precariously, and several of the yards were very nearly ruins.

I went first toward the quarterdeck. Seth Jeary still stood there, giving orders as calmly as if he had been taking a royal yacht for a gentle cruise upon a millpond, while the Reverend Thomas Eade was reading, or rather babbling, from the Book of Psalms. His words reached very few, but then, even the loudest preacher would have struggled to make himself heard above the din being made by Purton and Drewell, the *Cressy's* trumpeters. But as I stepped onto the stair up to the deck, a volley belched out from the upper deck of the *Oldenborg*. By some quirk of the waves, the gunfire swept the deck rather than the rigging. When I reached the top of the stair, the quarterdeck had been wiped out. The two warrant officers, two petty officers, two trumpeters and ten gun-crew who had been standing there a moment earlier were all felled. The deck was awash with blood, limbs and entrails. Over by the starboard rail the chaplain's head was pressed up against the torn, bloodied, head-less torso of Seth Jeary in a macabre bodily exchange. One man still lived, a good man of Wadebridge named Marrack. He looked at me imploringly and reached out his hand, but there was nought I could do for him: the whole of the left side of his body, from the waist down, had been torn off, and his blood was pumping hideously over the deck.

I turned back into the waist of the ship. There was no time to reflect that if I had climbed the stair a moment earlier – if, say, I had not stopped to order the release of John Bale – then I would have been struck down, and the parts of my body would now be lying there, apart and indiscriminate upon the deck.

'Mister Blackburn!' I cried. The Cressy's gunner turned from giving orders to his gun crews and saluted perfunctorily. 'You have the watch upon the quarterdeck, Master Gunner. But I implore you – be careful where you tread.'

As Blackburn went to take up his new post, I strode toward the fore-castle, bellowing encouragement to my men as I passed. 'Keep up your fire, Cressys, for God and the King! A whore and a beef dinner to the crew that brings down a yard!'

'And what for bringing down a mast, Sir Matthew?' cried Turnage, a cheerful lad from Rotherhithe. 'An entire whorehouse, perchance?'

'Bring down a mast, Turnage, and you can have your choice of the Whitehall bawds!'

The boy nodded determinedly and set to the swabbing of his piece with a vengeance. As I turned, I was aware that someone had come up and stood next to me. I half-expected it to be Phineas Musk, who had been on my shoulder in so many fights. But of course it could not be Musk. It was John Bale.

The regicide had armed himself with a pistol in his left hand and a cutlass in his right. He brought up the latter in the time-honoured warrior's salute.

'Thank you, Sir Matthew,' he said.

I simply inclined my head; what words could I say? How could I bring up my own sword to salute a king-killer? I could see the men in the gun crews all around me staring furiously upon the spectacle before them. Many of them were Cornish, and thus royalists to the very core. The older ones had taken wounds for the king this man had put to death, the younger ones had known their fathers fall in the same cause. But as John Bale and I made our way forward to join the battle at the forecastle, I reflected to myself that both the civil war and the execution of Charles Stuart were a long time ago, and no amount of bitter memories would do anything to repel the horde of Danes massing to overwhelm the *Cressy*.

* * *

I stepped onto the forecastle at much the same time that the first Danes appeared on it, from the bow-end above the beakhead. One of them raised his musket, but had no time to fire it before Julian Carvell buried the point of a half-pike deep into his belly. Fifty or sixty Cressys were massed on the deck in front of me, but it was plain to see that coming against them was a wave of a hundred or more Danes.

Kit Farrell presented himself before me. His shirt was in ribbons and his chest and arms ran with flesh-wound blood; despite the cold, he was bathed in sweat. He looked with profound suspicion and hatred upon the form of John Bale.

'Sir Matthew,' he said, 'we need to bring up men from the lower batteries to reinforce us. We can't hold against them for long, sir.'

I was loath to acquiesce. The relentless bombardment from our heaviest guns was wreaking havoc on the *Oldenborg*'s hull and undoubtedly gave us the best chance of victory. Moreover I was reminded of something that my uncle Tristram had once told me when we were exploring the ruins of Ampthill Castle, and I asked him why such fastnesses possessed spiral staircases.

'You only need one man to hold a space this narrow, young Matthew. What is the point of having more men behind, when they cannot bring their weapons to bear?'

I looked at the throng of Cressys ahead of me, and realised that simply piling up more men behind them would have little effect. I looked to starboard and saw that the *Faisant* had finally shrugged off the attentions of the *Nonsuch*, now reduced to but a shattered and drifting hulk, and was beating up into the wind; she would be up with us within half a glass, and then it would be impossible for us to fight both sides of the ship. Finally I looked across to the *Oldenborg*, and to the great holes that our shot had already blasted open in her hull, exposing the naked frames from which the planking had been torn away –

A thought came to me. Whether it was the thought of a genius, a lunatic or a dead man would only be established in the outcome.

'No, Mister Farrell,' I said, 'hold here for as long as you can with the men that you have. And when the Danes retreat, pursue them back across *their* hawse.'

'When they retreat, Sir Matthew?'

'Indeed, I pray that will be so. But if I am mistaken, Kit, then for God's sake, do not yield the ship to those fellows!' He nodded. 'Kellett, there!' I cried. 'Orders for Mister Blackburn and the helm, then for Mister Lanherne and the armourer!'

I barked my commands, then turned and made to go below. 'Sir Matthew,' said John Bale, 'I do not know what is in your mind, but I desire to fight alongside you, if you will permit it.'

There was no time to deliberate. 'I will permit it,' I said.

On the main deck, our great guns had fallen silent. Under Martin Lanherne's direction, cutlasses, pistols and half-pikes were being massed on the deck, ready for issue to the gun crews. Lanherne, a veteran of war on both sea and land, saluted at my approach, despite a resentful sneer at the regicide beside me.

'Reinforcing the forecastle, Sir Matthew?' Lanherne asked.

'Not so, Mister Lanherne,' I said. 'Draw the larboard guns inboard, as far as we can bring them. Then assign the men by their quarters to mass behind the third and sixth gunports.'

The boatswain of the *Cressy* nodded and barked his orders, which were repeated along the deck. Men hauled on tackle and pulled the great culverins inboard. They were well practised in the manoeuvre, and performed him both expertly and swiftly. And as they undertook their task, the ship's movement revealed to all the notion that was in their captain's mind. Having endeavoured for so long to adjust the helm to prevent us coming side-by-side with the *Oldenborg*, the helmsman and the others who would be assisting him to bring the whipstaff across were now striving for precisely the opposite end. The distance between the two hulls was closing.

Lanherne ordered men to their places. Bale and I took up positions by the sixth port, almost amidships, although I had to crouch beneath one of the timber knees that supported the upper deck. Treninnick, MacFerran and half a dozen others stood by us, waiting for the moment.

Closer...closer...the two hulls struck, and in that moment I raised my sword, bellowed 'Cressys, forward!' and pulled myself through the port hole, leaping from our hull across the few feet of icy sea-water far below and landing on the main gun deck of the *Oldenborg*. I thanked God that she was slender-built and not a great English slug with tumblehome, else the hulls would never have come close enough for me to make the leap. John Bale landed behind me, and through the other great hole in the side of the Danish ship came Martin Lanherne. We advanced, picking our way past deserted guns and tackle and over the remains of slaughtered Danes. Behind us came an ever-increasing wave of Cressys. For a few moments the deck before us was deserted, but Montnoir and Captain Rohde must have recognised the danger at once. Shots rang out from the fore and aft hatchways and ladders as the defenders of the *Oldenborg* rushed downward, attempting to retake the deck before we could get enough men onto it.

'Lanherne,' I cried, 'the fore ladder! The rest of you, with me!'

The Cressys divided according to the ports by which we had left our own ship. Lanherne and his men rushed forward, immediately exchanging fire and crossing swords with the Danes before them. I ran for the aft ladder. That was the most direct way to the enemy's quarterdeck: to the colours which I wished to see hauled down, to Captain Rohde, and above all to the Seigneur de Montnoir.

Chapter Nineteen

The Danes attempted to form a phalanx to protect the foot of the aft ladder, but their numbers were too few. I led the onrushing Cressys directly into them, swinging my sword viciously and feeling it strike flesh and bone. At my side, John Bale was a revelation. It was as though all of his pent-up miseries and broken dreams suddenly had an outlet. He cut and thrust with unrestrained brutality. A Dane came at him with a reversed musket, intending to use it as a club, but with a great roar Bale swung his sword and cleaved the man's head in two.

All around me my men were showing their worth, screaming their battle cries of '*Kernow!*' and '*Cressy!*'. Treninnick was worth his weight in gold in such situations, for few could match the phenomenal strength this strange, bent creature had developed during years in the tin mines of his native land. He wielded a half-pike as lightly as most men wield a dagger, spearing one man and instantly withdrawing the pike to wind another with the blunt end before bringing the weapon sharply over the man's head and pulling it hard against him to break his neck.

A tall, red-headed young man wearing better clothes and a sash stood before me. I recognised him from my reception aboard this very ship: Rohde's lieutenant. He wielded a cutlass commendably well, but evidently had little idea of how to acquit himself against an opponent bearing a long, straight, thick-bladed sword of earlier times. He swung diagonally for my shoulder, the classic cutlass move, but I was too tall and my blade was up too soon. My parry left him defenceless and enabled me to swing my sword sharply into his right shoulder. He dropped his weapon and stumbled away toward the stern, screaming in agony and trying to hold the nearly-severed arm to his torso.

My foot was on the bottom rung of the *Oldenborg's* aft ladder. I looked up and saw daylight, which was blotted out in the next instant by the dark shape of a man pointing a musket downward. An old matchlock, by the looks of it, slow of firing. I brought up the flintlock pistol in my left hand and shot him through the heart.

Up, and out onto the upper deck, followed closely by Bale and then the rest of my men. A half-pike came at me, but I was then still young enough to step smartly aside before it could bury itself in my stomach. The point tore my shirt and scratched my flesh, but I was now battle-hardened enough to regard such wounds as barely worthy of the name, no more than the merest flea bites.

The situation was clear to me. As I had hoped, our unexpected opening of a second front had forced Rohde to divert men from his boarding attack on the *Cressy*. That, in turn, allowed Kit and his men to rally: they were already crawling over the *Oldenborg's* beakhead, my lieutenant at their head, advancing inexorably on the Dane's forecastle. Meanwhile, Lanherne's men were starting to fight their way out from the fore ladder. Rohde had concentrated his main strength in the waist of the ship, rather than dispersing his men fore and aft to try and repel the two attacks. And as I looked away to starboard, it was clear what was in Rohde's mind. He did not have to defeat us; did not have to force us off the ship. All he had to do was play for enough time for the *Faisant* to come up and attack the *Cressy* upon her unprotected starboard side; Blackburn still had our upper deck guns manned and was still firing high into the *Oldenborg's* rigging, which was in as torn a condition as ours, but I knew there would be almost nobody below decks. And the Dutch ship was now very close indeed. One more tack and she would be roughly at the edge of her range for loosing off a broadside. If we were to prevail, we had to prevail quickly.

'Bale!' I cried. 'Take half the men with us – attack the Danes in the waist!' The regicide nodded and complied immediately. Now there were no resentful looks or hateful stares from even the most royalist of the Cressys: whatever else John Bale had once been, he was a formidable fighter and a born leader. 'The rest of you, with me!'

Onto the quarterdeck stair, with Treninnick and others clambering directly above the elaborate carvings adorning the bulkhead beneath the quarterdeck rail –

It was hot work now. Rohde had massed a formidable party on the quarterdeck, perhaps as many as fifty men. I parried, cut, slashed and thrust with all my strength. Now I experienced once again that strange feeling, peculiar to battle. The conscious mind closes down. In its place comes a heightened state, at once more aware of and more oblivious to all else around: the state of battle frenzy that the North Men of old called 'berserk'. I took wounds – a sword's point sliced into my arm, an unknown weapon bruised and bloodied my head – but they were as pinpricks. I gave better than I got, my grandfather's sword cleaving a path before me. A path set directly for the motionless figure, cloaked in black, who awaited me near the stern rail: the Seigneur de Montnoir.

A huge bearded Dane, naked to the waist, came at me with an axe, the very image of the Viking warrior. But an axe is a clumsy weapon, fearsome yet inflexible. He swung for my neck, seeking to decapitate me, but the very act of pulling back his arm exposed his undefended chest. I thrust my sword up, beneath his rib cage, and saw the astonishment in his eyes as his body slid off my blade and onto the deck.

'Bravo, Sir Matthew,' said Montnoir, raising his sword. 'You are becoming a considerable inconvenience to France and to me.'

'Not as inconvenient as I propose to be when I kill you, Montnoir.'

Our blades clashed. There was little space: Cressys and Oldenborgs were tightly packed all around us, all fighting their own battles to the death. Thus Montnoir and I could not exercise the refined moves of the training-yard. This was not an arena for feints, sidestepping and other such niceties. Instead we made short, sharp thrusts and low cuts, making more use of wrists and elbows than shoulders. A clever slashing attack from him brought his blade nearly to my neck, but my own came up in time. We stood there for what seemed an eternity, his cold eyes barely inches from mine as he tried to press his steel past my own and into my flesh. I pushed him away and countered with a bold thrust for his heart, but he defended briskly.

'Sir Matthew!' I recognised Ali Reis's unmistakeable Moorish speech; but he had been with Kit's party – 'The Danish captain has fallen, sir! Lord Bale has done for him!'

I felt a confusion of emotions: poor Rohde, as good and honest a fellow as one could wish to meet, felled by the sword of a foul regicide. Yet Rohde was my enemy, and Bale now my ally, and surely I ought to rejoice at my enemy's fall?

I looked at Montnoir. The usually imperturbable Frenchman was tiring and breathing heavily; but so was I. 'Surrender the ship, Montnoir!' I ordered.

'Surrender your own, Sir Matthew,' said the Knight of Malta, pointing his sword to starboard.

The *Faisant's* larboard battery fired. Several shots struck the undamaged starboard side of the *Cressy*. I saw Gunner Blackburn ordering men to move across from our larboard battery to the other side; but that was his last act on this earth. The *Faisant* fired again, and a great splinter of planking beneath the starboard rail of the *Cressy's* quarterdeck broke away. It pierced the Master Gunner's chest and drove his body over the other rail into the sea between *Cressy* and *Oldenborg*.

Montnoir took advantage of my distraction and attacked, thrusting directly for my head. But Ali Reis's half-pike knocked his sword away, and the Moor and two other Cressys faced down the Knight of Malta. Montnoir stepped away to give himself space to meet his new assailants.

'Reis,' I said, gasping for air, 'orders to Mister Farrell –'

'Begging pardon, Sir Matthew, but the lieutenant is wounded, sir. A bad one. Don't think he can give or take orders.'

Kit – oh God, Kit –

That was all the time I had for reflection. I ran to the quarterdeck stair and leapt down into the ship's waist. The Cressys clearly had the upper hand now, John Bale marshalling their efforts –

There was a crack like the very thunder of doomsday itself. I looked up and saw the mizzen mast of the *Oldenborg* topple. Master Gunner John Blackburn's elevated sakers and minions had paid him the finest posthumous tribute possible. Laniards and halyards snapped. The topyard broke away and the sails tore, the sound of ripping outdoing and silencing the hubbub of war. Timber and canvas alike fell in a great mass onto the quarterdeck, shattering the rails and planking. A great gun, an eighteen-pounder or thereabouts, fell over the side, its tackle entangling the limbs of one poor soul who was dragged after it. Any man on the quarterdeck directly beneath the falling mast would have been crushed in an instant. And my last sight of the Seigneur de Montnoir was in that exact spot in that exact moment, with sword in hand, fighting off the assault of my two Cressys. Then the remnants of the mizzen and its sails covered the quarterdeck like a shroud, and nothing moved beneath.

I turned and continued my run to the forecastle. Kit was there, slumped against a nine-pounder, Julian Carvell crouched over him and placing a makeshift bandage over what was clearly a bad wound in his gut.

'Sir Matthew,' said Kit, weakly, 'have we won the day?'

I replied with a heavy heart: my old friend, the saviour of my life, seemed not long for the world. 'Against the Dane – aye, Kit, we have, although his colours still fly. But unless we can man the *Cressy* again, I fear the Dutchman will assail an empty ship.'

'Then they must not face an empty ship, Sir Matthew.'

'No, Lieutenant. They must not.' I turned. 'Lanherne, there! Withdraw our men back to the *Cressy*, over the hawse! But as you do so, fire the *Oldenborg*!' The bluff Cornishman nodded and set about his duty. 'Carvell, get Lieutenant Farrell back to the *Cressy* and to the surgeon. Reis! MacFerran! You men, hereabouts! With me, to defend our withdrawal!'

With a dozen or so men, I stood at the head of a phalanx covering the retreat of the Cressys. The remaining Danes were too exhausted and too cowed to offer much resistance; and when the first wisps of smoke emerged from below, where my men were firing pitch- and tar-barrels, most of the enemy became concerned only with saving their own lives by getting into the long-boats that the *Oldenborg* towed behind her. Nevertheless a few brave or foolhardy souls were still fighting, and I realised that several of them were defending against the ferocious onslaught of one man: John Bale.

'Bale!' I cried. 'Enough! Evacuate the ship! We need to man the *Cressy*!'

He seemed not to hear me, consumed as he was with redemptive blood-lust. But at last he withdrew and joined us as we steadily backed toward the beakhead of the *Oldenborg*, then made our way across the web of cables and shrouds onto our own ship.

The *Faisant* was up with us now, and fired off another broadside which principally mauled what remained of our sails and rigging. The main mast was riddled with shot, and I prayed that it did not fall as the *Oldenborg*'s mizzen had. But with men ordered aloft and struggling to adjust our yards and canvas, Lanherne, the senior officer remaining after myself, was already doing his utmost to con our damaged hull away from the *Oldenborg*, where the flames were now licking out of the lower gunports. Although a proof of our victory, this created a new danger for the *Cressy*: if the Danish ship's magazine blew up before we had put enough water between us, we might be devastated by the same blast. Having witnessed the Dutch flagship *Eendracht* blow up at the Battle of Lowestoft a few months before, I had no wish to be at the centre of such a dreadful apocalypse.

I ran down to the main gun deck of the *Cressy*. My men knew their business, and without orders from any officer, they were already running out the starboard guns. 'Gun captains!' I cried. 'The Dutchman, there, thinks that we are weakened – that we can give him no welcome! Let's show him the hospitality of the *Cressy*!' There was a cheer at that.

The lad Kellett appeared at my side: I was relieved that he had survived the battle with the *Oldenborg*. 'To the after ladder, boy – you will have to relay my orders to the lower deck. Get down there and tell the gun captains that when they hear your command to give fire, they are to unleash hell's own wrath against the Dutch!'

'My command, Sir Matthew?'

'Aye, lad. Your command. For the next five minutes, you are the Master Gunner of the *Cressy*, Mister Kellett.'

The lad smiled brilliantly and saluted. 'Aye, aye, Sir Matthew!' He ran off and scuttled down the after ladder as fast as his legs would carry him.

The *Faisant* fired again, but her broadside was already ragged. No doubt the States-General of the United Provinces had not loaned one of their best ships and crews to the King of Denmark; probably quite the reverse. Therein lay my hope for the survival of my shattered ship and exhausted crew.

My gun captains had adjusted their angles of elevation. The barrels were swabbed, the canvas-covered charges and balls rammed home, the linstocks readied over the touch holes. 'Steady, lads,' I shouted, 'await the downroll...wait...wait...' I saw Kellett's face at the after hatch. He raised an impudent thumbs up. 'Wait – *give fire!*'

The starboard broadside of the *Cressy* fired. Standing in the midst of a cannonade is at once one of the most thrilling and frightening experiences a man can ever have. The fuses and then the mouths of the muzzles belch flame and smoke. The air becomes acrid, and for seconds on end it is impossible to see at all. The nearly unbearable noise of the firing is succeeded at once by the thunderous sound of the guns recoiling and the tackle pulling taut. And at once the gun crews set to the task of reloading, of preparing to run out the guns to fire again.

I went to the nearest gunport, both to breathe fresh air into my lungs and to see the effect of our broadside upon the *Faisant*. And what an effect it was! Confident of an easy victory over a disordered enemy, the Dutch captain had closed to barely two hundred yards. Consequently almost all of our shot had hit home: there were already several holes in the hull, and – thanks be to God, we had holed her just below the waterline, too! Even so, a valiant captain and crew would have shrugged off such wounds and responded in kind at once. But the *Faisant* did not fire. Instead, she began to move away. Men went aloft; the frigate put on more sail. At first I feared she was turning back downwind toward the mast-fleet, perhaps calculating that we were in no condition to sail to the aid of the merchantmen: which would have been true, if the Dutchman had but the gumption to attempt it. Instead it swiftly became clear that the *Faisant* was running. One good English broadside, and perhaps the dire warning provided by the sight of the *Oldenborg* in flames, had been enough to put her to flight. She fired a couple of desultory volleys from her stern chasers, but they did us no harm.

Or so I thought, until I returned to the upper deck. John Bale had been laid upon the deck. Most of the right side of his torso was gone. 'A thousand-to-one chance,' said MacFerran, who was kneeling beside him. 'The very last shot the Dutchman fired.'

I kneeled. The regicide looked at me and gripped my hand tightly, imploringly.

'All I did was for England,' John Bale said in a strangled, nearly inaudible voice, almost coughing upon each word. 'For the England I wished to see. But that perfect England was a false hope, Quinton – the falsest of hopes.' Blood trickled from the corner of his mouth. 'Better, then, to die for the imperfect sort. Tell my wife. Above all, tell my son. Tell them that John Bale served England, and died for her.'

'Yes, you have served England,' I said. 'Once for ill, now for good.

And you have served Sweden too, I think, in helping to save it from the designs of Lord Montnoir. By freeing me, you opened Count Dohna's eyes to Montnoir's true nature. You prevented –'

Bale did not allow me to finish, for his eyes had narrowed at the name I mentioned. 'Dohna?' he whispered, struggling for some last vestiges of breath. 'But Dohna is –' He coughed, and the dark blood oozed upon his lip and chin. 'Dohna is –'

His eyes stared hard at me, as though they were trying to complete the sentence that his mouth could no longer utter. But the eyelids did not blink, and I knew then that John Bale lived no more.

I bowed my head as I would to my superior in rank. 'Farewell, My Lord Bale,' I said.

Chapter Twenty

We effected running repairs off the Swedish isle of Marstrand, in the lee of the gaunt, forbidding fortress that dominated it. Then we committed to the deep the bodies of our departed shipmates, with myself playing the part of chaplain and reciting the prayers for the dead. At length the *Cressy* and her consorts proceeded to sea once more. We made but slow progress past the Skaw of Denmark, out of the Sound and so west, towards the Dogger Bank and England. The wind remained westerly and the mast-ships continued to struggle against it. We sighted many Dutch fishing craft, but were too wounded and too encumbered by the mast fleet to contemplate an attack upon them. Conversely we sighted several Dutch capers upon the horizon, two of which darted in impudently to see if one of the mast ships might happen to straggle, but even in her damaged state, the *Cressy* proved too formidable a deterrent to the ambitions of the brave crews from Harlingen, Stavoren and the like.

I made regular visits to the cockpit where Phineas Musk and Kit Farrell lay, both still thankfully alive. The former was swiftly out of danger from Lydford North's stab wound in his side and restored to his accustomed self: 'Not the first scars Musk has borne for you Quintons,' he growled, 'and I doubt if they'll be the last either.'

But Kit remained oblivious to all around him, by turns unconscious and delirious, until on the fourth day after the battle the surgeon reported to me that he was lucid and seeking a word with his captain.

'Well, Mister Farrell,' I said, remaining formal while others were in earshot, 'despite all, it is not yet time for you to depart this world.'

'God is merciful, Sir Matthew.'

Kit was not usually so devout; he claimed to have had his fill of the canting Puritanism that stifled his neighbourhood of Wapping when he was a child. But the prospect of death makes all men devout, as I knew from my own experience.

I sat by him. He was pale and thin – or at least, thinner, for Kit was a sturdy fellow - but he was strong, and seemed set fair to live.

'I rejoice in your recovery, Kit,' I said, and prayed I was not premature: he was still weak, and infection might yet fit him for the grave-shroud.

'And I give you joy of your victory, Sir Matthew, although you purchased it at a heavy price.'

'True, my friend. Many good men perished, yet seemingly for nought. A ketch out of Leith tells me this morning that we still have no formal war with the Danes. If this is the kind of battle we fight when we are notionally at peace, then God spare us all the sort we will have to fight when war does begin.'

In fact, there would be no war with the Danes for some months more. I later discovered from my brother that both the Danish King and my own were content to accept the explanation that Captain Rohde had attacked the mast fleet on his own initiative, hoping thereby to avenge our alleged perfidy at Bergen, and that valiant officer's death in the battle ensured that he could not testify to the contrary. (As lies went, it was of a piece with that which I perpetrated in my letter to Lord Arlington, informing him with profound sadness that Lydford North had fallen heroically in battle against England's enemies.) Moreover, King Frederik hardly wished it trumpeted that he had been browbeaten by the Seigneur de Montnoir into lending him one of Denmark's greatest men of war merely so that the Knight of Malta could pursue a personal vendetta; and of course it suited my King to delay a war against a third powerful enemy for as long as possible, certainly until after a summer's campaign which, we all prayed, would bring us the decisive victory that we had so nearly achieved in the previous year. If, that is, we could triumph over the Dutch fleet and its brilliant new commander, Michiel De Ruyter, before the French and the Danes could bring their full forces against us: in that event, the failure of my embassy to Sweden would hardly matter.

'Sir Matthew,' said Kit, 'I fear I have not behaved well toward you on this voyage, and I was intemperate upon the matter of the gentleman and the tarpaulins. My judgement was clouded by the Maiden Ter Horst; I must needs apologise to you.'

'In great heaven's name, Kit, *you* apologise to *me*? It is I who should apologise to you! You defended me admirably when we were ambushed in Gothenburg, and brought the *Cressy* down to ensure my release from Montnoir's prison, yet all that concerned me was the punctilio of the Lord High Admiral's instructions! I have been a very monster of ingratitude, Kit.'

He looked upon me curiously, and I thought for a moment there were tears in his eyes. 'And I was but a lovelorn young fool. At our last meeting, after we were released by the new Landtshere, Magdalena turned only angrily and told me the truth, in the few words of seafarers' argot that we shared. Her father had sent her to spy upon us, Sir Matthew – to spy on the doings of Lord Conisbrough and the *Cressy*, through me. She was to have attempted the same upon you, but it seems that word of your fidelity to your wife has reached even Gothenberg. That was why she appeared to take to me so quickly. I was nothing more than her dupe.'

'I am truly sorry, Kit.'

'A lesson learned, I think, Sir Matthew. And not the only one either. It was presumptuous beyond measure for me to believe myself ready for command. You have had to be an ambassador, to deal with the likes of the High Chancellor and the Landtshere, and you can take such dealings in your stride because you are born to consort with such men.'

Whereas who am I? Plain Kit Farrell of Wapping, who was merely a Master's mate only four years past.'

'You do yourself an injustice, Kit. You will make a fine captain one day, and that very soon. Wars create vacancies, my friend, and are ever a happy season for young men in search of promotion. Think upon it – if a shot had carried me away in the late fight, you would have been the captain of the *Cressy*, and I do not doubt that you would have pursued the battle with the *Oldenborg* to the same conclusion. The King and the Duke of York always promote in such cases, Kit.'

He smiled. 'Then I have to wait for you to be killed in battle, Sir Matthew?'

'I trust not, Kit. When we return to England I will see to it that your name is entered in the Lord High Admiral's book of candidates for command. Who knows, perhaps before this war is done I will be able to toast Captain Farrell, and give him joy of his first command!'

* * *

When we were still some thirty miles east of Yarmouth's shore by my reckoning, we encountered the sixth rate *Laurel*, under orders to take the mast-fleet up to Sir William Warren's timber yard at Deptford while we proceeded to Chatham for repairs. Thus relieved of its burden, the *Cressy* made a safe landfall, the reassuring bulk of Covehithe church's lofty tower plainly visible upon the Suffolk shore. We anchored, ostensibly to take on water, but in truth to accomplish a more secret purpose: under cover of nightfall we landed the coffin containing the body of John, Lord Bale, along with a small party of loyal men who had orders to convey it to Derbyshire, to his widow and their son. I know the mission was completed, both because the men reported back to me while the ship lay at Chatham, waiting to be paid off, and because by chance I found myself in those parts years later, when travelling to Manchester to investigate the possibility of investing in some mines about that god-forsaken place. There, in the corner of a windswept village churchyard overlooked by a great stark ridge of limestone, lay an overgrown grave with a marker that was already fading fast, so often was it lashed by the prodigious rains and frozen by the terrible winters common to those parts. It bore no name, only the initials JBB, which no passing wayfarer would comprehend but which I knew to stand for John, Baron of Baslow. Beneath the initials, this legend had been inscribed:

> *Quid eram, nescitis;*
> *Quid sum, nescitis;*
> *Ubi abii, nescitis;*
> *Valete.*

The servant attending upon me that day, who had no Latin, was curious as to the meaning of this singular epitaph. Thus as a drizzle came in over the hills to the west, I translated the lines for his benefit:

> *What I was, you know not;*
> *What I am, you know not;*
> *Whither I am gone, you know not;*
> *Farewell.*

Back aboard the *Cressy*, the morning after Bale's body was put ashore, I steeled myself to compose the letters duty bound me to write to my Lord High Admiral, recounting our fight with Montnoir and the gallant *Oldenborg*, as well as the deaths of so many valiant men of the *Cressy*; and, more painful still, the letters that compassion bound me to write to the mothers and widows of Jeary, Blackburn, Eade and the rest. The writing paper in my cabin had been a casualty of Dutch gunfire, but I knew I had a small stock at the bottom of my sea chest, which had survived unscathed. As I took out a parcel of linen shirts, something fell onto the deck. I stooped and recognised the small volume that Count Dohna had given me at our parting: the *Commentarii de Bello Gallico* of Caesar, tome the seventh. I was about to replace it in the chest when some instinct made me study the book more closely. Perhaps I sought a diversion from the grim task ahead of me; perhaps I wished to summon up recollection of a more carefree time, when the young Matthew

Quinton had studied the *de Bello* upon the knee of his uncle Tristram. In any event, I properly contemplated the crest upon the binding, as I do again now, tracing its outline in the leather with my ancient finger. The armorial achievements, which I had taken at a glance to be those of the Count Dohna, were plainly something quite other: the unmistakeable crossed keys and triple tiara of the Bishop of Rome, as we good Protestants were supposed to call him. The successor of Peter, Supreme Pontiff and Pope, as he called himself. The spine bore the legend *Bibliotheca Apostolica Vaticana*. Somehow, the count had appropriated this copy of *de Bello* from the papal library itself.

My puzzlement drew me to open the cover. Dohna had written upon the flyleaf. The message was in Latin, and as I read the faded words once again, all these years later, I feel again something of the shock and thrill which coursed through me that March day in the year of grace, 1666. For some reason, too, I suddenly called to mind what I had taken to be an empty boast of that singular little man, Lieutenant-General Erik Glete: *I obey none but High Admirals of Sweden, anointed sovereigns of The Three Crowns, and God Almighty.* Well, then. It was suddenly apparent to me that Glete had been privy to a great secret, and he had kept it with considerable aplomb.

Strange. Now I even seem to hear the echo of my own laughter, too: the unstoppable laughter that began there in the great cabin of the *Cressy* off the coast of Suffolk, when my astonishment turned finally to realisation.

At last, I knew why Count Dohna's hands were always gloved.

The inscription upon the yellowing page before me, written in precisely the same hand that wrote the inventory which I had read so recently, of weapons to be supplied to we Royalists in 1649, reads thus, duly rendered into my own tongue:

> *For my most honourable and gallant friend, Sir Matthew Quinton.*
>
> *Let the lessons of our brief acquaintance be these.*

Imprimis, sovereigns should trust not in false, flattering prophets who delude them with insinuations of a kingdom in peril and of duty to a twisted distortion of faith; who persuade them, indeed, that only their own presence, incognito, in their former realms will prevent pretended evils coming to pass.

Secundo, valiant knights should not assume that a man is defined by his garments alone.

I will remain, my dear Sir Matthew, a true friend to you. Remember, then, that you can ever depend upon the soul you knew as the Count Dohna, but who is known unto God as the sometime Queen of the Swedes, Goths and Wends,

Christina R.

Historical Note

Elements of the plot of *The Lion of Midnight* are based upon fact. In particular, both the size and importance of the mast-fleet that returned from Gothenburg in 1666 (actually in December, not February) are drawn directly from the historical record: Pepys's diary details his desperate concern for the fleet's safety, while the names of the ship masters and exact information about the size and dimensions of their cargoes can be found in the state papers at the National Archives, Kew. The Swedish embargo on tree-felling and the French acquisition of much of the remaining stock took place essentially as described. The battle of the *Cressy* against the *Oldenborg* and the *Faisant* is also based closely upon a real event. In May 1667 the *Princess* (Captain Henry Dawes), a Fourth Rate of similar size to the fictitious *Cressy*, was returning from Gothenburg having already fought off an attack from a Dutch fleet of no fewer than seventeen ships on her outward voyage. Off the coast of Norway she encountered two men-of-war that had been hired by the Danes from the Dutch. I have used the real name of one of these, the *Faisant*, but my *Oldenborg* was a far larger ship than the other of Dawes's assailants (and is somewhat larger, indeed, than the real *Oldenborg* that was in the Danish fleet at the time). Dawes was killed after an hour, his left thigh blown apart by a cannonball, but before he died he uttered the words that adorn the beginning of this book and which were for many years held up as an example to British naval captains: 'For God's sake, do not yield the ship to those fellows!'. The lieutenant took command, but lost both of his legs and had to give way to the master, who was killed in his turn. The gunner then took command for the remaining three hours of the engagement until the Danish ships finally stood away. Given the slaughter aboard the *Princess*, first-hand accounts of this engagement from her are inevitably lacking, so I have conflated elements of her battle during the outward voyage. This proved to be the only serious naval action undertaken by the Danes after war belatedly broke out between them and Charles II's three kingdoms in September 1666; they actually proved to be much less of a threat than many contemporaries of them expected them to be, although matters might have been different if they had undertaken the invasion of Orkney that they seriously contemplated.

The 'golden age' of Sweden lasted from roughly 1610 to 1710. The campaigns of her warrior king Gustavus II Adolphus, *der Löwe von Mitternacht* to his German enemies, won her vast new territories, despite her tiny population and limited natural resorces. Although Gustavus's intervention in the Thirty Years War was ended abruptly by his death during the battle of Lutzen in 1632, his generals continued to win triumph after triumph in the name of his daughter Christina, who succeeded to the throne at the age of five, and later under her warrior cousin who succeeded as Karl X. Queen Christina converted to Catholicism and abdicated in 1654, spending most of the remaining thirty-four years of her life in Rome. Most, but not all: she returned to Sweden twice, in 1660-1 and 1667, on both occasions to chivvy a reluctant Riksdag (and High Chancellor Magnus De La Gardie) into paying her the full allowance stipulated in her abdication settlement. This remarkable document signed over to the departing queen extensive estates, including entire towns and islands, but also permitted her to retain the full title and status of a ruling monarch, with sovereign rights over her own court (a situation that she rendered notorious by ordering the summary execution of her aide the Marchese Mondaleschi in her presence at the palace of Fontainebleu in 1657). Christina was indeed keen to ensure Sweden's neutrality in the second Anglo-Dutch war, but not entirely for the noble and disinterested reasons I have placed in her mouth; neutrality meant that she stood a better chance of receiving the full amounts of the revenues from her Swedish estates.

Christina's two return visits to Sweden following her abdication were entirely public events, but the Vasa dynasty as a whole had a long tradition of adopting aliases and going unrecognised among ordinary people. Christina's penchant for disguising herself as a man was notorious and formed the basis of the plot of the 1933 Greta Garbo film *Queen Christina*, which otherwise played fast and loose with the historical record. However, the male pseudonym of Count Dohna was adopted by the queen in both the film and in real life, and her astonishing horsemanship is reflected in all accounts of her life. There were persistent rumours of an affair between Christina and Count Magnus De La Gardie, although by the time in which *The Lion of Midnight* is set their relationship had become considerably more antipathetic than I have made it. Christina had other lovers of both sexes, including the Cardinal Azzolino mentioned in this book, although many – or perhaps all – of these relationships might have been platonic. I chose only to hint at the widespread beliefs that Christina's sexuality, or indeed her very gender, might have been ambiguous; indeed, in recent years she has become something of a cult figure among the transgender community.

There are many biographies of Queen Christina. I relied primarily on the newest available in English, Veronica Buckley's *Christina, Queen of Sweden*, as well as on the older *The Sibyl of the North* by Faith Compton Mackenzie and *Queen Christina* by Georgina Masson; for some unaccountable reason, however, I decided to forego the biography of her by Barbara Cartland. As for the title 'King (or Queen) of the Swedes, Goths and Wends', that continued to be borne by Swedish monarchs until the present incumbent, Karl XVI Gustaf, modified it to the simpler 'King of

Sweden' at his accession in 1973; nevertheless, the heraldic device of the 'three crowns' remains the emblem of Sweden and her sovereigns. There is no castle of Vasterholm, but my descriptions of its interior are based on those of Kalmar Castle; conversely, Lackö is a real place, about twelve miles north of Lidköping and ninety north-east of Gotebörg, and is still very much as it was in the days when it was the seat of Count Magnus De La Gardie, *Rikskansler* or High Chancellor of Sweden. However, I have taken considerable liberties with its internal layout.

Queen Christina did sell a vast arsenal to the royalists in 1649, and the inventory of weapons given in this book is faithful to the record. However, the agreement was negotiated solely by Patrick Ruthven, Earl of Brentford and Forth, one of the most colourful but underrated cavalier generals of the British civil wars. Ruthven, upon whom the character of Lord Conisbrough was partly modelled, had lived in Sweden for many years, was a favoured drinking partner of King Gustavus Adolphus, and had a daughter who was one of Christina's favourite ladies-in-waiting. Ruthven was also a cousin of the tragic Earls of Gowrie, whose story I recounted in my non-fiction book *Blood of Kings: the Stuarts, the Ruthvens and the Gowrie Conspiracy.* I have taken a slight liberty by placing the famous James Graham, Marquess of Montrose, in Gothenburg in May 1649; he did not arrive in the town until November, shortly before embarking on the final, tragic expedition that led to his defeat at Carbisdale, betrayal in Assynt and execution in Edinburgh. Montrose was hanged, drawn and quartered by forces loyal to his arch-enemy, the Earl of Argyll, who was also ostensibly fighting on the same side in the name of King Charles II. At the restoration of the monarchy in 1660 Montrose's remains were given a grand funeral in Saint Giles's Cathedral, Edinburgh, where they rest just across the nave from those of Argyll.

The character of John, Lord Bale of Baslow, is based on a real person, Thomas Grey, Lord Grey of Groby, who was actually the sole peer to sign the death warrant of King Charles the First. Unfortunately for my purposes, Grey died in 1657, so I had to create a fictional alter-ego for him; the epitaph upon Lord Bale's grave can be found at Castleton in the Peak District, not too many miles from the fictitious church-yard where I located the regicide's burial. The characters of Peregrine, Lord Conisbrough, and Lydford North, are entirely of my invention. However, there was indeed an English embassy to Sweden at the time when *The Lion of Midnight* is set, and it had precisely the same pur-pose as that which I have assigned to Conisbrough's, namely to try and bring Sweden into the second Anglo-Dutch war on Britain's side. This embassy was entirely public, though, and was of considerably longer duration: Henry Coventry, brother of Sir William Coventry, secretary to the Duke of York (who appears as a character in *The Blast That Tears The Skies*), served as ambassador to the court of the Three Crowns from August 1664 until recalled in the summer of 1666. Several travellers provided detailed accounts of Sweden at almost exactly the time when *The Lion of Midnight* is set. The most illustrious of these was Bulstrode Whitelocke, the Commonwealth's ambassador to Christina's court in 1653-4, not long before she abdicated. The second volume of White-locke's journal, recounting his meetings with the queen, is well known, but the first volume provides much valuable information on the city of Gothenburg and the nature of the country. (Whitelocke's difficult voyage to Gothenburg also provided much material for the account of the *Cressy*'s stormy passage in Chapter 1.) I also called upon the *Survey of the Kingdome of Sweden*, published in 1632; Bishop John Robinson's account of Sweden in 1688, published by the Karolinska Förbundets in 1996; and the unpublished account of the country in the 1670s by William Allestree in the National Archives, Kew, SP9/125. There are also a number of good modern histories of this period in English, nota-bly Paul Douglas Lockhart's *Sweden in the Seventeenth Century*, Robert Frost's *The Northern Wars* and Anthony Upton's *Charles XI and Swedish Absolutism, 1660-1697*.

The *Nonsuch* of Kinghorn was an actual Scots privateer of the second Anglo-Dutch war, and her captain was indeed an Andrew Wood; however, I have invented the latter's descent from the famous Sir Andrew Wood, the subject of Nigel Tranter's novel *The Admiral*. On the other hand Kinghorn is no more than fifteen miles from Largo in Fife where Sir Andrew had his estate, so it is entirely possible that he might have been an ancestor of my privateer captain. The remarkably successful story of the Scots privateers during this war is little known, but it is splendidly told in Steve Murdoch's book *The Terror of the Seas: Scottish Maritime Warfare 1513-1713* (2010), to which I contributed the foreword. And there really was a dog entered on a ship's books as 'Mister Bromley' so a captain could claim the wages, albeit not until 1675.

Late seventeenth century Gothenburg was every bit as cosmopolitan as I have made it out to be: although dominated by those of Dutch descent, like my fictional Landtshere Ter Horst, it had a large English community that included Arthur Rose, a carpenter who became a burgomaster of the town, and Francis Sheldon, the shipwright who later built one of the mightiest men-of-war of the age, the ill-fated *Kronan*. There was an even larger Scottish community, perhaps the most remarkable member of which was the man known to the Swedes as Hans Makleir, who had been a respected merchant in Gothenburg for over forty years. His alter ego was that of Sir John Maclean, baronet: a Maclean of Duart on Mull, he emigrated at the age of sixteen but subsequently provided substantial assistance to both the exiled Charles the Second and his tragic lieutenant Montrose, as a result of which he was rewarded with his hereditary title. Considerations of space and the demands of the narrative precluded the inclusion of the likes of Sheldon and Maclean as characters in this book, but they represent an almost forgotten strand of history, the deeply-rooted connections between seventeenth century Britain and Scandinavia.

Acknowledgments

Much of the plot of *The Lion of Midnight* was finalised during a very productive research trip to Kalmar and Gothenburg in February 2011. The superb exhibition of artefacts from the wreck of the great Swedish flagship *Kronan* at the Landsmuseum in Kalmar is much less well known than that for the *Vasa* in Stockholm, but should still be a 'must-see' for anyone interested in seventeenth century naval history. (However, I cannot entirely recommend landing at Kalmar's tiny airport in an ancient turbo-prop aircraft during a snowstorm.) The excellent city museum and maritime museum in Gothenburg contain a great deal of useful material on the history of the city in the seventeenth century (notably the huge scale model in the former), while my account of the funeral of Lord Conisbrough at the German church is drawn from a visit to it on a day as cold as that described in this book. A special thank you to the wonderfully friendly and helpful staff at the splendid Slöttshotel in Kalmar.

I am especially grateful to Professor Steve Murdoch of the University of St Andrews, whose work on Scottish and Scandinavian history in the seventeenth century was a major inspiration for the setting of this book; our conversations over the occasional dram provided stimulating food for thought, and I trust that my inclusion of one of the ships and men mentioned in his book *The Terror of the Seas* has won me a longstanding

bet of a liquid nature! I owe another great debt to the Swedish historian
Jan Glete, whom I knew and whose remarkable quantitative work on
European navies in the entire early modern period, and in particular
his excellent accounts of the Swedish navy, provided much material for
this book. Jan Glete's relatively early death in 2009 was a tragedy for
naval scholarship; the character name of General Erik Glete is by way
of a belated and inadequate tribute to him (although the polite and
thoughtful Jan shared no physical or personality traits whatsoever with
his namesake). As ever, Richard Endsor and Frank Fox provided invaluable assistance with the design, layout and armament of seventeenth
century warships; particular thanks to Frank for unearthing a rare con-
temporary gun-list of the Danish navy, showing the precise distribution
of ordnance of various sizes to the ships of the fleet.

The decision to set this book against the backdrop of Sweden's 'golden
age' probably owes a great deal – subconsciously, at least - to the time
in the 1990s when the A-level History curricula in English schools were
rather more flexible and varied than they are now, and I was able to inflict
on several successive classes an eclectic mixture of topics which included
the alleged 'military revolution' of the seventeenth century and also 'the
Swedish question', 1560-1721. In truth this was really two questions
which tended to be set alternately, variants on 'why did Sweden rise?'
and 'why did Sweden decline?'. The students did not complain; indeed,
they seemed positively to enjoy the experience, and the relative ease
of being able to prepare for such predictable lines of questioning contributed to many of them obtaining outstanding results. For my part,
I thoroughly enjoyed teaching fascinating, if slightly offbeat, topics to
interested and enthusiastic students; I developed an abiding interest in
the history of Scandinavia and am still in touch with some of the alumni
from that era, several of whom I now look upon as friends.

As always, I owe several debts of gratitude, notably to David Jenkins,
my agent Peter Buckman, and my publisher Ben Yarde-Buller. My
partner Wendy provided the first critical assessment of this, as of the

preceding books in the series, and gave me invaluable advice and moral support. Thanks to all, and to the readers who continue to enjoy – and in many cases, comment positively upon – 'the journals of Matthew Quinton'.

J D Davies
Bedfordshire
November 2012